# PRAISE FOR *MR. AND MRS. DIXON HIDE A BODY*

"A dark delight from the very first page. Combining suspense with black humor, *Mr. and Mrs. Dixon Hide a Body* is a riveting, unexpected, exploration of a toxic relationship. I adored this book."

—Mary Watson, #1 *Irish Times* bestselling author of *The Cleaner*

"*Mr. and Mrs. Dixon Hide a Body* is a comedy of errors in which all the errors lead to murder. It takes the tropes of a domestic thriller and turns them on their head into something hilarious and off-kilter."

—Tasha Coryell, author of *Love Letters to a Serial Killer*

"Deliciously dark. Holdich proves that some marriages are more dangerous than murder in this gloriously twisted thriller."

—L. M. Chilton, author of *Everyone in the Group Chat Dies*

"Holdich's out-of-the-ordinary, cozy-adjacent novel is recommended for readers who enjoy marriage revenge stories with eccentric characters."

—*Library Journal*

# ALSO BY JENNIFER HOLDICH

*Julie Tudor Is Not a Psychopath*

# MR. & MRS. DIXON HIDE A BODY

A NOVEL

JENNIFER HOLDICH

Cover design by Faceout Studio, Molly von Borstel
Cover images © GreenSkyStudio/Shutterstock, ariadna5/Getty Images, Leontura/iStock, graphicarts73/Shutterstock



Published by Sourcebooks Landmark, an imprint of Sourcebooks
1935 Brookdale RD, Naperville, IL 60563-2773
(630) 961-3900
sourcebooks.com

Cataloging-in-Publication Data is on file with the Library of Congress.

Printed and bound in the United States of America.
PAH 10 9 8 7 6 5 4 3 2 1

*For all the writing groups, especially Tuesday Night Writes and Cardiff Writers' Circle, & everyone who gives up their time for creative endeavors.*

# CHAPTER ONE

"DOESN'T IT GO ANY FASTER THAN THAT?" I ASKED, AS THE CHANDElier descended from the ceiling at glacial speed.

The contractor rubbed his chin. "Aye." He pressed the switch on the wall and the speed increased to iceberg.

"Any more?"

He nodded and pressed the switch again and I could actually see it moving, but anyone standing under it would have plenty of time to get away if they needed to.

"Have you ever seen one just drop from the ceiling and fall to the ground?" I asked.

"Nah, it's got a safety cord, would stop it if the chain broke. Safe as houses. Anyway, better slow it down, don't want to burn the motor out and leave it hanging halfway." And that we could agree on. "The top speed's for emergencies only," he remarked as the chandelier returned to its glacial dignity, but he didn't elaborate on the kind of emergency you might encounter.

"So, has nobody ever had a chandelier drop on them?" I wanted to make absolutely sure before I abandoned the idea.

"You've been watching too many *Midsomer Murders.*" He chuckled, and I nodded. I had. I was going to have to find another way to kill my husband.

---

On the days when I felt it was worth making an effort, I would haul laundry up and down the stairs, beneath the portraits of the ancestors, under the gaze of their ghosts, past the priceless antiques, around the chairs so valuable no one dared to sit on them, and into the washing machine that had a room all to itself. I'd dust the spots Mrs. Billings had missed and tidy until I didn't know where anything was. Then I'd vacuum until I bashed my knee or tripped over the hose. After that, I would return to the laundry and iron until I damaged one of James's Egyptian cotton shirts, which wasn't usually more than two or three shirts in.

Then, I'd flop onto the sofa, craving a whodunit, or three, and as I watched them, my mind would wander to the parts of the house I hadn't touched: the grime in the ancient carpets in the unused bedrooms, the dust in their heavy velvet curtains, mothballs in the wardrobes harboring the old, old clothes from long-dead former residents. I'd reflect, in dismay, on the herculean task I would never complete and the knowledge that I would never truly be mistress of this house. My enthusiasm would evaporate.

But that was just on the days when I felt it was worth making an effort. Most days, I would leave the cleaning to Mrs. Billings; unconcerned about the quality of her work, I would merely shift from my bed to the sofa and watch TV for much of the time, the long stretch of hours broken into manageable segments by morning chat shows and afternoon thrillers.

My only break from the TV would be time spent at my sewing machine, if I had a particularly good idea for a new dress or skirt or top. As I stitched, my mind would wander, not to the state of the house but to the parting of ways of James and me and how much longer it would be until I could put into play the perfect murder and inherit his wealth.

When James and I first got engaged and I moved into Langley Hall, I sold the house I had inherited from my mum, an old thatched cottage in the middle of our village, and invested all the money in his cryptocurrency business. All of it.

Years later, I decided enough of this marriage was enough and I asked him for my money back, along with the gains I had made, only to be told that of the £350,000 I had invested, I would only get around £20,000 if I cashed it in now.

Apparently, you had to leave it for many years to get the fortune promised at the end. I asked a few more times over the years, but I was always told, just a little bit longer.

"Think of it more like a pension plan than short-term savings," James said to me.

Apparently, we had discussed all that before I invested and, apparently, I said I understood. James had money because he was paid for managing the currency, but we investors had to bide our time.

I couldn't leave with only £20,000 of the inheritance my mum had left for me, and I had no realistic means of supporting myself—after years of not working, my job prospects were limited. So I had no choice but to wait until either it was worth something or I could claim the equivalent under the terms of our prenup.

"Hasn't anyone ever taken their money out sooner?" I asked.

"Not without making a huge loss," James said. Then he looked thoughtful. "Maybe I should make it clearer in the contract, then people wouldn't be so confused. I'm having to explain it all the time."

So I continued as I was.

Most days, around half past five, whether I was making an effort or not, I'd rise from the sofa and shimmy over to the kitchen, where I'd concoct nothing more technical than a Meal to Share from Marks and Spencer. For health and safety reasons, I am forbidden from making anything from scratch.

An M&S ready meal was the peak of fine dining for us. On a more average night, I'd slide fish fingers under the grill, and into the oven would go a trayful of oven chips. I'd microwave some frozen veg and serve it all out. Sometimes James would come home and eat it; sometimes he wouldn't, and I'd either put his in the oven to keep it warm or throw it straight in the bin, depending on my mood.

When he was here to eat, it would be like attending a work meeting. He'd ask me about tasks he had set while I fussed about nervously, wondering if he was going to catch me in a lie:

"Did you get Mrs. Billings to iron the curtains?"

"Yes," I said. No, that was a ridiculous task, I wouldn't demean myself, or her. He couldn't tell if they'd been ironed or not.

"Did you count up how many new roof tiles we need?"

"Yes," I said. "I've made a note of it somewhere." No, that was like trying to count the stars, but that was often the point of these tasks. We needed a professional to come and look at it properly.

"Has the surveyor's report arrived yet?" he asked me one evening through mouthfuls of chicken nuggets, potato waffles, and peas, clearing his giant plate in minutes.

"Not yet," I said, taking my time over my stingy portion. Ever since James decided I was putting on weight, he insisted I eat from a child's plate with plenty of space visible around the edges. He says portion control is the name of the game.

"Chase them up, will you?" he said of the surveyors. "What's taking them so long?"

What was taking them so long was the fact that there was no surveyor's report.

On our estate is a small, private graveyard with a mausoleum. It was once attached to a chapel which belonged to the house. The chapel no longer stands, but the graveyard is still consecrated ground, and the mausoleum houses the remains of the aristocrats who once inhabited this stately home.

When James bought the house, tumbledown and unlived-in for years, he was advised to keep an eye on the mausoleum. In days gone by, the river had been rerouted and it now ran within damaging distance. More recently, a sizable part of the nearby woods was chopped down, causing drainage issues in that corner of our land and threatening the mausoleum further. The time had come for a survey, and the task of arranging it had fallen to me.

But there was a problem: James insisted we use a company run by a couple from the village, Euan and Samantha Saunders. I had gone to school with them, and they had bullied me mercilessly through every year.

I was an outcast at school: firstly, because of being poor, and secondly, because, while I was not alone in living in a single-parent household, I was unique in not knowing who my dad was. It was a goldmine for Euan and Samantha.

My mum always said I must've inherited my mad, blond hair

from him because no one else in the family had locks like mine. I spent my childhood staring whenever I saw a bushy-haired man, looking for other similarities between us and trying to work up the courage to ask him if he was my father, but I never did.

To this day, the sight of Samantha and Euan turned me back into that same girl they tortured mercilessly, and they hadn't evolved much further themselves. The last time they had been to Langley Hall, they had made unnecessary trips to the house together, asking to use the toilet, asking for glasses of water, insisting on coming in to pour it themselves. Turning up as and when they felt like it because I had to make allowances for their medical condition—they both had the same one. Talking about how "it's alright for some" and "there's no justice." We all knew they meant more by that than the fact that I lived in Langley Hall.

There were smirks and looks exchanged, loud laughter whenever I walked away. I tried to tell myself they were just jealous. True, I had my health, while they had their medication, but there is only so far that sentiment can take you.

"I thought we might try a different company this time," I had said to James when he first raised the issue of the survey.

But he said, "Shop local," and that was the end of the discussion.

I shouldn't be made to feel uncomfortable in my own home—aside from when James was there—so I put the matter on hold until I devised a strategy to make myself comfortable when they were around. To date, no such strategy had presented itself.

As a stopgap, I went down to the mausoleum and I gave the walls a good shove myself. I leaned on them with my full weight and I kicked the corners. I wandered among the trees along the riverbank until I found a good, sturdy branch. I took it back to the mausoleum and whacked the walls with it. I ran at the door with it, like a battering ram. Nothing moved, not so much as a pebble fell, not even a little bit of crumbling.

So it seemed rock solid to me, and I told James the surveyors had been and they had said it was fine and they would send their report in due course. That, I felt, deferred the problem for another five years, by which point, hopefully, James would be in there himself. For now, I just had to wait for him to forget about the report.

I put it to the back of my mind as I returned to Project Kill Your Husband, looking through cupboards and drawers for innocuous household items that would suddenly present themselves as the perfect murder weapon, knowing that out in the countryside beyond there was a plethora of toxic plants. If only he would let me cook for him properly.

# CHAPTER TWO

"HOW MUCH?" JAMES SAID, AS I POURED MYSELF A BOWL OF CORN-flakes. "A serving is thirty grams."

He put the kitchen scales down in front of me, but I didn't use them; I already knew what thirty grams looked like. It was a tiny bite of breakfast.

I put a few back in the packet.

"Now you've had your fingers all over them," he said. Well, I was the only person who ate them. He watched closely as I poured the milk, lest I got greedy with that as well.

"Don't forget they're dropping off my dry cleaning today," he said, as he stuffed toast into his mouth and headed for the door. Before he left, he looked back at me. "You should get your glands checked," he said. "You're putting on weight like nobody's business."

For all the chips, nuggets, and fish fingers James shoveled down his neck, he hardly ever put on a pound; he was almost as thin as when we first met. The only signs of the passing of twenty years were a few gray hairs and a sightly receding hairline. Otherwise, he had the same smooth complexion, the same bright blue eyes, and the same pointy face, although more and more I was thinking he looked fox-like.

I didn't top my cornflakes up immediately after he'd gone. I'd fallen for that before, taking out forbidden snacks as soon as the door slammed, only for him to return minutes later and catch me, mid-Monster Munch.

He nearly tore the house apart looking for more. He ripped open the kitchen cupboards and cabinets, he yanked a drawer right out and cutlery scattered across the floor. Then he went into the lounge, where he pulled the door on the dresser so hard, he damaged the hinges.

"Where is it?" he shouted at me.

"There isn't any more," I whimpered.

"Tell the truth, Daisy!" he yelled.

"I am! Grocery delivery brought it by mistake and I didn't tell them."

He calmed down after that and collected his things to leave again. "I'm only doing it for your sake," he said, as he picked his keys up. "You know that, don't you? The doctor told you not to eat that stuff."

The doctor didn't say that as such. It was just a generalized comment about a balanced diet, many years ago, when it mattered.

So, before I indulged in more cornflakes, I watched from the window as he went to the garage, then drove away in his Audi. Then I ate them there, keeping an eye out in case he came back.

Later, I would eat a bag of Monster Munch—of course there was more! I had a hiding place that James knew nothing about.

As luck would have it, the dry cleaning arrived while I was still eating my forbidden flakes, only a few minutes after James left; he must have passed the van on the road. I carried it upstairs, but instead of hanging it in the wardrobe, I took it to my sewing room and sat down at the table there.

A lot of girls these days don't learn, or don't like, to sew. When I was growing up with my make-do-and-mend mother, I preferred foraging, which was another area of my mum's expertise. We'd spend long afternoons out in the fields and forest, picking bits and pieces to augment our meals with. I could confidently eat my way through a British hedgerow.

But I didn't like sewing: learning to attach a button, darn a hole, outfit your secondhand Sindys with garments made from outgrown clothes that were already hand-me-downs themselves. And have your playmates recognize their own discarded apparel on my secondhand Sindy dolls.

Sometimes people would bring us material that would otherwise have been thrown away. They'd hand it to my mum saying, "I know you work miracles with fabric, Lorna, so I thought you might like this." It saved them the trip to get rid of it.

If my mother resented being used as the local recycling center, she never said so, not even the time it led to a flea infestation. She'd bring whatever they had donated into the house, hold it up to the light, and say, "Now, what shall we make with this, Daisy Daydream? A nice sun hat?"—to a particularly threadbare floral duvet set with little left of it. "A skirt?"—to a rich, flowing pair of russet curtains.

I hated to wear her homemade creations. I was once caught out in a pinafore, reincarnated as a waistcoat and skirt, and another time was spotted wearing next door's old curtains as a T-shirt and shorts combo.

But where I walked steeped in shame, my mother used to wear her creations with pride.

"In years ahead, Daisy," she'd say to me, "people will envy us for the riches we can make from a few old rags."

These days, now that I can walk into any shop and buy whatever I want, I enjoy sewing. It takes me back to evenings with my mum, cutting and stitching, pinning and patterning, chatting about school—mine or hers, we went to the same one—with Radio 2 in the background. After she died, I started wearing the clothes we had made again; they reminded me of her. Where before I only saw shame in wearing my schoolmates' castoffs, now I appreciated the skill that went into repurposing them.

People wondered if I might leave the village after my mum died. I was generally ostracized there, due to an incident some years before, but I meant to go on living in the place I was born and raised in and where my ancestors, for centuries before me, had lived. So, I stayed and I walked out in the clothes made of their own discarded items and I felt their eyes following me, and I felt hostility and I carried on.

Now, James hated me to wear anything that cost less than £1,000 in public. If a garment didn't have a designer label on it, if it hadn't been modeled by an A-list celebrity, if it didn't cost at least as much as some people's monthly income, it wasn't good enough for him. While I couldn't entirely avoid the designer clothes, I wreaked havoc with my accessories. As we headed out to a networking event, I'd often risk his wrath by draping myself in something he last saw protecting our privacy in a front-facing window. I liked to see how long it was until he noticed.

And I think every girl should learn to sew, not because I think every girl ought to be out wearing her neighbors' old bed linen, but because if you can't sew, how are you going to do this:

I carefully unpicked the seams on James's shirt. Then, with the precision of a master tailor, began to sew them back up, just a tiny bit tighter. I would enjoy seeing his discomfort later, as the material strained in all the wrong places and he tried to compensate for it by standing up straight and sucking his stomach in. Let's see which of us needs to get their glands checked.

I stitched away, daydreaming about my plans for James. When he shuffled off this mortal coil, it had to look like an accident. He is a lot bigger than me and I wouldn't be able to move the body, so I would have to raise the alarm and have the corpse taken away for me, no hard questions asked.

So hard was I concentrating, I nearly jumped out of my skin when the big bell, from the main door, rang. I opened a window and looked down into the driveway. Mrs. Billings was standing outside—it was gone ten o'clock!

"Cooee!" she shouted, waving up at me. "I forgot my key!"

James doesn't know I've given her a key and he wouldn't approve, but I'd known Mrs. Billings all my life and she had one to our old house in the village, for emergencies, so I gave her one when I moved here. It didn't seem right not to, and anyway, I thought it would be handy in case I was out when she came to clean. But, it transpired, I was never out.

"I'll be down now," I said. Then I scrambled for some clothes—shop-bought jeans and T-shirt for now—and ran down the grand staircase, across the regal entrance hall, passing the partial Elizabethan suit of armor and the family tree with just James's and my names at the top. It had replaced an ancient tree, started by the branch of the family that came before me, the Penneys.

Their names had cascaded down from the founding marriage in the fourteenth century, a long list of Richards, Eleanors, Edwards,

Catherines, Margarets, Mabels, Henrys, and the occasional Hugo, to the final Lord Ashbury, the last of the direct line, who died when I was at school.

When James installed the new family tree, he bought us our own coat of arms as well, from a company in Nevada. He had it carved and mounted above the front door, and that made me angry: my ancestors, who had built this beautiful house, obliterated and replaced with cheap rubbish.

I was a descendant, but I had no position or power over what happened to Langley Hall. I was from an illegitimate branch who never featured on the tree, in the history books, or at the time of the wealth distribution. I had no claim on the house.

For centuries, Langley Hall, situated just outside the village of Upper Iffley, had been the jewel of the West Country, standing in the middle of its estate, deer grazing on the grounds in front.

Upper Iffley sits on the River Iver, about fifteen minutes' drive from the town of Tippington, or forty if you're on the bus, and around an hour from Bristol. It's an old, old village, with an entry in the Domesday Book, alongside Lower Iffley, which was deserted during the plague in the fourteenth century so that only Upper Iffley remains.

In the center is a village green with a duck pond. The church, the pub, and the village shops are huddled around it. The streets leading haphazardly away from the green are rows of thatched cottages, one of which I grew up in. Farther out are houses made from stone, with slated roofs, then brick with tiled roofs, becoming progressively more modern, until you reach the new estate on the outskirts of the village. The people living there are considered foreigners by us locals, but it is still a small village—you can walk the entire perimeter in about half an hour.

If you take the road out of Upper Iffley toward Tippington, a ten-minute stroll will bring you to edge of the Langley Hall estate. From there you can stand on the pavement opposite and admire the crenelated walls and turret of the house, which make it look like a castle from a distance.

The original house was built in the fifteenth century, but all that remained of that were the walls of the great hall, which was now the entrance hall. Subsequent generations had added to it, and it rose up and sprawled out, so that there were arched cloisters around the ground floor and more windows than I could count on the upper floors.

"Our ancestors lived there, Daisy," my mum would say to me. "That's why our surname's Langley, after the hall."

It gave me a fascination with the house. Time after time I went to the mobile library that came to the village on Wednesdays and borrowed a book called *The Story of Langley Hall*, along with *The Ghosts of Langley Hall*, both out of print now. I read about all the former residents, wondering which I was descended from. When the books were withdrawn, Mrs. Harris, the librarian, gave them to me, tattered though they were.

After Lord Ashbury, the last lord of the manor, died, it was inherited by a very distant relative in Australia. He didn't fancy swapping Helios for heritage and promptly put it on the market, where it stayed for years, neglected and unloved. A storm broke the windows and they weren't repaired. Tiles slipped from the roof and weren't replaced. The turret began to crumble. The house became somewhere local teenagers dared each other to visit at Halloween. Then James arrived, incredibly rich and looking for a home in the country and a wife with which to found a dynasty. He made a start at restoring it, and all the windows at least had glass now.

When he found me, of noble blood but impoverished, it seemed like a perfect combination, like days of yore when up-and-coming bourgeoisie would marry aristocrats who were on the way down, combining wealth with lineage. But there was more work than he anticipated. Progress stalled and his plans came to nothing. From time to time we still had to chase teenagers away.

And in the end, James didn't value old things; the fact of my ancestry meant less to him than I'd thought; he was only concerned with the future, and the original family tree was torn down and replaced with this barren shrub. There was space on it for a football team of children and generations ad infinitum, but try as we might in the early years of our marriage, children never came.

We went to the best fertility specialists money could buy. James passed his tests with flying colors, while I was poked and prodded and monitored and injected, but children didn't come. Heads were scratched and shoulders were shrugged. I was taken on a luxury holiday, to see if something as simple as rest and relaxation would help, but still, children didn't come.

Eventually, we realized we were throwing good money after bad, and I had failed in my purpose to continue the family line. The tree remained blank, the paper yellowing and curling at the edges. We stopped talking about it, then we stopped talking about anything. James went out every morning and I stayed in. Langley Hall and Mrs. Billings became my world.

As the years went by, James saw the last chance of a new line disappear and began to tighten the purse strings and create all sorts of rules. I'd outlived my usefulness and failed to perform. We began to sleep in separate rooms. He started monitoring the bank accounts to see what I was spending money on, and he halved my allowance. He began watching what I ate, which had the effect of making me want to eat more and more. He canceled my TV subscriptions so that all I could watch was basic TV or the shows I already owned on DVD, mostly whodunits.

Mrs. B knocked on the front door again. "Are you there, Lady Langley, love?" My name is not Lady Langley. It is Daisy Dixon, née Langley, and I live in Langley Hall, but Mrs. Billings won't be moved on the subject of how to address me. I reached the front door, and with some heaving and ho'ing, opened it.

Every Monday and Thursday, Mrs. Billings comes to clean the rooms James and I live in, while Mr. Billings keeps the garden in order. However, Mrs. Billings's days were flexible, she came and went largely as she pleased, and that week she had moved it to a Tuesday so that she and Mr. Billings could go to an agricultural show over on the other side of Bristol on the Monday.

Every spring, contractors come to clean the chandeliers in the ballroom, in which James takes a particular pride, although we haven't used it for years. The rest is left to fend for itself, other than the odd day, aforementioned, when I come over all domesticated.

Mrs. B entered, unraveling her headscarf and heading for the kitchen. "Everything alright?" Her curly gray hair sprang out and she looked around her, as if seeing the house for the first time. She was small and slight, her eyes were hazel, her nose was long, and with her head always forward from her shoulders, it sometimes made her look as if she were sniffing her way around.

"Fine thanks, just lost track of time," I said, and I followed her to the old kitchen, a big room on the ground floor where, in days gone by, they served up elaborate banquets for the English aristocracy. Apparently the Duke of Wellington had once visited. Now, with a working sink, kettle, fridge, cooker, and microwave, it was primarily used by Mr. and Mrs. Billings and saw the preparation of tea and biscuits, or the occasional Cup-a-Soup. The kitchen James and I used was a small modern affair on the first floor adjacent to our lounge.

"I suppose you'll want me to get straight on?" Mrs. Billings said, looking at the kettle. "Thing is, I can't stop to make the time up; we've got Silver Surfers after this." Mr. and Mrs. Billings were midway through an adult education course teaching them how to make the most of the internet.

"No, that's fine." I filled the kettle, took two mugs from the mug tree, Miss Marple for her and *Death in Paradise* for me, and dropped a teabag into each one. "You go when you have to. Leave the vacuuming if you don't have time."

I poured hot water over the tea bags, and Mrs. Billings took a packet of ginger nuts out of her bag.

"My turn, isn't it?" I said and she nodded, unpacking crisps and chocolate as well. Her handbag was huge, more like an overnight bag—all the better for hiding things in. I took my phone out of my pocket and transferred £10 to her account under the reference "Bits and Bobbins" so that James thought it was sewing supplies when he checked. It was more than the snacks had cost, but the difference was never remarked on and I could afford it.

James gave me an allowance of £250 every month, which may sound like a pittance against the tens of thousands he was earning and was less than it used to be, but all I had to spend it on was sewing supplies, contraband treats, and knickknacks that Mrs. Billing pilfered from us on a weekly basis. Everything else was paid for me.

"I don't know why you have to be so cloak-and-dagger about it," Mrs. Billings said, as I took possession of the biscuits. "You're a grown woman. You should just say 'I choose what I eat and I choose to eat ginger nuts.' Or Bourbons or Jammie Dodgers or whatever."

I nodded and "Hmm'd" vaguely. Mrs. B wasn't fully aware of the subtle nuances of James's and my relationship.

We sat at the old refectory table. Mrs. Billings took a small container of sugar out of her bag and spooned some into her drink. The previous year, the contractors cleaning the chandeliers had angered me and I'd swapped the sugar for salt. Unfortunately, I forgot to swap it back after they'd gone and the next day Mrs. Billings became unintended collateral. She would never forget the lessons of last year's spring clean.

Next, she pulled out a carton of milk, broke the seal, and poured for both of us. That was the legacy of a much earlier faux pas.

We'd hardly started on our drinks when the back door opened and Mr. Billings entered. He stood on the mat and pulled one of his boots off.

"Sole's coming away from the upper, Brenda. It's letting water in," he said to Mrs. B. She rose from the table and went to have a look at it.

"That's done for," she said. "You'll need a new pair. That's going to cost."

Mr. B sighed heavily and I wondered if it would help if I offered him some overtime.

"Got a pair of old trainers in the van," he said to Mrs. B. "That'll do for now. Keep me feet dry at least." And he marched off to his van, in one boot and one sock, which must have been soaking within a few paces. He returned a minute later with his trainers and an old Tesco carrier bag, the flimsy plastic type we used before bags for life were common. He put the old boots in the carrier and changed into his trainers. Then he shuffled back into the garden, leaving the boots in the bag by the door, the "danger of suffocation" warning staring me in the face.

I thought about holding it over James's head and watching as his breaths grew smaller, until he breathed no more. But I'm not a total fantasist; James would have no trouble at all in reaching up and lifting me off before I did any damage. He wouldn't miss more than a breath. I'd need to get him really drunk first or drug him with something, but James rarely drank in the house and if I had something to drug him with, I'd have done it long ago.

"One day our ship will come in," Mrs. B said, as she watched Mr. B cross the lawn. "I have no doubt about that."

Mr. and Mrs. Billings had a nest egg she sometimes alluded to, and one day soon it was going to allow them to retire in comfort. But until then they were slaves to James's dime. "Penny for your thoughts, Lady Langley, love?" she asked, turning back to me as I stared at the bag.

"I was just thinking about another biscuit," I said.

"You dig in." She pushed the packet toward me. "There's not a scrap on you," she said, which wasn't strictly true. She continued on a different subject, one I didn't really like. "I saw the Newmans in the King's Head the other day. They're not happy about the farm—they're going to see about taking legal advice."

The Newmans were tenant farmers on the farm on the west side of our estate. They'd been there for generations, and no one could imagine the farm as anything else. No one except James, that was, and a company that wanted to build warehouses on the fields, which for hundreds of years had grown barley or wheat or corn or grazed sheep. They had made an offer to buy the land. The Newmans had made a counteroffer, but they couldn't match the warehouse people, and the fact that those fields are the first thing you see of Upper Iffley, as you approach it from Tippington, didn't sway James.

"No farms, no food," Mr. Newman had said when he came to discuss it.

"No warehouses, no internet shopping," James replied. "We can manage without one farm." Then he slammed the door in Mr. N's face. And there things stood between us and the Newmans. Secretly, I agreed entirely with the Newmans, but business is business and money is money, and as things stood, everything was James's.

When the tea had been drunk, the supply of biscuits dented, and the village gossip imparted, Mrs. Billings rose stiffly from her chair and said, "Anyway, Lady Langley, better show willing," then she shuffled up the stairs to the rooms on the first and second floors that James and I used as living quarters.

While she cleaned, I shut myself in my sewing room and finished the seams on James's shirt, which took me up to Mrs. B's finishing time. When she had gone, I had a rummage through the drawers to see what she had taken.

Mrs. Billings is a kleptomaniac. I usually put something out for her to pinch; I have a collection of cheap knickknacks that I buy especially for this purpose. It usually satisfies her light fingers and keeps her away from the priceless antiques. Usually, but not always; I once found a figurine of a shepherdess with a lamb and a basket of flowers that was supposed to sit on the ledge that ran along the landing of our second floor in a charity shop in town, priced up at a fiver.

But sometimes I forgot to leave an offering and I had to go looking to see what she took. Just a corkscrew this time, no big deal. We had five—four now. I put a new one on the shopping list in case James noticed.

Then it was time for lunch, and *Bargain Hunt*, after which I returned to my sewing and took James's trousers in slightly at the waist; I resisted the temptation to take one of the legs up. The secret to successful trickery is not to overplay your hand: You only have to go a little bit too far to give yourself away.

I left it there for the time being. I still had the jacket to do and that, with its lining, was a more difficult job. But he wouldn't be wearing it until the next day. I would come to it fresh in the morning.

After that, I spent some time on the other project I had on the go: I was making myself a cocktail dress from a selection of frocks I had found in local charity shops. I had a small bet with myself that I would blend the different colors and fabrics together so well, James would never know I had made it with my own hand. Although half the fun was seeing his face at the moment he realized.

Then I was tired. By my standards it had been a busy morning, and for now death was beckoning in the form of another murder mystery. It had been quite some time since I'd bothered the little gray cells of Hercule Poirot, and there was a whole series where I couldn't remember whodunit.

# CHAPTER THREE

ON WEDNESDAY MORNING I WOKE TO THE SOUND OF JAMES SLAMming around in the lounge and smiled, knowing he was looking for his keys, which I had hidden behind the stereo cabinet.

"Daisy, help me look," he shouted and seconds later we were both marching around the flat, upending cushions, peering behind cases and stands, which is quite a boring activity when you know the object you're looking for isn't there, although I did find a scrunchie that had gone missing a year or so before.

Later, when he got home that night, he would find the keys in a jacket pocket, which he could have *sworn* he'd looked in.

Eventually, he went to the small cupboard that housed the keys for his classic cars, along with a spare for the garage.

"I haven't got my house keys," he shouted as he left. "Make sure you're in when I get back." I would be. "And don't forget we have to be out by eight tonight!" was his parting shot as he raced out of the front door. We had one of his networking events that night. "And you need to look like you're married to a successful fucking businessman. At least shave your fucking legs."

The door slammed shut, then opened again. "And make sure you're wearing something that was bought in a shop!" The door slammed once more and he was gone.

I pulled the bed foward and added another line to my tally of days. Like any good prisoner, I kept a countdown to the day I could be set free. I'm twenty years into this marriage, but I didn't start the tally until after the first decade; it took me some time to fully fathom my situation. I have to wait for the end of my sentence because we have a prenup.

When James first mooted the idea of a prenuptial agreement, not long after we got engaged, I found it rather hurtful, as if he thought I was in it for the money.

But he said, "It's for both of our benefits. So that if the worst happens—and I'm sure it won't—we both know what to expect and it can all be dealt with without acrimony. We'll have children by then; it would be good for them if everything went smoothly. It's like insurance: It's there in case the worst happens, but it's usually a waste of money."

I still wasn't keen—it felt like admitting defeat before we'd even started—but I took his point about the insurance and I was excited about children, so I agreed to it.

When I told Mrs. Billings what we were doing, she suggested I have my own solicitor go through it, instead of relying on James's.

"It's not that Lord James would do you wrong," she said, "but those solicitors can be sly foxes. They could stitch you up good and proper, and there'd be nothing either of you could do about it."

I didn't have money for my own solicitor. By then I'd moved into Langley Hall and sold my mum's house, and all the money from the sale was tied up in James's cryptocurrency. I didn't want to ask James to pay—it would make it sound as if I didn't trust him—but Mrs. B was very set against me signing it without advice.

"I told Lorna I'd keep an eye out for you," she kept saying of my mum; Mrs. B lived across the road from us when I was growing up, and she and my mum had been friends for as long as I could remember. In the end she persuaded a lawyer who lived in one of the new houses on the outskirts of the village to look at it for free.

He read it over and he didn't think it was nearly as good as James's lawyer had thought. He sent him an email.

"This document gives everything to Mr. Dixon from the beginning to the middle to the end. It leaves Miss Langley in an unfair position and treats her as no more than a lodger."

My blood ran a little bit cold when I read that. It felt critical of James himself, and I hoped this could be sorted out between solicitors without him seeing it.

My solicitor continued and asked for various changes, including a clause that if at any time I chose to leave, I would get at least the market value of my mum's house at that time.

James's lawyer rejected all of them except one I had asked for, whereby I could choose the decor when the bedrooms were renovated.

In particular, they objected to the idea of giving me the market value of my house.

James's lawyer said that would be unfair to James because if he had to provide me with that amount from the investment, it could be at a time at which the value was low and he would have to make up the difference. Plus, why would he give the market value? I could wait until property values were high, then jump in and make a killing; it would be like signing a blank check.

I didn't like that either; it made me sound like a gold digger.

Then my lawyer said, "He's meant to be a billionaire, for god's sake! Why is he quibbling over a few thousand?"

And this went back and forth for a while, until James's solicitor said they could write in the clause about the house, but for the amount I sold it for, not the market value, and only after twenty-five years of marriage, take it or leave it. Of course, I could cash my investment in at any time, but I may get back less than I invested if I did that too soon. Although that was not what I remembered James saying to me when he took my money.

Next, my lawyer gave me some advice.

"If I were you," he said, "I'd walk away from the whole thing. Run, actually, don't walk."

But I was young, I was in love, and I wanted to get married. Plus, I had no money and nowhere else to live. And anyway, we were going to start a family. The terms became much more favorable then.

So, that was the length of my sentence, twenty-five years. At that point, if my investment was worth the same, or more, as my house, I would take that. If it was worth less, James would have to give me the amount I had sold the house for.

Tally done for another day, I made my way to my sewing room and set to work taking in James's jacket.

It took me well into the afternoon and my back was stiff by the time I finished, but it would be well worth it to see James later, standing up straight, sucking his stomach in, surreptitiously testing the give around his shoulders, which I had left as they were because I wanted him to think his stomach had expanded, not the rest of him.

He would eschew food and would look sheepishly at a glass of whiskey in the moment before he slugged it down.

Then I went for the required shower and grooming processes. It was especially important for me to look the part that night because this was a crowd James had been trying to get in with for a long time. Many of them would be from the far end of Somerset, almost Devon, and we didn't see them in this neck of the woods very often. James thought they were the gateway to an untapped seam of business from the South West and the south coast, if he could only pin them down long enough to get their investment.

Once washed and groomed, my flyaway hair straightened into submission, I opened my wardrobe and chose a dress. I went for a sleeveless gray silk creation; I knew James would approve, simply because it cost nearly two grand and I'd never worn it before. It was rather tighter than it had been when I first bought it; I should've let it out when I was taking James's suit in.

Finally, hair and makeup complete and a suitably expensive pair of earrings in place, I added the finishing touch: a delicate gray-blue scarf, made from a tablecloth I found in a cupboard here when I first moved in.

"Love your scarf!" I imagined the other women saying. "Who's it by?"

And James would try to control his apoplexy as I smiled sweetly and said, "Daisy at Dunelm Mill."

James was later home than he had planned to be after work, which was all the better for me. It meant he would take the first shirt he was handed and wouldn't swap them if he didn't like the fit.

"Your shirt's gaping," I said to him as we were about to leave, admiring the way the buttons were straining. James stood up straighter, breathed in, and pulled his jacket around his middle, struggling to bring both sides together. I might have gone a bit too far with that.

He stared at me and held the car keys out. "You're driving."

I knew it was coming, but I still felt the pang of a woman condemned to a long evening of small talk and mineral water.

"Why don't we get a taxi?" I asked. But the one and only village taxi driver finished for the day around seven o'clock, and to wait for one from town took so long you could usually have walked more quickly.

"Sorry, darling." James shrugged, but he wasn't sorry at all.

We drove with a retro station on the radio. James was engrossed with his phone, so he didn't comment on my choice of music, but as we reached the outskirts of town he put it away and looked at me.

"I'm really concerned about your weight," he said.

"I can go and get some tests," I said. "For my glands." A trip to the doctor's would at least be a trip out of the house.

"I think there's more we can do ourselves first," he said. "We can have a look at some lifestyle tweaks to see if there's anything you could be doing differently."

Come to think of it, it wouldn't do me any harm to go for a walk now and then, I could live with that, but James continued.

"I'm going to get some cameras set up around the house, to see what you're doing, and maybe we can get to the bottom of what's causing you to put on so much weight."

"You're going to watch me in the house?"

"I'm just going to keep an eye on things. I'm sure there's a simple explanation for your weight gain, and once we know what it is we can deal with it."

Yes, there was a simple explanation and that was the problem. Not only would he find out about the snacks, but he would find out about Mrs. B's stealing, and it would be the end of her employment.

"You're putting cameras in all the rooms?" I asked.

"All the ones you use, to start with."

And if I started using other rooms, those as well, no doubt.

"But you'll be able to see what I'm doing all day," I said.

"You're not doing anything you wouldn't want me to see, are you?" he asked. "You know I'm only doing it for you. For your health."

I looked at the scene in front of me: houses, lampposts, garden walls. There was nothing I could drive the car into that would reliably kill James and leave me unharmed. I continued driving safely down the road; we would both reach our destination in one piece.

The truth was, I was never going to kill him. I loved to daydream about it, but in reality, I didn't dare. I would get caught and spend the rest of my life in prison, of that there was no doubt. If I wanted to be out of this marriage, I would have to leave.

Before it had felt like failure to leave with nothing, no fortune, no children, no house, no money, but right there and then, it suddenly felt like freedom. Faced with having my every move monitored, none of it mattered. I was ready to leave. And I still had the cryptocurrency to come in the future; I only had to manage for a decade or two. It seemed easy in that moment. By the time we got to the party, I was riding high on the joy of a good decision well made.

The venue was a house on the nice estate on the outskirts of town, where all the properties were set far back from the road, with drives you could turn a lorry around on, mature trees hiding the house from public view, and large gardens stretching back to the fields beyond. The houses weren't on the scale of ours, but they were better maintained, every room was usable, none had damp patches spreading across the ceiling or hundred-year-old wallpaper hanging off the walls.

I turned the car into the drive, packed with other cars, and circled around looking for a space, but it was already full. I turned the car to leave the drive and park in the street.

"You can get in there," James said, as he realized what I was doing.

I looked to where he was pointing. "It won't fit there," I said.

"There's loads of room, fold the mirrors in."

"If I have to fold the mirrors in, it's too small. How are we going to get out? With my enormous backside? I'd get stuck. They'd need to get a crane to hoist me."

"It would be a memorable night, though," James said.

We parked in the leafy avenue outside, James harping on all the time that there was plenty of space on the drive.

As we approached the house, I could see exactly what kind of party we were getting ourselves into. People stood stiffly against the walls in formal dresses and penguin suits, holding drinks to their chests, hardly moving as waiting staff offered canapés and more drinks. This wasn't the kind of do where people had a drink and a boogie, it was a networking event, where business people guffawed loudly at jokes that weren't funny and swapped business cards while their spouses and partners loitered until they could go home.

We rang the doorbell and waited until a suited gentleman let us in and herded us into the chamber of doom, where no music played and little was said.

But it was early. Whiskey, port, cognac, prosecco, and wine flowed. Someone asked for a schooner of sherry and caused quite a kerfuffle; a bottle of Harvey's Bristol Cream was eventually pulled out from the depths of a cupboard and dusted off.

"Mineral water, please," I said when my turn came.

"Still or sparkling?"

"Sparkling." After all, this was a party.

When I turned round with my drink, James had vanished, leaving me standing on my own. I looked around, wondering if there was anyone there I knew from the village and if that would be a good thing or a bad thing, but the people here were all new to me.

"Are you Mrs. James?" A tall, stocky woman with a 1980s backcomb and a home counties accent appeared beside me, a bottle of wine tucked under her arm, a glass of the stuff in one hand and a bottle of water in the other. "Are you James Dixon's wife?" she clarified, and I nodded.

"I'm Margery, your charming hostess."

I smiled. "Lovely to meet you. Yes, I am Mrs. James: Daisy."

"Drink?" she asked, tipping her head at the wine bottle tucked under her arm.

I shook my head. "Thank you, but I'm driving."

"Can't you get a taxi?" she asked, then seemed to think again. "Oh no, unless you booked it six months ago, I suppose you probably can't. Maybe just a little one?" She nodded at the wine bottle again. "It's going to be an awfully long night without."

Regretfully, I shook my head. "I'd rather not risk it."

"Well, if you're ready to meet the other wives sober…" she said and pushed me toward one of the groups of women. "Ladies!" she chirped. "This is Daisy."

"Hello, Daisy," one of the women said. She was perfectly, expensively, designed; not a cell in her body looked natural.

"Daisy is married to James Dixon, our cryptocurrency entrepreneur," Margery said, and this aroused some interest among them.

"Do you mine for cryptocurrency yourself, Daisy?" another expensive-looking woman asked.

"Are you a billionaire as well?"

"Can you teach us how to do it?"

"My husband put £600,000 into your husband's cryptocurrency empire. When are we going to see it back? I thought it was meant to grow like billy-o."

I laughed nervously. "I leave all that to James."

"But how do you get money out?" she asked. "My husband wanted to make a withdrawal, and he was told he had to leave it."

"You have to leave it quite some time," I said, happy to have been asked a question I knew the answer to. "Think of it more like a pension plan."

"That's not what he said when we put the money in," she said.

"I think he's updating his blurb, to make it clearer."

"What do you do all day if you're not involved in the business?" the first wife asked. "Do you have a job?"

"No," I said.

"Are you on any committees?"

"No."

"Do you have children?"

"No," I said.

"We're looking for someone to help with the Fun Run, contacting the council about road closures and so on. Is that something you could do?"

That sounded well beyond my organizational capabilities. I couldn't imagine myself contacting people and making arrangements for things that were actually going to happen. I think I visibly quaked.

I'd had enough. I'd been briefly buoyed up by the knowledge that within twenty-four hours, I would have left all this behind me, but now flight was starting to win the fight or flight dilemma. "Where is the toilet?" I asked.

Margery gave me directions and I stayed there, looking at sewing patterns on my phone to while away the evening. I even had time to look at a few crochet designs—I still had the needles from a failed project in years gone by, and I had ideas about trying again—before someone hammered on the door, shouting, "Are you going to be much longer?"

Reluctantly, I left the bathroom and went in search of more water, which I found in a neighboring room, where a stash of drinks and nibbles were set out on tables waiting to be dispensed to the guests.

I peered at a platter of canapés. There were no labels to tell you what they were, and I was wary. I looked around for a wrapper. There was a pile of the Lidl packets that they had apparently come in and little flags with descriptions written on attached to cocktail sticks nearby, but they were all in a heap.

I tasted a canapé. It was something fresh and fruity, watermelon. I tasted another. That might have been fish; I ate two. I tried a different one and ran out of luck: beetroot! Gagging, I looked around for somewhere to spit it out.

"Ah, so you've found Aladdin's cave!" a man's voice boomed behind me, and I turned to see a portly man with white hair and a red face, probably older than sixty but younger than eighty, at the door. He looked familiar, but I couldn't place him. Maybe we were related and I was seeing myself in him. It had been a long time since I'd looked at an older man and wondered if he was my dad, but I peered at him as he scanned the plates on the table, trying to spot a likeness, until he turned to face me and I was forced to swallow the beetroot down.

"Aladdin's cave?" I asked.

"You've found the treasure!" I still didn't get it. "You've found where they're stashing the food. I knew there must be more than that piffling little morsel they brought round." He picked up a wrapper. "Lidl's are the best. Margery always knows where to shop."

In contrast, James would have a fit if he knew he was eating Lidl canapés; he probably thought they were all handmade that morning by Margery's personal chef. The man reached for one.

"That's beetroot," I said, just before he touched it.

He recoiled. "Horrible."

"Watermelon," I told him, pointing at the first one I'd tasted.

He took three and wandered over to the drinks, where he poured himself a generous slosh of vodka and mixed in some Coke. He waved the bottles at me.

"No thanks," I said.

"Something else? What's your poison?" he asked, swapping the vodka and Coke for bottles of wine, one red, one white.

I shook my head again. "I'm driving."

"Oh, a wee one won't hurt," he said.

"That's what Margery said," I told him.

"Margery knows what she's talking about." He waved the bottle of white dangerously close to my glass, which was empty by then. "I won't tell if you don't. You can't be expected to get through a night like this without a drink."

That was also pretty much what Margery had said.

"Here, have a few of these." He began piling canapés up on a plate. "And one of these." He tipped white wine into a glass. "You'll feel much better with a full stomach and a decent drink. As long as you stay within the limits." He took my empty glass and shoved the food and drink at me. I took them from him.

I hadn't thought I needed to feel better, or rather, I knew I would feel better when I was on my way home, but I thought I would just have to wait for that moment to arrive. Yet as soon as I stuffed a canapé with some kind of paste in it into my mouth, to my surprise, I did feel better. At least, I felt like the man was giving me permission to eat, when James would have said the four I'd already had were four more than enough.

I ate the whole plateful.

"Who are you here with, then?" the man asked as he chose the next canapé. "You're not with that yuppie-type, are you? The whipper-snapper in the dinner jacket?"

"All the men here are in dinner jackets."

"The one with the virtual money. The cryptocurrency. Right piece of work he is."

"Yes, I'm with him," I said.

"Don't you get involved in that cyber money."

It was a bit late for that.

The man nodded at the glass in my hand. The wine was still untouched, but after all that food, a mouthful wasn't going to hurt. A mouthful mind, not a whole glass. So I took a mouthful, but a mouthful isn't much and it's true you can have a drink when you drive, within the limits; that is the law.

So I finished the glass and it was chilled and delicious and the man had been right, I did feel better, but I shook my head when he refilled it and I put the glass down on the table.

"You'll be fine," he said. "Let your hair down. Most people here are having a miserable time."

It was nice to know no one here was enjoying themselves, but even so, I told him no thank you. Instead, I fetched a fresh glass and filled it with water.

I wanted to ask him about James—most people thought James was wonderful—but I was stopped in my tracks by a banshee howl.

I jumped a mile in the air and looked around to see who was being killed or where the monster was attacking from, but the man calmly put his hand in his pocket and took out his phone. The noise was his ringtone. "Better take this," he said, and he left as my heart rate began to return to normal.

He was gone for now, but I resolved to find him later and ask him more about James. Maybe he'd like to join me in plotting murder.

I'd had enough of canapés, and I couldn't stay in that room all evening. I prepared myself to go back into the fray, but who would I speak to? What would I say? How much longer did we have to stay here? The night seemed discouragingly young.

"Oh, there you are!" Margery was at the door. "Do come through, Lennie's about to make a speech."

"Well, I wouldn't want to miss that," I said, whoever Lennie was.

Margery vanished and I eyed the glass of wine I had declined. Nobody would know. But I walked away.

Lennie, it transpired, was the man I had just met in the refreshments room and what he had to tell us about—at length—was that he had been leading a campaign to raise funds for a nearby hospice, and they had finally reached their target. He pulled one of those enormous checks out from behind a screen and handed it over to one of the other guests. There was much applause, although it was for just over £1million, an amount that most of the people there could have handed over without a second thought.

With the presentation over, everyone, except me, arranged themselves into groups: huddles of business men and women and separate cliques of their partners arranged in some kind of hierarchy I couldn't decipher and couldn't penetrate. I roamed from group to group, looking for my tribe, but no one paused in their conversation and said, "Oh, hello, Daisy, come and join us." No one moved to let me in.

James was in the center of a group of middle-aged men, laughing and speaking with loud voices; they were all holding their wrists out, comparing watches.

"Nearly two hundred thousand," I heard James saying.

"Two hundred and fifty," the man next to him said, rotating his wrist so everyone could get a good look.

"Four hundred," said a third, and I put a curse on him: *May your watch always run five minutes late.*

Clearly that group wasn't where I was meant to be; my watch was worth just under a grand. I stood alone in the middle of the room, ignored by everyone except the waiting staff, who had to walk around me. I was uncomfortable, I was nervous, I was wondering how I was going to get to the end of the evening.

It takes approximately an hour to process one unit of alcohol. It must have been at least an hour since I had that drink. At least. I made my way back to the room, where the food had been taken away, but the drink I had declined was still on the table. I glugged it down, but it wasn't cold anymore, so I tipped a splash in from the bottle in the chiller, just a taste, so I could have the memory of that first glass.

My head was still as clear as day, but I didn't feel better, the way I should have done. I looked at the bottle of wine again, just one last gulp? I tipped the neck toward my glass, but then, no, maybe I needed more food, that was a better idea. I went to look for some.

As I turned to leave the room, I saw James in the doorway, watching me. He walked away.

I headed back out into the party, but the only food remaining was scraps. So I returned to wandering around, lingering on the fringes of various groups, hoping someone would let me join them. Ignored, I went to wait in the toilet again, until, at last, just before midnight, James was banging on the door. His work here was done.

"Let's go," he said, marching past me, tugging at the buttons on his shirt. "How much have you had to drink?"

"Not much," I said, but on reflection, I didn't think it would be a good idea for me to be in charge of a car. I was pretty sure I was within legal limits, but I didn't usually drink anything if I was going to drive and I wasn't confident about doing so. I couldn't tell him that, though. Instead I said, "I'm really tired; can you drive?"

"No, I've had half a bottle of whiskey. Is that glass all you had? Can you touch your nose?"

Well, of course I could.

"Can you walk in a straight line?"

I could.

"There you go, then. We're not going far."

He started walking toward the front door and I followed, taking my phone out of my bag. James would not be happy if I suggested phoning a taxi, but if one was already on the way, he might agree to wait. If… There was never a taxi available if you hadn't booked it decades in advance, but it was worth a try.

I dialed Rich from the village, who was known professionally as Upper Iffley Private Hire, but predictably, he had finished for the night and it went straight to voicemail.

Then I called the taxi service from town, who answered but told me, "Sorry, we've got nothing all night. We start again at six in the morning."

James was not going to go for that.

"Daisy!" he called from the drive, and I hurried after him.

"Is there anyone here from Upper Iffley who could give us a lift?" I asked.

He looked around at people emerging from the house. I was born and bred in the village. I knew all the residents, except a few in the new-build houses, and I was confident there was no one.

"Someone driving past Langley Hall?" I asked. "They could drop us off."

"Do you want to ask them?"

I didn't really, but I turned to approach the nearest couple. James grabbed my arm.

"Don't," he said. "We're not begging for lifts in the middle of the night because my wife can't stay away from the bottle. You can walk straight, you're talking normally, just be careful."

The fresh air did me good, and I felt clearheaded by the time we reached the car. I had a bit of a wobble at the end of the drive, but that was because my stiletto heels were unbalancing me. I was especially glad now that I hadn't parked in the tiny space James wanted me to maneuver into when we arrived.

As I started the car, the radio blasted out. James had ignored it on the way there, but now, as we pulled away from the curb with the sound of KC and the Sunshine Band filling the air, he leaned forward and switched it off.

"I was listening to that," I said, turning it back on. I hate to drive in silence.

He turned it off. "No, you weren't."

I turned it back on. "It helps me concentrate."

He turned it off again.

I turned it on.

Off. On. Off. On. Off.

I gave up and began to drive, at a funereally slow pace, away from the house.

"Pick up the speed," James said. "Nothing looks more suspicious than driving like a learner."

So I drove slightly faster and we got out of town with no incidents. I began to feel happier; I was on the way to my bed and in the morning, my freedom.

Annoyingly, there were overnight roadworks blocking our route home, so we had to take a detour through Great Beadington, our neighboring village, but eventually we came to the other side of that wretched backwater and were heading toward Upper Iffley. I felt relief flooding through me, just a few more minutes and we'd be safe. There was just one final obstacle: This road was haunted.

"If you pull the visor down and look in the mirror, you'll see the ghost of a monk in the back seat," I said. "Half the village has seen it." I do love a ghost story.

"There's no such thing as ghosts, Daisy. Half the village hasn't seen it."

"Have a look if you're so sure. There used to be a small monastery here. It was closed down by King Henry VIII and his crew." That much was true. "The monk tried to stop them taking all the gold and silver and was hacked to death in front of the altar. Now he appears to travelers on this road, haunting the back of their cars, wanting their jewelry and watches. The more expensive the better."

I saw James glance surreptitiously down at his watch. I looked up to the rearview mirror and gasped.

James's head twitched toward the back seat, but he remembered himself in time. "Stop messing about," he said.

"Have a look then. Do it and prove me a fool if you're sure."

"For god's sake."

He pulled the visor down and yelled as something small and hairy, with many legs, fell out into his lap. The shout made me jump; I turned my head and accidentally accelerated when I should have watched where I was going and braked.

There was a heavy thud, and we lost some velocity. The steering was wrenched out of my control, and the car started to slide this way and that. I had a glimpse of something flying up into the windshield as the airbag blew up in my face.

# CHAPTER FOUR

THE CAR JUDDERED AND SLOWED BEFORE IT STOPPED COMPLETELY.

I held my hands up in front of me; they were shaking. I stared at them, half expecting to see blood.

"Clutch," James said, pulling the handbrake up.

"What?"

"Put the clutch down."

I looked at him, then at the floor for a moment, confused. Then, "It's down," I said. The clutch and the brake were still pressed as far down as they would go from my belated emergency stop. James took the car out of gear, and I let the pedals up. The airbag was already deflating and we sat for a moment in silence, looking at the cracks across the glass in front of us, radiating out from the central point of impact. A spider's web of cracks, you could say.

I stared at my hands, unable to stop the shaking. My breath was loud and uneven. James stared straight ahead, his face blank, his hands wedged between his legs.

"We killed a rabbit," I whispered.

"A rabbit?" James said. "That was a hundred times the size of a rabbit."

"A badger?" I suggested.

"It was too tall for a badger."

"A deer? Oh no."

The sign for deer crossing wasn't for another mile or so, but they could definitely be on the road here instead. A deer could easily have jumped out in front of us. "What if it's still alive and it's injured?" I asked. "What if it's got a fawn waiting for it?" It was the right time of year.

I wanted James to say, "I think it will be alright; we weren't going fast. I'm sure it will get up in a minute and run off with just a few bruises." But he didn't and we sat for a moment longer, until what James actually did say was:

"We'd better go and see what you've done."

I watched with dread as he opened his door and got out. As he exited, a toy spider lay harmlessly where he had sat.

James is scared of spiders. I used to find it endearing, now I just found it ridiculous. I'd put it there ages ago, for another occasion as auspicious as this one and then, for one reason or another, hadn't sprung my trap. I'd forgotten about it until the moment it fell from the visor.

My legs were wobbly as I made my way round to the front of the car. They nearly went from under me when I saw James crouched over a shape in the road. Fragments from the headlight cover lay around, shattered like glass, reflecting the glow of the uncovered lamp in a thousand tiny sparkles. The bumper hung loose, touching the ground. The shape had two legs and ears at the side of its head, and it was wearing clothes. It was a man. I screamed.

The man groaned.

"He's still alive!" I said, almost hysterical with the gladness of not having orphaned a fawn and the terror of having hit a human. "I'll call 999."

James held up his hand. "Great idea if you want to go to prison," he said. "They'll want to breathalyze you and you've been drinking."

"I only drank a bit. I was careful."

"You want to test that theory against a breathalyzer, do you? I saw you knocking back half a bottle."

"No, I didn't. We have to call an ambulance," I said, but I was nervous about a breathalyzer. I had been careful, I was sure, but my calculations weren't scientifically tested.

Maybe my panic would metabolize it more quickly and bring the reading down? Maybe they'd take that into account when they decided if I'd been safe to drive? Maybe, maybe, maybe.

"There's someone coming!" I yelped, as headlights appeared over the hill a mile or so away.

"Turn the lights off, then help me get him in the car," James said.

"What? We can't move him. You're not supposed to move injured people."

"Get him in the car. We'll take him to hospital." He grabbed the man's upper half, but I couldn't bring myself to move. "Daisy!" The headlights flashed again, and I grabbed the man's legs.

"Hush, hush," I said as he cried out in pain. "It will be alright. We'll get you to the hospital."

We turned our lights off and stuffed him in, then waited for the other car to appear at the top of the slope, my heart racing. But the car didn't materialize and a moment later, I saw the beams heading off to the right.

I exhaled. "They're going to Little Beadington." I pointed at the lights as they faded into the distance.

I heard James let out a "phew," then he made his way to the front of the car and pulled the bumper fully off. "Help me clear this up," he said.

Whoever would have thought that in a match between a human and a car, especially a high-end model, the car would have come off so badly? Together, we picked up the pieces of the smashed headlight. A satchel, presumably the man's, lay in the road as well. James picked it up and flung it at me.

"I'll drive," James said and made his way to the driver's seat.

I got in beside him, clutching the bag. After the flurry of activity, I found myself reacting to the shock; I felt cold and queasy. I heard the rasping breath of the man in the back seat. I looked up into the mirror—no monk—and then behind me at the man.

I shone the light from my phone on him to see if his eyes were open and realized his head was bleeding. I realized something else as well: The man was Lennie.

"Oh, Lennie," I said to him, biting back tears now. "I'm so sorry."

He grunted. I didn't know if he was replying to me or if he was just in pain.

"It was an accident," I said. "Really. We'll get you to a hospital and get you patched up. You'll be as good as new."

He stared at me; he looked unconvinced.

I tried to cheer him up. "I can help while you're in hospital. I can run errands. I could water your houseplants if you have any. Do you have a pet? I could feed it. I could walk a dog. I volunteer at the donkey sanctuary." I used to. I looked after a donkey who was also called Daisy, but she left to be a companion to a race horse and I never bonded with another donkey in the same way, so it petered out.

Lennie continued to stare at me, the blood trickling close to his eyes.

I remembered we had a cloth in the glove box for wiping the windshield with. I took it out and gave it to him to stanch the flow. He didn't seem to know what to do with the cloth, either that or—worse—he wasn't capable, so I had to twist myself round and hold it there for him.

"Would you like me to phone someone for you?" I asked.

"No, he would not," James butted in. "He wouldn't want people to see him like this. He wouldn't want to worry them."

"Wouldn't you?" I asked Lennie. "Most people would." Although truth to tell, the last person I would want if I'd been in an accident was James. I wouldn't want him hanging about, asking if it was time to switch off the life support yet.

I waited for James to turn the car round and head back toward town, to A&E, but, headlights on low beam, he continued away from Great Beadington, toward Upper Iffley and Langley Hall.

"The hospital's the other way," I whispered.

"Daisy, what are we going to say at the hospital? We found this man in the road, and just by coincidence, our headlight is smashed, so is our windshield, there's a dent in the bonnet, the bumper's come off, and we've both been drinking. And whatever else we haven't noticed yet."

I hadn't thought about that, but I was sure that, if we did the right thing, we could still smooth it over. Accidents happened, mistakes were made. That's what the coroner said last time.

"The best thing would be to get him into the house and have a proper look at him," James continued. "He might not need to go to hospital at all."

I looked back at Lennie, doubtful.

"Look how fat he is," James said. "I expect all that blubber cushioned the impact."

"His breathing doesn't sound very good."

"I bet he's like that all the time."

I would have bet he wasn't, but I kept my mouth shut as we approached the house.

Once the car was safely parked in the garage, I tucked Lennie's bag under one arm and we hauled him back out of the car and into the house, not an easy job to do in a cocktail dress and heels. I fell halfway across the drive.

James snapped at me, "Stop messing around!"

We dragged Lennie to the drawing room and laid him out across the dust cover over a chaise longue, his bag on the floor next to it. He lay, shivering, his eyes half-closed, his skin pale, but the blood didn't look so bad now, just a cut on his forehead, and no broken limbs sticking out at sharp angles.

His eyes opened fully and he began to speak. I couldn't hear what he was saying.

"Water?" I guessed. "I can get you some water."

He tried to speak again.

"Cup of tea?" I tried. "You look cold." I draped my jacket over him. "Are we going to call an ambulance now?" But I knew from the look James gave me that the answer to that was no.

"Why don't you go and get the first aid kit?" he asked me.

"I don't think we have one."

"A glass of brandy then, maybe?" James said. "I think we have some somewhere. We can revive him with it."

Well, I hadn't seen that technique on *Casualty* and some might say enough alcohol had already been consumed for one night, but I wanted to be out of the room and away from them as much as anything. I headed for the kitchen and started looking for supplies. I knew we didn't have anything as sensible as a first aid kit, but somewhere in this house we did have plasters, antiseptic, painkillers, maybe a bandage or two, and perhaps something we had bought years ago and forgotten about that would now come into its own. And James was right: We had brandy.

I returned a few minutes later with gauze, Vaseline, aspirin, a bottle of Courvoisier, and a blanket as well to find James rising from the chaise longue. He jumped when he saw me but recovered himself.

"He's gone," James said, somberly. "I was checking for breath."

I gazed down at Lennie, his eyes closed, his body motionless, his skin waxy. He looked very peaceful.

"Are you sure?" I asked.

James nodded.

"No," I said. He couldn't be dead. Only a few minutes before, James had told me he might not even need to go to hospital. He'd had his eyes open. He'd tried to speak. I'd only been gone a few minutes. He couldn't have gone from that to this in such a short time.

I knelt down beside him, searching for signs of life. I couldn't find anything: no breath, no pulse. His neck was all loose, maybe because it was relaxed now, in death, or maybe he'd damaged the bones or the windpipe.

"Oh, Lennie," I whispered. *I'd killed him.* I looked at James. I was close to tears.

"Don't start," he said. "We need to sort this out. I've got work in the morning."

"You're going to work tomorrow?" I was surprised.

"Of course I am. We have to behave as if everything is normal."

"But what are we going to do? We can't leave him here. Mrs. Billings is due in the morning. Shall I cancel her?"

"No, don't cancel her; *everything has to be normal.* Do you want to go to prison?"

Of course I didn't, but, "I won't go to prison if it was an accident," I said. "He just stepped out in front of us. I didn't have time to react."

"How are you going to explain the fact that, instead of calling the emergency services, you put him in the car and drove him home?" James asked.

"That was you."

"And you."

James looked around the room as if he was going to tidy him into a cupboard or something. "We'll have to bury him," he said.

I shook my head; I didn't have the strength, physically or psychologically.

James ran his hands through his hair. "Eric Billings digs in the garden, so that's no good, not unless we want him coming up with the potatoes next year. We'll bury him in the copse; no one goes there," he said. Then, "Better idea, we'll put him in the graveyard… No, we'll put him in the mausoleum. Of course, the mausoleum!"

"But it's for family!"

"Then, welcome to the family, my man," James said. Then to me: "Go and get changed."

I thought about telling James I'd changed my mind and that, on reflection, yes, I did want to go to prison, more than I wanted to dispose of Lennie's body in the middle of the night. At least then I would sleep again one day. But I'd done whatever James told me to for years—at least when I was in sight of him—and it was a hard habit to break.

I ate what he told me to, I wore what he told me to, I went where he told me to, and now I buried what he told me to.

I stepped out of my stilettos and went to get changed.

---

We hoofed the body out of the back of the house, through the garden, through the little copse that separated the main house from the burial area, and into the graveyard that contained the mausoleum, tripping over stones and sinking into holes as we went.

James wore a rucksack that contained a number of large keys. He hadn't been sure which was the right one, not having had cause to unlock the mausoleum before.

The building stood in the far corner, a stone structure with a gabled roof and sculptured angels at the corners. In the graveyard, around the mausoleum, were the last resting places of more distant family members and the occasional favorite servant. The river ran alongside it by the edge of the graveyard and off toward Upper Iffley.

On the side walls were the names and dates of all the people interred within. Most of them had been rendered illegible over the years from the weather and the lichen. The only names that could be read clearly were Lord Ashbury's and the two lords immediately before him.

I imagined James wanting to add Lennie to the list. "Phone an engraver," he'd bark at me on his way out one morning. "And make sure they spell it right."

"We should've used Mr. Billings's wheelbarrow," I said, regaining my breath as we dropped the body at the wooden door framed by decorative Roman-style columns and rested for a moment.

"Now you tell me." James opened the rucksack and started trying the keys in the lock. It took a few goes, but eventually it opened, the stiff metal sounding loud in the night as it ground against itself.

"What if someone hears us and comes to see what's going on?" I asked, wincing at the creaking hinges as James heaved the door open.

"Who's going to hear us?" he said. "We're miles from anywhere. It's the middle of the night."

"But what if they do? It's a public right-of-way, someone could be passing." There was a public footpath running through the field. "An insomniac."

"We'll lock them in here as well, in that case." He stepped back from the doorway. He put his hand in his pocket, took his phone out, and used it to shine a light into the cavern. "After you," he said.

I hovered on the edge, inhaling the fetid odor that came from inside, and took a pace backward.

James stepped past me into the interior and shone his phone around. I thought about taking him up on his own threat and locking him in there…

That would be quite the conundrum when they were found: James in the mausoleum, probably at the door, having died trying to claw his way out, and Lennie, battered and bruised, outside.

But I was too slow; he came back out and started hauling Lennie by the shoulders.

"Help me. Come on."

For the last time, I picked up Lennie's ankles, and we moved him in.

We always referred to the building as the mausoleum, the whole village did, but really, it was more of a huge walk-in tomb. The coffins were all on shelves along the walls, the oldest at the back. I could hardly see those and I didn't want to: after centuries they couldn't be much more than sticks and bones. Nearest the door was Lord Ashbury and it made me shudder because I'd seen him in the village when he was alive, and I remembered him as a posh and affable old man.

We got Lennie over the threshold and dropped him on the floor, toward the middle, then we hurried back out, locked the door, and made our escape.

Back at the house we saw Lennie's satchel lying by the chaise longue.

"We should've taken that with us," James said, but we would've risked dropping things out of it again, leaving a trail of evidence to follow from the house to the mausoleum. Instead, exhausted, we put it in a cupboard in the drawing room.

I took my makeup off, brushed my teeth, changed into my pajamas, and got into bed on autopilot, the shock setting in and making me numb. But in bed I lay awake, thinking about the moment of the accident, Lennie's lifeless face, the trip to the mausoleum. I thought of us running back from the graveyard, stumbling over the uneven ground, trying not to run into trees in the dark, and I thought about how I wasn't going to be leaving James the next morning after all.

# CHAPTER FIVE

I DIDN'T GET UP WHEN JAMES DID THE FOLLOWING DAY. I LAY IN bed, my eyes closed, delaying the moment I would have to rise and face reality.

I heard him a couple of rooms away, going through his usual routine as if this were any other morning and not the morning after our lives changed out of all recognition—and Lennie's as well. He went into the main living area and began banging about in his usual manner; he sounded like he was looking for something. I thought back, trying to remember if I'd hidden anything from him the night before. My memory was hazy on the details; mostly my thoughts were of images of the scene, the airbag flying up in my face, the toy spider on the passenger seat, Lennie lying in the road, on the back seat of the car, on the chaise longue, his eyes closed, his skin pale.

For all that I could and couldn't remember, I was sure I hadn't hidden anything. For once, it was the furthest thing from my mind. He must have mislaid whatever it was without my help.

"Daisy, have you seen my phone?" he asked, barging into my room. I sat up in bed and looked around.

"No."

He began opening drawers and looking under the furniture. I stood up and shook the duvet out, thinking back to when I'd last seen him with it, but I hadn't been watching that closely. And anyway, he hadn't been in my room.

"Call it, will you?" he said, standing up.

I took my own phone from the bedside cabinet, scrolled down to his name, and pressed call. I put it on loud and we waited as the ringing began. One ring, two, three... We listened for the hum of his phone in reply.

"It's not in here," I said, as the bedroom remained silent. When voicemail kicked in we left the room and I dialed again.

In the main house we couldn't hear it. I tried a third time as we roamed through every room we'd been in the night before, our necks stretched long, as if that would help.

"When did you last see it?" I asked.

"Can't remember."

He headed to the lounge and opened his laptop.

"What's my number?" he said, opening up a "find my phone" website, and I read his number out to him.

James tutted. "It says it's here somewhere." We both looked around us and for a final, hopeless time, I tried calling him. Nothing. "Have a look for it while I'm at work," he said. "I'm already late."

"I think if there's one occasion on which you can be late, this is it," I said.

"Yeah, so that everyone remembers I did something out of the ordinary the morning after that man went missing. Brilliant idea. And make sure you check there's nothing out of place before Mrs. Billings comes."

Then James took a key from the bureau and opened up the case that contained the keys for his classic car collection. He lifted one out.

"What are you doing?" I asked.

"Well, I can't take the Audi. It has an enormous dent in the hood, a crack in the windshield, a smashed headlight, and no bumper."

He left, and from the window I could see him crunching across the gravel to the garage. A few minutes later he emerged behind the wheel of a classic 1940s Rolls Royce, roof down, looking every bit the part with a driving cap, goggles, and gloves.

I drank a cup of tea and gazed out of the window, watching to see if the police were coming yet, even though I knew that was impossible.

I dressed and began tidying the house, remembering what James had said about making sure nothing was out of place before Mrs. Billings arrived. After all he had done to clear up the accident the night before, the least I could do was to hold the fort at home. I stopped when I realized nothing would look more suspicious than to present Mrs. B with a show home, instead of the bombsite she was accustomed to. So I messed the room back up again and settled down to watch an episode of *Agatha Raisin*, an old favorite that I could speak the words along with. For once, it didn't calm me.

I began another lap of the house, but it would be strange for me to be wandering round the house in my nightwear when Mrs. Billings got here, so I went to have a shower. By the time I'd finished, Mrs. B had arrived.

"Hello, Lady Langley." Her voice floated across the room as I entered the old kitchen. She was sitting at the table going through the contents of a brown leather satchel. Lennie's satchel. "Is this yours, love?" she asked me, holding up the bag. I remembered hiding it away.

"Where did you find that?" I asked, my voice slightly shaky.

"In the drawing room," she said. "Looked like it had fallen out of that cupboard on the back wall. The catch on the door isn't working; it was hanging open."

Those pieces of furniture were meant to be examples of flawless craftsmanship; even after centuries, the catches should be working. I tried to think back, wondering if we'd not closed it properly, but it was pointless. She had the bag now, and it was clearly too late to complain to the cabinetmaker about the catch. Then I felt a stab of panic, wondering if we'd somehow not closed the mausoleum door and if Lennie was lying half in, half out. But I remembered clearly James turning the key in the lock before we made our way back.

"Is it yours?" Mrs. Billing asked again.

I shook my head. "James's." Why was she going through it?

"Thought it was Eric's," she said. Eric, Mr. Billings to me, usually carried his property around in carrier bags. "Interesting pages he's got in here." Mrs. Billings pushed the sheets of paper I'd seen the night before toward me. "Is he writing a book?"

I flicked through the papers and, yes, it looked as if Lennie had been working on his autobiography.

"James is writing his memoir," I said. "He thought it might be interesting, local boy done good and all that."

"I didn't know he'd met Winston Churchill," Mrs. Billings said. "He doesn't look old enough."

He wasn't old enough.

"I think he means a different Winston Churchill," I said. "Quite a common name really."

I shoved the pages back into the bag and put it on the floor, propped up against a table leg, out of her sight. But that didn't mean out of her mind.

"What's this?" she asked, reaching down. She raised her arm and, pinched between her thumb and forefinger, was the bloody cloth I'd held against Lennie's head in the car. I think I stopped breathing.

Yet, having nearly brought about the end of the world, Mrs. Billings went on to save the day. "Has somebody had a nosebleed?" she asked. "You should soak it in water."

Gratefully, I took it from her, also pinching it between my thumb and forefinger, and turned on the tap.

"Cold water for blood," Mrs. Billings said. "Soak it in cold water for a couple of hours, then put some Vanish on when you put it in the washing machine. That'll get rid of it."

"Thank you," I said. Thank you, thank you, thank you, *thank you*. I turned the hot tap off and the cold tap on. I didn't think we had any Vanish, though, or any other kind of stain remover. James always bought new stuff if anything got stained. "Cuppa?"

"Please, love," Mrs. Billings said. She said no more, but she didn't take her eyes off the bag as I nudged it farther out of the way, set the kettle to boil, and put the biscuits out. I ate one, then I ate another in one bite. Then another. I hadn't eaten breakfast and I was starving. As soon as I ate one biscuit, I found I couldn't stop.

"Cravings, Lady Langley, love?" Mrs. B asked me, with a glint in her eye, although she must have known almost as well as I did how unlikely that was. The chances of cravings became less every day; I was at an age where every time I had to take my cardigan off, I wondered if this was the first hot flash.

"Peckish," I said. I couldn't tell her I hadn't had breakfast—that would be so unheard-of. It would be enough on its own to bring the police running round. Mrs. B grabbed a couple for herself before there were none left.

Then she turned the radio on. The Billingses listened to a local community radio station while they worked and that was what it was tuned to. They were playing requests; we listened to a recent chart topper, followed by Frank Sinatra, then an eighties classic, and then, the news bulletin, a national overview, followed by an update for the county. My blood ran cold as I heard the headline for the local news.

"Concern is growing as to the whereabouts of TV personality Lennie Green, who was last seen at a charity event near his home in Great Beadington."

Mrs. Billings leaped to her feet with a speed I didn't know she had and turned the volume up. She stood there, hovering over it for the rest of the item, but there wasn't much more.

"No one has seen or heard from him since he left the event, which family say is out of character. Police are asking him to make contact, or for anyone with any information to come forward."

"Goodness me," Mrs. Billings said, looking white as a sheet. "I hope he's alright."

"Did you know him?" I asked, wincing at the past tense, but Mrs. Billings didn't notice.

"Not personally, but he was quite the heartthrob when I was a young girl. Been a fan all my life."

"Was he famous, then?" I reminded myself too late: *is* he famous. That could be why he'd looked familiar when I'd first seen him.

"Oh yeah. Probably before your time," Mrs. Billings said. "He must be getting on a bit now. I do hope they find him safe and sound. Done all sorts for the area."

Mrs. B took another biscuit to steady herself after the shock. She offered the packet to me, and I trembled as I reached for it.

"Are you alright, Lady Langley, love?"

I nearly broke. Suddenly, I wanted to unburden myself, to tell Mrs. Billings what had happened the night before, how it wasn't my fault and how James had made me help him hide the body. I wanted to have her forgiveness and her reassurance that it wasn't that bad, I wasn't to blame and everyone would forgive me. Even Lennie's family. In fact, I wanted her to say we'd all end up the best of friends.

But she'd only just heard about Lennie, and she'd need time to come to terms with it. Plus she thought he was only missing. It would be quite a leap for her to come round to the fact that he was dead and buried, on our estate, and we all had to move on. She might not be ready to take such a pragmatic view; the initial shock might cause her to do something foolish, like telling the police. An action she'd come to regret, I was sure, but not as much as I would. So, I kept my guilty conscience to myself; I'd wait until she'd learned to live in a world without Lennie.

And anyway, the previous night James had risked everything for me. I was the one who had run Lennie over, I would have been in the firing line if we'd been caught, but he had taken control and saved me from myself. After all, I'd been about to call 999. It would be ungrateful of me to let the cat out of the bag and get us both in trouble. I couldn't just think of myself now.

Instead, I said, "Yes, yes. Still a bit tired from last night, heavy night." I corrected myself: "No, it wasn't. I didn't drink. A late night last night. Late, but not heavy." We fell quiet as the radio presenter warned us of busy traffic and delays.

Mrs. Billings looked at me for a moment, then said, "You're looking peaky if you ask me. Maybe you should go for a rest."

"Maybe."

Drained from the stress of the morning, I left Mrs. Billings to finish her tea and biscuits, although I was usually there to the end, willing her to stay and chat longer. I took Lennie's bag to my room and shoved it to the back of the wardrobe.

Next I took a pottery cherub out of Mrs. Billings's drawer of loot and carried it through to the lounge, where I put it on a small table behind the sofa. Then I turned the TV on and waited, staring at *This Morning* without hearing a word as Mrs. B bustled her way around for a couple of hours.

While I waited, I realized where James's phone might be. The last place I had seen him with it was in the mausoleum, just before we hauled Lennie's body in. I thought he had put it in his pocket after that, and I remembered him leaning over the corpse for a while. The chances seemed high that he had dropped it in the mausoleum.

Which got me to thinking about Lennie's phone. At that very moment it could be on the premises, emitting its little rays for the police to come and track him down. At any minute it could ring and that very memorable ringtone could rip through the house. Or the graveyard, if it was in his pocket, as it had been at the party. Could it? I wondered. Was it loud enough to be heard through the mausoleum walls? It would terrify anyone who did, especially if it rang at night.

I didn't want to go back to the mausoleum; I wanted to just tell James where his phone was and let him go and get it. He could look for Lennie's at the same time. *But* if Lennie's was in that mausoleum and it rang, I did not want to bet my freedom on the likelihood of it not being audible from outside. And the news bulletin had said concern was growing. It seemed fair to think Lennie's nearest and dearest would be calling him.

Still, it might be in his bag. I waited until I heard Mrs. B revving up the vacuum cleaner, then I ran to the bedroom, where I pulled the bag out of the wardrobe and tipped the contents onto the bed. No phone. I checked the bag for pockets and compartments. Nothing. I shook it again. Nothing. I stared at his memoir, a set of keys, a cigarette lighter, a few pens, a blue inhaler, willing it to materialize, but it wasn't there. I stuffed the items back into the bag and the bag back into the wardrobe.

As I came out of the bedroom Mrs. B uttered a "Toodle-oo!" and left the building. She couldn't have made a very good job of the vacuuming—I'd been in there less than five minutes—but I watched from behind the curtains as she and Mr. Billings left in Mr. B's van, and I let out my breath.

Back in the lounge, the first thing I noticed was the pottery cherub. My heart sank. Putting knickknacks out for her wasn't a foolproof plan. She'd taken something other than the sacrifice offered before now, but I was starting to think there were only two places Lennie's phone could be.

I put the cherub back in the drawer for another day, then I took the key to the mausoleum and headed out. Across the garden, through the copse, and into the graveyard. I scanned the neighboring fields for farmers or walkers. There was a tiny figure a few fields across, but it was moving away. Lucky for me it was a weekday afternoon. These fields were often crawling with ramblers on the weekend, and dog walkers at dawn, but now it was quiet.

I spent some time standing outside the door before I could bring myself to open it: What would Lennie be like now? Would he have putrefied? It seemed soon for that. Would rats be munching on him? Possibly. Would I catch plague or something from going in there? Also possibly. Would Lennie have come back to life and be looking for revenge? This was the least likely of the scenarios, but it was the one that gave me the shivers and had me lingering out there taking deep breaths, standing up straight, and thinking of the ancestors, also interred in there, who would be wishing me well.

I wondered if I really had to do this, or if, in fact, I could just wait until James got home and point him in the right direction, but every time I was about to give up and go back to the house, I remembered the ringtone and stayed put. I took one final deep breath and inserted the key.

This time, when I opened the door, daylight lit the scene inside, enough to be able to see the coffins on shelves lining the walls, some intact, some buckling, and Lennie, slung on the floor between them. I stepped back.

I couldn't do it.

I had to do it.

I looked again at Lennie, sprawled as we had left him. He looked somewhat less beatific now, his face had already begun to sink into itself. I stepped back…

I took a lungful of the spring air outside and I darted in. James's phone was by Lennie's shoulder, easy to find; I put it in my back pocket. Then I patted Lennie down, found nothing of interest, and darted back out. I began to push the door closed but stopped. I had to admit to myself that I hadn't checked his pockets properly. And I could not go back to the house and forget about it if I hadn't done a thorough job.

It took a few goes. I couldn't take a breath in that space, so I had to step outside every time I needed to inhale, but eventually I had been through all of his pockets thoroughly. No phone. What I did find was his wallet and a small address book. It seemed a bit old-fashioned, now that everything is online, but I supposed Lennie was of that generation.

I also found one of James's business cards. He must have given it to him at the party, although it looked quite old and battered. I took it to be on the safe side, best to sever all connections. Apart from the connection that was him lying in our mausoleum. I took the address book, the wallet, and the business card, but there was no phone.

I hurried back to the house, feeling the foul air of the mausoleum clinging to me, then on to my next job: finding what Mrs. B had taken.

I went all over the living area, I searched high and low, I even searched in places I was sure Mrs. B couldn't reach. There was nothing that wasn't where it should be, but I was confident that she hadn't left empty-handed. That had never happened.

In hope rather than expectation, I took a walk around the main house, praying she had spotted an antique that might look good on her mantelpiece, but there were no gaps in the arrangements, no spots missing their dust, no dark rectangles on a faded wall. Now it made sense that she had said she thought Lennie's bag was Mr. B's: she thought she was about to be caught taking the phone.

I went back to the bedroom and took Lennie's bag out of the wardrobe. I would hide it where I hid my snacks.

It is a little-known fact that Langley Hall has a priest hole, a relic from the days in which to be a Catholic priest was a very daring career choice indeed. It was shown only to the summer visitors who paid for a tour and I was on one of those tours, more than thirty-five years ago now.

Normally, adventures like the Langley Hall tour would be beyond the means of my mum and me when I was growing up, but in the summer I turned eleven, she won £50 in a village sweepstake. Langley Hall was our first port of call, obsessed with it as we were.

We arrived just in time for the tour, and within minutes we were amongst a group of around ten, following an excited guide upstairs, where we saw four-poster beds in rooms with painted ceilings, a ballroom like the one Cinderella danced in, a library with more books than our mobile library had ever seen, and cases full of jewelry. Finally the guide stopped on the staircase and asked:

"Who knows what a priest hole is?"

My hand shot into the air; this had been in the book from the library. "It used to be illegal to be a Catholic and if you had a Catholic priest in your house and he was found, he would be executed. So they made hiding places for them."

"That's right," the guide said—I knew it was right! "Back in the sixteenth century Catholicism was punishable by death, but people didn't want to abandon their faith, so the priests came to their houses to say mass and they created hiding places for them, in case the authorities came. Those places were very hard to find. Can anyone see where it might be?"

We all looked around for a clue, until the guide crouched down, pressed a panel on one of the stairs, and the step, along with the step above it, lifted to reveal a hidey-hole.

"Would anyone like to get in it?" she asked, and I did not need to be asked twice.

There was room for me, at the age of nearly eleven, to stretch out comfortably.

"But can you imagine how cramped it would be for a full-grown man?" the guide said. "And he could be in there for hours while the soldiers searched. It must have been pitch black." She partially dropped the stair back down. "Is it dark in there?"

"A little bit," I said. There was still a fair amount of light getting in, but I got the picture.

"He'd be able to hear the soldiers stomping up and down; he'd hear their voices. And if the householders were taken away, he could be stuck in there indefinitely. Possibly forever."

She lost her grip on the step then and for a few seconds I had the full priest hole experience—she was right, it was pitch dark—until she managed to lift it back up and was relieved to find me smiling.

That was one of the last tours. Lord Ashbury died the following winter, Langley Hall was never reopened to the public, and its secrets faded from memory.

In recent years, that remarkable piece of history had been used for hiding snacks from James and, now, evidence from a crime. I put Lennie's satchel and the treats Mrs. Billings had brought that morning inside and closed the priest hole up again.

The effort drained the last of my energy from me; this was the busiest day I'd had for years. And the most stressful, but there was one more job to do. I took the clothes we'd been wearing that night, all dry clean only, and set them to soak, with the stained cloth, in cold water. A couple of hours later, I put them on a hot wash.

After that, I retreated to the sofa and thought about how, if I did kill James, I knew now I could hide him in the mausoleum, if I could think of a way to get him down there. But that was a question for another day. I typed out a WhatsApp message: "I can't cook tonight, I'm too tired. Can you get a takeaway, please?" and pressed send. From my pocket, James's phone beeped on receipt of the message. Oh yeah.

# CHAPTER SIX

IT RAINED TOWARD THE END OF THE AFTERNOON, SO I PUT BUCKETS out in all the top-story rooms where they leaked. That was the routine when it rained in this house. Meanwhile, in town, James was unable to get the roof of the Rolls Royce up. He arrived home soaked through, telling me the upholstery would have to be cleaned, possibly replaced.

Neither of us felt like eating much and the Potato Smiles I'd bought seemed inappropriate now anyway, so we had toast while we waited for the evening news to begin, needing to know where they were with the search for Lennie. Watching the news was not normal for us, but there was no one around to witness it.

"Where did you find this?" James asked, checking his phone for messages.

"In the mausoleum. You dropped it when you were in there last night."

"You went down there by yourself?" he said. "Didn't think you had it in you. What about these?" He was looking at the wallet and the address book.

"Same place. I found them in Lennie's pockets."

He spent a moment paging through the address book, then picked the wallet up and looked inside. He pulled out a bank card, then another, then a library card and a bus pass. He found a £20 note and pocketed it, as a reflex action when he saw money. Then he put the wallet back down where I had left it.

Then I gave him the bad news about Lennie's phone being missing, I didn't tell him I thought Mrs. Billings had taken it. He didn't know she stole things, and I didn't want him to know; it would almost certainly lead to a sacking, and Mrs. Billings needed the job, while I needed our chats and snacks.

"Where have you looked?" he asked.

"In his pockets and in his bag."

"I'll look in the car."

Of course; why didn't I think of that? We paused the TV and I followed him to the garage. I watched, filled with hope, as he searched the car for a phone. Twenty minutes later the car had been searched several times and there was nothing.

"Don't panic," he said. "He could have lost it anywhere. What did you do with that bag he had?"

I hesitated.

"What?"

"I put it with his body," I fibbed.

"Good. You're sure the phone wasn't in it?"

"Absolutely sure."

We went back to the lounge to watch the local news. Lennie's disappearance was the lead story, along with a look back at his career, which was varied and mostly successful, spanning the sixties, seventies, and eighties, with a small blip in the nineties. Now that he was all over the news, I realized I had seen him on the odd TV show. He'd fallen out of fashion for a while and had, apparently, been involved in a number of disastrous business deals that, at one point, saw him homeless. He had a renaissance around the turn of the century, following an appearance on a celebrity reality TV show, but had then drifted into retirement, living in a cottage in Great Beadington. From there he headed up a number of local charities. His life after showbiz, it transpired, had been devoted to good works.

In contrast, I divided my time between watching TV and plotting to kill my husband, and James managed investments no one could get their money out of.

His neighbors were out in force, singing his praises and praying for his swift return, harping on about how it was the not knowing that was the worst. I hoped they'd be able to come to terms with the not knowing; the alternative didn't bear thinking about. Although we were going to have to atone somehow—you can't just run someone over and forget about it.

A neighbor wiped away a tear. Did she know something she shouldn't? "It's just not like him," she said. "He's usually in by ten o'clock with his hot chocolate and his slippers."

"He's the center of this community. It won't be the same if something's happened to him," another said.

A man stepped up. "Japanese knotweed in his garden," he said, "and he's refusing to do a damn thing about it. It's taking thousands off the value of my property."

"Dangerous words," James said. "If the police decide to progress the case, he'll be a prime suspect."

Oh lord, if that neighbor was blamed, it would mean that not only had we killed a local hero, but someone else would go to prison for it. I wondered at what point I would draw the line and confess on behalf of us both.

The reporter turned to a young man, standing next to him. The caption on the screen said: "Anthony Green. Son of Lennie Green."

"If you're watching this, Dad, please get in touch," he said. "If someone's kidnapped him, please let him go. He has children and grandchildren."

"He has children and grandchildren," I repeated to James, who didn't react. Now that the adrenaline was wearing off, my thoughts turned to Lennie himself, how nice he'd seemed at the party and how it had all ended for him, as he was on his way home for hot chocolate and slippers.

"Slow news day," James replied, unconcerned and unremorseful. "Who would kidnap him, for god's sake? We're safe. Even if that phone turns up, it's not been here; we would've seen it if it had. So why would they link it to us?"

When they finally did shut up about Lennie, the next item on the news was an in-depth analysis of an under-elevens football fundraiser, so James may have had a point about the slow news day.

The wallet and the address book stayed on the coffee table for the rest of the evening, while we flicked from channel to channel, never settling on anything, and I drank a couple of glasses of wine to relieve my stress. It went to my head, and it made me go to the loo three times, as they were quite large glasses.

Eventually, around midnight, James looked at Lennie's property and said, "We can't leave these lying around. Put them in the case with the car keys while we decide how to get rid of them." He meant the case where the keys for his classic cars were kept. It had a lock, so no one—and by that I mean Mrs. Billings—would come across them by chance. I swayed my slightly drunken way over and did as he said. Then we both went to bed, at which point, I couldn't find my hairbrush. I never did see it again.

Over the following days we learned, via the local news, that the police really didn't have a clue where to start. No one had noticed Lennie leaving the party that night. He was caught on camera walking down the drive, his bag over his shoulder, and turning left into the street. He had later been seen, on CCTV, cutting across the high street toward the bus station, where he waited for the late-night bus that ran from Tippington all the way to Bristol, with Great Beadington in its path. From the camera on the bus, we saw him boarding and chatting with the driver as they drove along. At one point, he put his hand in his pocket and took out his phone, so we knew he had it then.

He alighted just outside the village, not far from where we had hit him; we must have been close at the moment he was stepping down from the bus. That was where the trail went cold. It was a short walk to his house, but there was no CCTV in that rural spot. Hooray!

As a result, the police were concentrating their efforts in the small area from the bus stop to his house. That made sense, but I hoped they weren't going to be searching the ground too closely. We'd picked up as much of the smashed headlight as we could, but in the dark, in a hurry, on that night, pieces must have been missed. I had no doubt a forensic search, if they chose to do one, would find more. I wondered how many pieces they needed to be able to identify the make and model of the car.

It all left me feeling slightly queasy. When I went to bed, I dreamt about folk in white suits crawling around the bus stop and finding… Lennie's phone!

---

The phone was all I thought of over the weekend. I continued to think about it as I waved James off to work on Monday morning and took stock of my snacks.

If Lennie had dropped his phone somewhere between the bus stop and his house, it would remove it from our list of things to worry about. It wouldn't matter if it was found or not. It was easy to believe a man walking along that path, in the dark, after a few drinks, could have dropped it into the grass that lined either side of the path, and it was just far enough from the first row of houses for the ringtone to go unheard when his friends and family tried to call him.

Was it? I wondered. Was I right about that? I clicked on to the online news for an update. I knew that didn't match my usual search history, but if the police came asking, would it really be so strange to look up a local celebrity who had gone missing? And if we had covered our tracks so well, why would they come anyway?

"Hope for the best, but prepare for the worst," James said of the matter. "It's the Cub Scout motto."

I didn't think it was, but I took his point.

There was nothing on the news that hadn't been there before. There was nothing new about Lennie, nothing about debris from a smashed Audi headlight cover, and nothing about the phone.

I typed Lennie's name into the search bar and hovered my finger over the "go" button. I pressed it.

The first few links were the same news articles I had just looked at. I worked my way down to the Wikipedia page, tapped on it, and looked at the information at the top: Leonard Patrick Green, born on 7 April 1949.

Now I knew his middle name was Patrick and that he was an Aries—useful to know for the mausoleum wall. I scrolled down to the personal section and read that he had been married for nearly forty years and had four children, he played in an amateur skiffle band, and was a member of CAMRA, the Campaign for Real Ale.

I was getting away from the point. I scrolled through more articles, looking for a clue as to what the police were thinking, but the pieces were all the same. I needed to see for myself: I was feeling the pull of the crime scene.

I'd heard about it many times on my dramas, the urge criminals have to revisit the site, and now I was experiencing it for myself. I needed to know what was and wasn't there. After all, even now, the police might be peering at a pile of teeny, tiny headlight shards and asking themselves, "What happened here?"

Or they might be picking his phone out of the hedgerow and saying, "Oh, here it is, no more need to search this area." Whichever it was, good or bad, I needed to know.

It was a risk James would almost certainly forbid me from taking if he knew; after all, there was nothing normal about me poking around on the shoulder of the road just outside Great Beadington, but if my mission were successful, the rewards would be immense. If I found the phone, I could kick it into view, to be found soon after by an unconnected passerby. If I found headlight pieces, I could scatter them to the winds.

Eyes fixed firmly on the prize, I grabbed the keys for my own

Fiesta that James supplied me with, so that I could run errands for him, and headed out.

---

Great Beadington is our neighboring village, of a similar size to Upper Iffley but less attractive. It only has a handful of thatched cottages, whereas Upper Iffley is stuffed full of them—the whole village is an absolute fire hazard.

Great Beadington has a large village green, but the surface is so uneven, you can hardly step on it without twisting your ankle. Its folk dancers can't move to a rhythm, its cricket team can't guard a wicket, and its amateur dramatics society can never remember their lines.

The village pub quiz team can't even beat ours when the subject is themselves. The question that stumps them is: "Who is believed to have stolen the third of Upper Iffley's original five church bells?"

The answer is: Great Beadington! In a scandal that must have rocked the South West of England back in the fourteenth century, natives of Great Beadington broke into Upper Iffley's church tower and stole one of the bells. That is why there are only four bells in our church and therefore a note missing from the scale. The Upper Iffley church bell fund, which was constantly running, was an effort to remedy this. There was no recorded instance of anyone from Great Beadington ever having contributed to it.

I drove along the road that we had driven down on the night of the accident. This time it was lined with media vans, stretching some way out of Great Beadington.

I made my way through the middle of the village and found a side street to park on. Before I left the car, I pulled my hair back and hid it under a cap. I wasn't well known there, but I was aware that

Mrs. Faulkner, from the Upper Iffley newsagent's, had a Beadington cousin, and Mrs. Chambers, from the small shop, knew another local business owner there. So, you never knew who you were going to run into, and my hair is quite distinctive.

I wore sunglasses as well for good measure. It was a sunny day, so there was nothing strange about that. Then I walked toward the center of the village, nodding and exchanging "Afternoon's" with strangers who were wandering aimlessly about, presumably looking for clues or news. I walked until I saw a media van parked outside the school. Farther down, I could see the beginning of the cavalcade I had passed on my way in and members of the press, congregated opposite one house.

I crept toward it and stood behind a van. This must be Lennie's abode. It was an old stone cottage in a terrace of cottages, all with large, well-tended front gardens. Lennie's had a cheerful red front door, but all the curtains were drawn, giving it a dour aspect. It wasn't far at all from the spot where we had run him down.

I stayed where I was for a moment, wondering how I was going to get past them all and out to the scene of the crime. I didn't want to get myself on TV; that would certainly give rise to a comment from James when we watched the news that evening.

Then I had a stroke of luck; it was home time at the village school. Within minutes, I was surrounded by primary school children and parents, some of whom were heading in the direction of the media vans.

I didn't go entirely unnoticed. Some of the mums glanced at me as they passed, and I heard comments such as "ghoul" and "rubberneck." But to the media personnel, I was just a middle-aged woman doing women's things. None took any notice of me.

I carried on, out of the village, keeping behind the news vans that lined the road. As I left the safety of the school crowd, I stopped and looked behind me every few paces. So far, so good, they were all looking in the opposite direction.

I stopped at the spot where I thought it had happened, or as near as I could get. There was no forensics. Whatever they had been looking for, they must have either finished or looked in the wrong place. Instead, there was a van parked there, crushing any pieces of headlight it crunched over better than I could have done. I looked up and down the road, to check that no one was watching, then I crouched down and began to search for the phone.

I looked around the vans and along the path. No sign of it. I looked in the long grass and under the hedge, automatically scanning for plants fit for foraging as I did so. It was a habit left over from childhood, but there is little on offer until autumn; I found nothing you can eat and I found no phone. I eased myself into the small ditch that ran below the hedge. I emerged with wet trainers but still no phone.

I searched a longer stretch of road, in case it had been thrown in the air when we hit him, and I looked under the vans but no sign of it. I crossed the road and did the same on the other side, unlikely though it was to have made its way over there. On that side I found a broken umbrella, a pen, and a water bottle, but no phone. I picked them up to throw away and looked under the vans again. Nothing.

It was time to give it up as a bad job. I was reluctant to leave without achieving what I had gone there to do, but the fact was the phone wasn't there; I could search for days and still leave empty-handed.

I wished then that I hadn't gone. If I hadn't gone, I could still imagine it was there, dropped by Lennie when he got off the bus, and that there was nothing for us to worry about. Now, I felt sure he had it with him when we arrived back at Langley Hall, and Mrs. Billings was looking more and more likely to be the last person to have seen it.

I tried to console myself with the knowledge that the news vans had probably neutralized any threat from the smashed headlight, but it was a scant consolation. Disquieted, I prepared to head home.

I looked back toward the village, remembering the dense clump of journalists outside Lennie's house. Not wanting to pass them again, I opened the gate and took the scenic route, through the fields, the sprouting acres of wheat and barley, and the bright yellow of oilseed rape, around the perimeter of Great Beadington, my trainers still wet and now uncomfortable.

By the time I got back to civilization, I was gasping for a drink, so I hobbled into the village shop for a bottle of water. On the way out I bumped into a young woman with bright pink hair, wearing a red T-shirt that clashed with it.

"Sorry," I said, stepping backward to let her in.

"No problem," she replied. "We've all got our minds on other things at the moment, haven't we?" She nodded her head in the direction of Lennie's street.

"I know," I said. "It's all I can think about." Which was true. I moved to step past her, but she shifted slightly, so that I would have had to touch her to get by.

"Did you know Mr. Green?" she asked.

"Not as such," I said, then, regretting that: "I suppose we all knew him in our way."

She nodded sadly. "It's been a shock, even for those who aren't from round here. Are you local?"

I shook my head. "Upper Iffley," I said, wishing straightaway that I hadn't.

"Local to the area, then," she said, although I couldn't really agree that I was anything but alien in Great Beadington. She handed me a business card.

"Emma Beddoe," it said. "Junior Reporter, Crime, *The Western Bugle Online*."

"Crime?" I said. It sounded like the press were one step ahead of the police.

"I cover anything," she told me. "I put crime on there because it's the most interesting thing I do. What do you think happened?"

"Abducted by aliens," I said; it seemed reasonable to think she wouldn't follow up on that. "I have to get going now."

"Let me know if you have anything you want to talk about," she said, finally stepping out of the way. "Love your T-shirt, by the way."

It was one I'd made myself, but it looked fairly normal. It was stitched from one of James's T-shirts and the only eccentricities were the orange panels I'd added along the sides, bright against the original deep blue, where I'd taken it in to fit me.

I drove home wondering whether to tell James or not to tell James about my afternoon. In the end there was so much I hadn't told him: the priest hole, Mrs. Billings's kleptomania, my plans to kill him, the bag, the surveyors, why break the habit now?

# CHAPTER SEVEN

ON THURSDAY MORNING I WAS MAKING MY WAY ACROSS THE HALL when there was a knock on the door. Not thinking, I went to answer it and had the fright of my life when I saw two police officers standing in front of me!

It didn't seem right, after I'd worked so hard to destroy evidence and had every intention of making amends in a different way. Had we missed something? It was possible, given the number of things there were to think of. Had they found the phone and tracked it back to us? Or sifted their way through a million splinters of headlight cover?

"Morning, morning," one of them said. "Nothing to worry about, we're just speaking to everyone who might have seen Lennie Green on the day he went missing. We were given your name by the party hosts. Can we come in?"

"I don't know anything about it."

"We just need to take a statement. Crossing the t's and dotting the i's."

I let them in because I didn't think I had a choice, and before I could stop them, they hung a left into the very room in which Lennie had passed. I followed them and took a dust sheet off one of the chairs, sniffing the air as I did for the telltale scent of death I had often heard of. There was nothing discernible, not to me at least. I watched to see if they were going to turn up their noses, but there was no reaction. I looked round to check they hadn't brought one of those cadaver dogs—that could have been a death blow to us—but there were no pets whatsoever.

"Have a seat," I said and they said "thank you" and took the sheet off the very chaise longue on which Lennie had expired!

"Everything alright?" one of them asked. He was tall and thin, with a very pasty complexion, but he said to me, "You're looking pale."

"Yes," I whispered. "Yes, I'm alright."

"Are you sure?"

"That's a very old piece of furniture," I said. They both stood up, and I tried to look as if that had solved all my problems.

In the end we went through to the old kitchen. The walk gave me time to take a few deep breaths and get my shaking hands under some control.

There I told them that it was true I had met Lennie at the party; I had been matching the labels to the canapés, and he was looking for a drink. I had a brief wobble here, remembering the drink he'd poured me, but I recovered myself and told them that he and I spoke briefly about canapés, then he'd left to answer his phone. I tripped slightly on the word "phone," but they didn't seem to notice. The next time I saw him, he was presenting a check for a charity. I had never seen him before, *or since*, I stressed to them.

"I didn't even know he was the national treasure, Lennie Green," I said. "I didn't know we'd had—no, we *have*—a national treasure called Lennie Green."

"Haven't you found him yet?" Mrs. Billings clattered into the kitchen, seeing the police officers and catching the end of the conversation.

"Not yet," the first officer said. "And you are?"

"Brenda Billings, head of housekeeping and lifelong fan of Lennie Green." She put her hand out and shook hands with the officers. "Why are you looking here?"

"We're just speaking to everyone who was at the same party as Mr. Green," the officer said, and Mrs. B looked at me.

"You never said you were at the same party," she said.

I shrugged. "I thought you knew. I thought it was obvious."

"But you didn't even know who he was when it was on the radio the next day?"

"I didn't realize it was him."

"Young people," Mrs. B said disparagingly to the police, although they were younger than me.

They said they had no more questions and asked where they could contact James. I gave them his mobile number and saw them out.

I flopped down onto the chaise longue, then remembering once more who the last person to lie there was, leaped back up again. I spent the rest of the afternoon replaying the interview in my head and wondering if they had thought "aha" at the moment I said Lennie *had* been a national treasure. Or if maybe everyone behaved like that when they were interviewed and they thought nothing of it. Or perhaps they weren't that experienced and had been overawed by the house. I should have spoken to them in the hall, where they would have had the Elizabethan armor and the empty family tree to take their minds off me. I could have told them about how there once was a beautiful decorated document which started in the fourteenth century and followed the family right down to Lord Ashbury and how James got rid of it.

To see James that evening, you would never have known there was anything to worry about.

"You can tell by how long it's taken them to get to us how far down we are on the list of priorities. It stands to reason. We'd never met him before that night. Why would we have anything to do with it?" he said, watching me microwave a bowl of Waitrose carbonara, the film of which had been pierced in front of him. Regardless, when I served it up, he peered closely at it, then he poked around at it with his fork.

"Not going on a killing spree, are you?" he asked. "I know this is your favorite MO." Finally, he ate it, after first swapping his plate with mine, then saying, "Double bluff" and swapping them back. I wanted to tell him that he needn't have worried: Revenge was a dish best served cold and that little bowl of pasta was piping hot.

Afterward, we decamped to the lounge to watch the local news. That evening, Lennie was a much smaller item, just a reminder that he was still missing and that the police would like to thank everyone so far who had provided camera footage; they were currently reviewing it all.

Then I had a thought: "James, we haven't taken the dashcam out of the Audi."

"Shit!"

Who would have thought there was so much to think of in the aftermath of a hit-and-run? The body had proved to be the least of our problems; there were cameras, phones, bags, and damaged cars to consider, all while acting normally. Next time, I'd draw up a checklist first. Not that there would be a next time. Unless the victim was James, which was something to think about. But I cast that thought aside. I had to concentrate on the matter in hand. We went running out to the garage to retrieve the camera.

Back in the house, James logged onto his laptop.

"Do you want to see it?" he asked. "Your best bits?"

No, I didn't, but he downloaded the dashcam footage anyway and played it back. You could hear me trying to get him to look at the ghost in the back seat as we wended our way toward the country lane. You could see the tail lights of the bus disappearing around the corner and Lennie at the side of the road—so maybe I did have time to notice him. He started to cross. At the same time, you could hear James's yelp as he pulled the sun visor down and the spider fell out, then a split second later, Lennie's horrified expression as he flew toward the windshield. The dashcam had a much better view than I had had from behind the airbag, and you could clearly see the horror on his face. For a time I was back in that moment, and I had to sit down.

If only I'd remembered to take that spider out. Or to play the trick when I first set it up. If only I hadn't forgotten about it.

"Any news on the phone?" James asked me, and I shook my head. "Keep an eye out for it. We'll get rid of the Audi this weekend."

As simple as that. An accident had happened, but it was being cleared up. It seemed wrong that such a big event could be laid to rest so easily, but I kept reminding myself that, once the immediate danger had passed, I would carry out some kind of penance for this.

---

James woke me before 2:00 a.m. on Saturday morning.

"Rise and shine," he said. "We're going to the seaside."

And he made me get up and dress and pack, as if for a day at the coast, although being only April, we didn't go for full beachwear.

"Bring these," he said, and he handed me the earrings my mum had given me for my twenty-first birthday. Puzzled, I started putting them on, but James said, "Leave them in the box."

"What for?"

"You'll see."

When we were ready, we climbed into the battered Audi. James told me to put the earrings in the glove compartment, then we drove, on dipped headlights, for more than an hour and a half to Brean Down, on the coast.

There, we drove the car off the road, onto the footpath, where cars are not supposed to go, and up to the top of the cliff. It was only just wide enough for the Audi, but at least we didn't have to worry anymore about the paintwork getting scratched. Then we went along the clifftop, which was slightly easier than the path but terrifying in case we made a mistake and went over the edge. Eventually, we stopped where the water below was deep. James took a cloth out of his pocket and wiped our fingerprints off everything he could think of. Then we got out and he wiped the doorhandles.

"Shouldn't our fingerprints be on our own car?" I asked.

"Not if we're going to say it was stolen and there are no one else's prints on it."

Then he reached inside, took the handbrake off, said, "Wrap your hands in your sleeves when you touch anything," and he made me help him push it off the cliff into the sea.

"My earrings!" I shouted, remembering them as it went over the edge.

"Exactly," James said. "When we report it as stolen, we can say it had items with sentimental value inside. It'll make it sound more convincing."

"But my mum gave them to me."

"Yes, so we didn't have to sacrifice an expensive pair. Win-win."

I didn't have words. They were the most valuable I had, worth more than all the jewelry he'd bought me combined. I hated him, I hated him, *I hated him*. If we'd been nearer the edge at that moment I would've tried to shove him over too. And I'd have told the police what I'd done, and I'd have told them why.

We walked down to the seaside and stayed out of view as we watched the sun come up and the town come to life. Then we walked up and down side streets, and James chose a place to tell the police we'd parked it when he reported it as stolen later that day, a spot that was secluded and untroubled by CCTV.

"They'll only give us a crime number anyway; they won't investigate it," he promised me, and that promise came true.

After that, we went for breakfast. I was exhausted by then, but I had to undertake a full day out, experiencing the wonders of Burnham-on-Sea because we couldn't go out for the day and be ready to go home by seven in the morning.

"Why didn't we just smash the lock on the garage and tell them we found it stolen when we got up?" I asked him. After all we didn't have external CCTV at Langley Hall, just an alarm for the living quarters to protect all his electrical gadgets. James put up cameras when he first bought the house, but a few years ago the subscription lapsed and he decided not to renew.

"In all the years we've been here, no one's tried to break in," he'd said. The worst had been the odd teenager on the grounds. "We've still got the box up there; that's enough to scare people off. Double bluff." James was a fan of the double bluff and in this case, so far, it seemed to be working. Maybe the place just looked too dilapidated to contain anything worth stealing.

We endured a day out until midafternoon, then we went to the spot James had chosen and he phoned the police to report the car as stolen. I managed to cry when we told them about the earrings. They were tears of fury. We got a taxi home and I cried all the way.

We didn't wait for the Audi to be written off before I drove James to the dealership to buy a new one. James only had insurance because it was less trouble to have it than to deal with the potential legal ramifications of not having it. In fact, he decided not to bother the insurance company at all; he just added another car to the policy.

"We don't want them looking too closely at the damage, do we?" he said. "Might turn out to be incompatible with a fall from a cliff."

And in the end, I got my earrings back. They found the car and pulled it out of the water. Someone was good enough to look in the glove compartment and phoned me to say I could go and get them; they weren't too badly tarnished. So all was well that ended well.

# CHAPTER EIGHT

OVER THE FOLLOWING WEEKS WE FELL INTO A NEW ROUTINE, EATING together in front of the TV, watching the news. We didn't usually watch the weather forecast at the end, but that night we both sat, finishing our chicken wings, as they predicted torrential rain within the next twenty-four hours.

"Better put some buckets out on the top floor," James said, and I raced around, putting down buckets, repositioning buckets, searching Amazon for more buckets, wishing James would just get the roof fixed.

I felt glad that Lennie was in the mausoleum, keeping dry.

That night, the buckets overflowed and the river burst its banks. It swamped all the nearby fields and swept devastation through some of the best gardens in the village, putting the annual flower festival in jeopardy. Elsewhere, the damage was worse and the local news crews entertained themselves for a day, wading through ruined kitchens and marveling at submerged cars.

"Good job we got the mausoleum checked out," James said. "A flood like that could knock it off its foundations if they weren't solid."

Oh, really?

---

The next morning, after James had gone to work, I made my way down to the mausoleum.

Well! The river covered half the graveyard, my trainers were soaked in seconds, and as James surmised, disaster had struck. One wall of the mausoleum had collapsed into the water, the two adjoining it were spread in pieces across the sodden grass, the door lay uselessly on the ground. The fourth wall was mostly standing, but the roof was at a forty-five degree angle, one end pitched into the ground. I looked down and saw a tibia floating in a puddle in front of me. I screamed.

Birds flew up from the nearby trees. I looked around to see who might have noticed, but on a Wednesday morning, in our personal graveyard, it seems no one can hear you scream. A closer look revealed shattered coffins, some halfway out of the mausoleum, and bones scattered everywhere. Some had made their way to the river and no doubt as far as the village and beyond. A jawbone, complete with teeth, was snared in the reeds. I wondered which ancestor it was. An Eleanor, or a Richard, or maybe a rare Hugo?

Our names were going to be mud when the authorities realized we'd unleashed an early Halloween on our neighbors, but that was the least of our worries. I crept up to what had been the door of the mausoleum and peered at what had been the interior, looking for Lennie. I couldn't see him.

---

I ran up and down the riverbank looking, but there was no sign of Lennie. I paced the graveyard, searching for any trace of him or his clothing. Not a sniff, although I did see a patch of meadowsweet, which is good as a natural sweetener, if only James would let me use it.

I followed the river downstream to the gate and through it. I crossed the road, which crossed the river, and went through the opposite gate into the field there and followed the public footpath along. No sign. At the end of the field, the river turned one way, the path another, and the rest of the riverbank was blocked off by bushes.

I walked farther, through the fields, until I could see the house and the garden of the west farm, with the Newman family out in it. Then I turned round and went home before they saw me.

Half an hour later I went back out and looked again, but still no luck.

All day, I kept going down there, but each time, there was no change. I found a stick and poked the skull in the reeds clear to set it on its way, but it sank and I realized that if I was going to do anything, I should have rescued it to be reburied.

It occurred to me that Lennie's body could still be nearby but stuck under the water, snagged on a tree root, ready to break free and float back up just as a walking group passed by. It would certainly be one of their more memorable outings.

I stood at the edge of the riverbank and peered hard. Where the water flowed by what had been the mausoleum, it was clear and you could see down to the pebbles on the riverbed, but not much further along it was deeper and murky. Anything could be under there, including Lennie.

There was nothing for it. I went back to the house, took a beanpole from Mr. Billings's shed, and put on a pair of boots that had been near the back door since before I arrived. I marched down to the river, checked there was no one around, and stepped into the water. The boots leaked. After a minute my feet were so wet there was hardly any point wearing them. I waded in deeper and water flooded over the top. I wanted to scream with the cold, but I kept my mind on the job and pressed on, poking around with the beanpole as I did so.

I prodded as gently as I could; I wanted to know where he was, but I didn't want to actually release his corpse from a tangle of reeds and send him on his merry way toward the village. I wasn't sure which I dreaded more: not finding him, but knowing he was out there, a disaster waiting to happen, or finding him and having to ask for James's help to hide him again. Still, I carried on along the river, the current pulling at me and the cold freezing me. What else could I do?

"Have you lost something?"

I jumped and turned to see a dog walker standing behind me, his pet wagging its tail beside him.

"My dog," I said. It was easy to look distressed.

"Oh no!" he said. "Do you think it's in the water?" I nodded. "Don't panic; they're natural swimmers. Do you have a photo? I'll put it on the village Facebook page. What's its name?"

"Tibs," I said, thinking of the tibia. "I've already put it on Facebook."

"What does Tibs look like?"

"He's a liver and white spaniel."

"That's a coincidence," the dog walker said, looking down at his own liver and white spaniel. "They're great dogs, aren't they? Good sniffers."

That comment left me all aquiver; a good sniffer was the last thing I wanted to meet.

"My friend has a dinghy, might make it easier to search," he said. "Do you want me to phone him?"

I shook my head.

"It's no trouble," the man said. "He loves dogs."

So he phoned his friend and his friend said he could be there in half an hour. I climbed out of the river to wait, water pouring out of my boots as I trudged up the bank.

"Do you know what happened to this?" the man asked, nodding at the mausoleum.

"Gravity," I said, and he seemed happy with that. Maybe he was new to the area and didn't know what a recent development the collapse was.

We stood awkwardly; I was shivering from my dip in the river.

"Do you live nearby?" the man asked. "Do you think you should go and get changed?"

I said that was a very good idea and plodded back up to the house. There, I waited a minute, then ran back down to the graveyard, waving my hands in the air.

"He's back! He's back!" I shouted.

"Tibs?"

"Yes. He was there waiting when I got to the house. Pretty muddy, I think he was in the water."

The man looked elated. "Well, that's good news! Where is he?"

"In the house. I'd better get back to him. Thank you for your help."

Thank you for nothing. I couldn't go back into the water now; I didn't have another story if I was caught. The only way we'd know about Lennie now was if he appeared. I went back to the house and put my clothes in to wash.

---

I decided not to tell James about the collapsed mausoleum straightaway. Or at all, if I could avoid it. He'd helped me clear up immediately after the accident, but that was in the aftermath of an unexpected, unforeseeable event that had sprung up out of the blue. This problem was caused by my failure to do what he had told me to do regarding the surveyor. I didn't expect a sympathetic response, and I didn't want to shatter our relative peace with the news that the local celebrity we'd buried privately was back in the public domain. Anyway, he wouldn't be able to do anything I couldn't, which at that point was to continue looking for Lennie.

I thought about tidying some of the bones up. I shuddered. Anyway, where would I put them? What would Mr. Billings say if he went down there and found a stack of human remains in a neat pile? Mind you, what would he say if he went down there and found them as they were? I spent a few minutes in front of the mirror, practicing looking surprised. In the event that this development did come to light, it would be best to be prepared to be caught unprepared.

I tried to calm myself with the thought that if Lennie and all the other bones were swept miles away, maybe as far as the sea, and if James didn't go down to the graveyard for at least five years, all would be well, the danger would pass. For a moment both of these things seemed possible, but then reality reasserted itself and "it will be fine," became an empty mantra I repeated to try to keep my panic at bay.

I spent the rest of the day going to and fro from the house to the river, to see if Lennie had turned up. Between searches, I tried to watch my usual TV, hoping it would relax me. After catching the end of *Bargain Hunt*, which was a repeat, I watched the lunchtime news, followed by the local edition. They started with an item about how a number of bones had appeared around the village as the river levels started to go down.

"We thought it must be from the churchyard, didn't we, Betty?" said Terry Chambers, husband of Betty, who ran the small shop and had found a shoulder socket at the bottom of their garden. "But when we went up there, there was nothing wrong at the church. The river didn't even get that high."

"It's a mystery," Betty said, twirling the bone around in her fingers.

The story was on the evening news as well. I watched it with James. By then more bones had been found, so the piece was extended, but it still featured the same interview with Betty and Terry Chambers.

I watched James as Betty Chambers once again declared the findings to be a mystery.

"No, it isn't," he said. I watched his expression change as everything he understood about the world—and about engineering—collapsed around him.

Without another word, he leaped from his seat and left the house. I followed as he raced across the garden and into the copse. When I came out from the other side of the trees, I saw him in the graveyard, holding up a skull, Hamlet-like. I'd never noticed before that he would make quite a dashing, if overaged, Hamlet.

He marched to where the mausoleum door had been and looked inside, presumably looking for Lennie.

He turned and saw me. "What in the name of fuckety-fuck has happened?" he shouted. "Daisy, where is that fucking surveyor's report?"

I stopped and pretended I couldn't make out what he was saying. He flung the skull away from him and marched toward me. "Did you hear me? Where is that fucking surveyor's report?"

"I don't think it ever came," I said.

He stared at me.

"Do you want me to give them a ring in the morning?" I asked.

Well, no, James did not want me to give them a ring in the morning. He made me aware, in no uncertain terms, that he did not want the surveyors anywhere near the place now.

"That report has suddenly dropped right down our list of priorities, don't you think?" he asked me. But it was good that he still believed there was a report.

"Help me look!" he said, and he marched along the riverbank on the same pilgrimage I had already made several times that day, looking for Lennie. I followed, wondering whether or not to tell him Lennie wasn't there. But James stopped, looking down into the water.

There was Lennie. Apparently, he had either broken loose from whatever had been holding him under or reached the optimum stage of decomposition to have risen to the surface. He looked rather different to the last time I had seen him; the fine weather we had been having had certainly done its work. James stood, hands on his hips, surveying the scene as if it were a minor spillage. I looked at Lennie again, took in the full state of him, eyes missing, holes in his skin. I thought I could smell the decay, although I was a fair way away from him. I began to gag.

"Don't," James said. I walked away from the riverbank and took deep breaths of fresh air. I waited for James to tell me what to do, because I was certain there would be something.

Sure enough. "We're going to have to move him," he said.

I turned. "How are we going to get him out?" I asked. And out in one piece? He looked to be delicately held together and we didn't want an errant arm floating off on its own.

"We don't have to get him out. We just have to get him away from this area."

I returned to the riverbank, where James was picking fallen branches from the ground and discarding them. There was little that was much more than a twig. He reached up and pulled at a branch, then let it go.

"Wait here," he said to me. "Don't let anyone come past." And I watched him walking back to the house, wondering how I was meant to stop anyone coming past.

Luckily, no one did and a few minutes later, James reappeared with a spade and a rake from Mr. Billings's tool shed. "Which do you want?" he asked me.

Not being sure what they were to be used for, I chose the rake, as raking seemed to be a less labor-intensive job, but it turned out it didn't matter, the plan was to use them to push Lennie's body out, away from the riverbank, so that the current would catch it and float him off and away, far from our land. Perfect. I had to give James credit for a good plan there.

And so we began, gently prodding the body free of the reeds and out to where we could see the water moving. Lennie swirled for a moment, then began bobbing gracefully away from us.

We followed with our implements. Now and then James would give Lennie a little poke to stop him catching on some shrubbery on our side, or I would reach over and rake him back in toward us if he floated too far toward the other bank. We kept an eye out for walkers approaching, but it was a quiet evening on the public rights-of-way.

From a distance, we must have looked like a couple of country bumpkins carrying out some country chore, as our ancestors had done for centuries before us. And so we made our bucolic way along, the birds singing, the breeze rustling the leaves on the trees, and the river running alongside us, carrying its gruesome cargo. "Row, Row, Row Your Boat" popped into my head, and I sang it as we went along. So well was it all going, James didn't even tell me to "shut the fuck up."

Then we came to the end of the field, where the road went over the river and on the other side the Newmans' farm began.

"Is this far enough?" I asked. After all, once it was under the bridge, it was, technically, off our property. In a manner of speaking, the Newmans' farm was our property, them being tenant farmers—for now at least, the dispute over selling it for warehouses notwithstanding.

"It's not far enough," he said. "We need to get him well onto the Newmans' land. Otherwise, it's obvious where he came from."

I took his point, but I wasn't keen on going much farther.

Lennie floated under the bridge and stopped. The water was quite shallow there, and he seemed to have caught on a rock. James sighed and waded in. He pulled at Lennie until he moved a little farther but no more.

"Help me," he said, and after some hesitation, I laid down my rake and made my way into the cold water, going in with my shoes and socks on, as James had done. I didn't realize before how much time you spend standing in cold water after you've killed someone. As on the night of the accident, James took Lennie's shoulders and I took his ankles, gingerly holding his trousers and being careful not to touch flesh. We moved him along under the bridge, his head tipping back and under the surface. I had to keep reminding myself it didn't matter; we didn't need to be careful of his head.

Before we emerged from the bridge, we checked that there was still no one to see us, then we pushed the body out into the deeper water. James climbed up the riverbank on that side and I went back for the spade and rake, then walked through the gate and across the road to join him.

We continued on our way, this time I had the spade, the job of pushing him away seemed like an easier one than raking him in. Soon we would be well away from Langley Hall, then the body could float free and come to rest wherever it rested, its origin forever a mystery. But first, we had to get it past the farmhouse.

There was no sign that anyone was in there, but we were still some distance away, so we couldn't see the downstairs rooms or if there was a car in the drive.

A minute later, we didn't need to.

"Evening." Mr. Newman was making his way from the far end of the field toward us. Normally, the sight of us taking an evening stroll through the countryside would attract nothing more than a wave and maybe a "don't see you out here very often." But the attempt to evict Mr. Newman and his family from the farm had left bad feelings; Mr. N's demeanor was hostile, and he was marching our way with purpose. "Anything I can help you with?" he called as he neared us, in a tone that sounded more like "Get off my land."

He stopped and looked at us, looking down at our wet jeans and trainers and up at the gardening tools in our hands. Then he saw Lennie. His jaw dropped. He drew nearer to get a better look: It was a sight you had to see to believe.

"Is that… Is that the chap they're all looking for?"

It was a fair question. With the state Lennie was in, even his biggest fan—Mrs. Billings—would have to look twice to be sure it was him.

"Where did he come from?" Mr. Newman asked, and simultaneously, we all turned and looked upstream, back toward Langley Hall. Mr. Newman looked again at the rake and the spade, but I never knew if he completely understood what we'd been doing with them because at that moment, James made a bad decision. He pushed Mr. N into the river.

He fell into the murky depths, the movement of the water sending Lennie bobbing to the opposite bank. James and I watched as Mr. Newman sank, then rose again, standing in water that only came up to his waist.

"What did you do that for?" he shouted at James, and Mr. N and I waited, both curious to hear the answer. James said nothing. So, Mr. Newman stepped up to the bank and tried to climb out, but the riverbank was steep and slippery there. He was going to have to make his way farther downriver. Or upriver, if he preferred to wade past Lennie and back in the direction of Langley Hall. Unsurprisingly, he went in the direction of his home.

Then James launched himself. He leaped off the bank and onto Mr. Newman. They both fell backward and under. A moment later, they emerged fighting.

Although he wasn't young, James was a younger man than Mr. N and he had kept himself in shape—the mind games I played with altering his clothes notwithstanding—but Mr. N was bigger and I knew from local gossip that he could handle himself in a fight. It was anyone's guess who would win. It would be decided by stamina, luck, and, maybe, a woman on the riverbank, holding a spade.

I didn't know what would happen if I weighed in on the side of Mr. Newman. The story up to that moment was already a difficult one to explain away, but Mr. N disliked James and this escapade wouldn't be doing anything to change his mind on that front. My mum and the first Mrs. Newman had always got on well. Perhaps a helping hand from me here would be enough for him to believe me if I said I knew nothing about how Lennie had got into that state and that James had made me float him down the river.

If I weighed in on the side of James, I would probably be in line with the "for better, for worse" part of my wedding vows, but James would still be a thorn in my side, and anyway I'd been looking for a chance like this…

I raised the spade and waited for them to come close enough to the bank. I waited, waited, waited, and as James's head came near, I brought the spade down as hard as I could and hit…Mr. Newman.

"Aargh!" I shouted in frustration as Mr. N wobbled. I hadn't hit him hard enough to kill him, or even knock him out, but it unbalanced him long enough for James to push his head under and hold it there, with me screaming, "Stop! You'll kill him!" even though I was sure that was the point.

But Mr. Newman wasn't done for; he rose again. James grabbed the spade from me and battered him until he ceased to protest and fell back into the water, where James held him down again.

I watched the spot as the body sank, hoping for Mr. N to rise up one more time, with renewed strength and fury, and put an end to James, even though that would be disastrous for me now. But Mr. N didn't rise up, and after a while it was clear he wasn't going to. Instead, bubbles rose and burst.

"You took long enough, he nearly had the better of me," James said.

"What have you done!" I shouted. "What have you done?"

"What else could I have done, Daisy? We couldn't just let him walk away."

"But you've killed him."

"And you killed Lennie Green. Looks like one begets another. I just wonder: Who's next?" And he gave me a look I didn't much like.

"There was no need. We could have told him something."

"What like?"

"I don't know. We were taking Lennie to the police station?"

James looked at me but didn't speak.

"You've killed a man!" I squeaked at him as he reached for the rake and calmly began shepherding Lennie's body past the spot where he'd drowned Mr. N—sunk for now but sure to rise up again soon enough.

"You've killed a man too," he said. "Come on now, I need you to check there's no one at the Newmans' house."

With my only other option being to go back to Langley Hall and wait for whatever would come next, I crept toward the house and peered over the fence. There was no sign of anyone being in, the house was quiet, twilight was starting to fall, and the windows were dark. There was no sound.

So we went on down the river, until Lennie's body was well away from Langley Hall. Then we squelched back in our wet clothes across the fields to the spot we had left Mr. Newman in.

"We're going to have to move him," James said. "Get him farther away from Langley Hall and closer to where we left Lennie Green. At least then it will look like an accident. It will look like Doug Newman saw him floating past and stopped to have a look, then fell in and drowned himself."

I sighed. I knew you couldn't just leave corpses lying around, but I'd had enough of moving them for one day. Then a light came on in the farmhouse, so we couldn't be shunting a body along in the river next to it. Even if the body would be below the surface, we would be above it, behaving in a way that would definitely attract curiosity and questions and would stick in people's memories.

Instead, we went back to Langley Hall, dried ourselves off, and waited until midnight. Then we went back down to the river, entering the water at the shallow bit that went under the bridge, and waded down until we found the body. There was still a light on in the farmhouse. I wondered if they were sitting up waiting for Mr. Newman to come home while we were dragging his body along the riverbed, which is not much fun but is easier than carrying a body across land. We left him close to where we had left Lennie and went home.

# CHAPTER NINE

THE NEXT MORNING, JAMES GOT UP AND WENT TO WORK, AS EVER, as if nothing had happened.

"You'll need to get back out there and look for his bag," he said as he left. It took me a minute to work out what he meant, but of course, James thought Lennie's bag had been in the mausoleum with him, so he now thought it was out there, evidence waiting to be found. I waved him off promising I would not rest until it was safely back in the house, then I fetched some early-morning chocolate from the priest hole, tucked away behind Lennie's satchel, and watched some cartoons for a change.

But the cartoons could not stop me from rerunning the events of the night before in my head, wondering if I could have done something differently, such as, be more accurate with the spade. Then I could've been a merry widow that morning, maybe even a local hero, depending on the tale Mr. Newman chose to tell, or believe.

Instead, I was involved in the death and disposal of not one, but two casualties.

I made myself go through the usual routine: shower, breakfast, sewing, and tea and biscuits with Mrs. Billings, trying to sound interested in the goings-on at the amateur dramatics society. As she talked, I kept an anxious eye on Mr. Billings and his shed, having realized we'd forgotten to check the spade for blood the night before, but he was busy with a trowel and a flowerbed, so it seemed we'd have a second chance at hiding that evidence.

Then a knock on the door, which Mrs. Billings answered before I could run away. On the doorstep were a young police constable and an older man wearing a tweed suit with a waistcoat and an old Victorian-style watch hanging by a chain from his top pocket. At the sight of the police uniform, my knees went a little weak and I wondered *how did they know so soon?* I'd have thought that even in the worst-case scenario, I'd still have a day or two of freedom left to me, at least until they found the bodies.

The police officer introduced himself as PC Applegate and the older man as Mr. Earnest Winkleman, who was the local coroner. The coroner! Imagine! Although it was not my first experience of a coroner.

"Are you the property owner?" PC Applegate asked me, and I wasn't sure how to reply.

"My husband," I said in the end.

The coroner did the rest. "You may have heard about a number of bones that have appeared in Upper Iffley?" He was smiling, so either it wasn't all that bad, or he enjoyed delivering bad news.

"I saw it on TV," I said, then taking my inspiration from Mrs. Chambers: "It's a mystery."

"Perhaps not quite such a mystery as it seems. I believe there's a graveyard attached to this property?"

I nodded; I didn't trust myself to speak.

"We think that's where they may have come from." He took an Ordnance Survey map from his pocket and began unfolding it. "I believe the river runs along the edge of it."

I nodded again.

"We'd just like to nip down and take a look?" he said, making it sound like something I could say no to.

I felt myself starting to shake. This was it. They were going to arrest me and lock me up for life.

"Don't you need a warrant to search the property?" Mrs. Billings spoke up.

"There's a public right-of-way through it," I said to her.

No doubt they already knew that from their Ordnance Survey, and I realized at that moment that there had never been a chance it was all going to go unnoticed. It was only a matter of time—and not a long time—before another dog walker strolled past the ruined mausoleum and on, back to his house, where he mentioned to his wife that the tomb up by Langley Hall had come down and there was a skull in the river. And the wife would look at the pelvis in their vegetable patch and say, "I wonder if that's where this is from?"

"We like to speak to you first as a courtesy," the coroner said.

"Are you going to arrest poor Lord Langley?" Mrs. Billings asked the police officer.

Or "Lady Langley" I thought, feeling the blood drain from my head.

Mr. Winkleman gave a short laugh. "Goodness me, no! It's time and tide will have shifted those bones, no one's being arrested."

"I'm just here as a precaution," PC Applegate said.

"A precaution for what?" Mrs. Billings asked, but we never got to the bottom of that.

Well, at least I wasn't going to be arrested. For now—Lennie and Mr. Newman were still out there somewhere—but I was still apprehensive as the "all will be revealed" moment approached. I kept imagining that somehow their bloated corpses might have made their way back upstream and would be found lying just to the side of a skull.

Nevertheless, I said, "No problem."

"Well, if you're sure, Lady Langley," Mrs. Billings said. "But we should go down with them and keep an eye on things."

"It's quite a walk," I said, thinking of her creaky knees and wondering if we'd have to get the wheelbarrow out for her, as we should have done for Lennie.

"I'll manage," Mrs. B said. And so she did, moving over the lawn, through the copse, and across the field to the graveyard with a speed and surefootedness that eluded her in the house. We picked up Mr. Billings en route, Mrs. B feeling sure this was a spectacle he wouldn't want to miss, and nor did he. I marched ahead of them, leading the way, practicing my surprised face as I went.

When Mr. Billings saw the toppled mausoleum, he whistled in amazement. "Never thought I'd see the day," he said. "Thought this would outlast the pyramids." He bent down to pick something up off the ground and rose with a small bone in his hand. He crossed himself and muttered something under his breath.

"Makes you wonder what's next," Mrs. Billings said, and she cast a wary eye back toward the house.

"When did this happen?" the coroner asked. "Are you alright?"

I closed my gobsmacked mouth. "Just surprised," I said. I think I might have overdone it. I hoped the dog walker wasn't going to appear and reveal that I'd known about it for days. And ask after Tibs.

The coroner asked me again when the mausoleum had collapsed, and I said I didn't know. He picked his way through the overgrown grass, scanning the ground for more bones as he went. Occasionally he would stoop and pick one up. He went to the entrance of the mausoleum and looked inside. I waited, breath baited, but he came away showing no sign of anything untoward. Or more untoward than he expected it to be.

He wandered to the riverbank, and we all held our breath in case he slipped in the mud and was washed downstream to the village, proving his own theory as to where things that entered the water here ended up.

But he didn't slip; he made his way back to us, a small collection of bones in his hands. "Yes," he said. "I think we've found the source. There's a fairly recent-looking coffin still in the ruins, do you know whose that would be?"

"That'd be the old lord," Mr. B told him. "He passed a few years ago."

"Thirtysomething years ago," I said.

"Aye," Mr. Billings said, "a few years."

The coroner nodded. "Well, that's the only one looks like it might be recent, so PC Appleby, I think we're done with your services after today, just as we expected." He turned to me. "Who's responsibility is it to maintain that building?"

I did my best to look shamefaced as I said, "The property owner."

"So, what happens now?" Mr. Billings asked as we made our way back to the house.

"The archaeologists come into it," the coroner said. "They'll gather together the bones and try to identify which goes with which. Then, they'll need a proper reburial."

"Will we be haunted?" Mrs. B asked.

"You'd have to ask the vicar about that," the coroner said. He turned to me. "Do you have a record of who was buried in that mausoleum?"

"It's on the wall, if you can read it," I said. We walked round to where the slab with the names and dates on it had fallen. It was there but in pieces.

"Never mind. We might be able to put it back together. If not, there'll be something somewhere. Maybe in the church logbooks, if we have an idea of the dates we're looking at."

And I thought of the original family tree, which, at least, would have given us the years. Mrs. B led them back to the house, with promises of tea and biscuits. I stayed a moment; I'd seen the skull James had thrown in anger the night before, still lying on its side in the long grass. I picked it up and examined it for damage. It had hit a rock and was fractured. There was nothing I could do, other than to set it carefully on its jaw beside the mausoleum.

"Sleep tight, Richard, Eleanor, Edward, Catherine, Margaret, Mabel, Henry, or Hugo. You probably didn't expect to see sunlight again," I said, before following the others back to the house.

After the Billingses had gone that day, I fetched the spade and the rake and gave them a wash, then I stuck them into the soil a few times to stop them looking too clean.

When James came home that night, he insisted we go back out and look for Lennie's bag and its contents. I told him I'd been out there looking countless times that day and I was exhausted, and in the end, he went by himself. That set the pattern for the following days, until he decided that wherever it was, it must be far away from Langley Hall.

---

"No one's seen Doug Newman for days," Mrs. Billings said on Monday morning. "Jo took the kids to karate last Wednesday evening and when she came home, Meg was there, but no sign of Doug." Jo was Mrs. Newman, Mr. Newman's second wife, and Meg was Mr. N's favorite sheepdog.

"Oh," I said, reflecting, with relief, on the fact that Meg hadn't been there that night. Would James have drowned her as well? I didn't like to think.

"He never leaves Meg if he's going to be more than a few minutes."

"Oh," I said again. "Do you think he's racked up gambling debts and run off?"

"That would be more than a few minutes," Mrs. Billings said, then: "Well, I'm not going to be the one to tell Jo. Still strange he didn't take the dog."

---

The archaeologists' plan was that they would set up a tent with a generator in the graveyard, and they would do as much as they could from there before taking everything to the university. There was a short delay while James tried to negotiate the bill we were liable for down. He thought it would arouse suspicion if he went meekly to the checkbook and paid up without a quarrel. So negotiations commenced, but he was soon convinced that this would keep the costs down as far as possible, and work began.

By now, a collection point had been set up in the village hall and people were bringing them, bone by bone, as they found them in their streets and gardens.

"It's quite a party," Mrs. Billings told me. "They've decorated the table and the box they're collecting the bones in. There's bunting all over the place. The church choir's doing a turn and the teashop's set up a refreshments stall, so you can go there and have a cake and a natter."

I wasn't the biggest fan of Mrs. Thorpe and Mrs. Thrussell from The Two Ts teashop; they had declined to take my cakes after my mum had died and I needed a bit of extra income. A lot of extra income, if the truth be told. And it wasn't due to their quality, I knew, because they took some from the local Brownie pack and they blended their ingredients with all the finesse of a cement mixer. I was no expert, but I'd been making Victoria sponges, just the odd one here and there, since before the Brownies were born.

"They're talking about having a raffle if it goes on into the weekend," Mrs. Billings continued. "To raise money for the church bell appeal. They might have some music and a little disco for the kiddies. They're calling it the Bone Bonanza and are thinking to mark it every year." She sounded quite excited by this addition to the village calendar, which presumably would fall between the May Day celebrations and the village fete in July.

"If they raise any money it should go to me. To pay for all of this," James said when a delegation came to the house to tell him, firsthand, about the collection for the church bells and to ask him if, given the link to the hall and grounds, he would like to make a contribution. So, far from being the recipient of the fundraising, James had to fork out another grand to avoid looking churlish. Regardless, the envoys were hardly able to conceal their disappointment at receiving only one thousand of the billions of pounds James had as they departed.

And he'd have been even more annoyed had he known that the generator the archaeologists set up was not all it could be and they began trekking up to the house, asking favors.

"Young gentleman wanting to use the electricity, Lady Langley, love," Mrs. Billings shouted to me when the first one knocked on the kitchen door.

I'm not sure James is going to like that, I thought, imagining he'd come to plug the generator in, which may not have gone well for our dilapidated wiring, but all the man standing in the doorway had in his hands was a kettle.

He was young, about thirty, muscular, with long blond hair and an Aussie-surfer style about him. He had colored string bracelets tied around his wrist. We'd called them friendship bracelets when I was at school; he must have had a lot of friends judging by the number he had. With that, he wore loose shorts, trainers, and a T-shirt that wouldn't have looked out of place hung up next to mine.

"Sorry to intrude," he said. "But I wondered if I could boil up in here, please? We blew a fuse when we tried to do it from our own power. It was just that bit too much for the generator."

"Of course," I said, standing back to let him in and gesturing to the nearest socket. As he saw the full splendor of my outfit—a T-shirt made from other T-shirts, it was a wardrobe staple, and a skirt made from an old throw—he stared, astonished.

"Kaboolu?" he said.

"What?"

"Are your clothes from Kaboolu? I've never seen anyone else wearing Kaboolu clothes before. Where did you find them?"

I'd never had a reaction like that to my clothes. He sounded almost impressed, and it was a minute before I answered. In my befuddlement, I nearly said, "Yes, Kaboolu," but I recovered myself and told the simple truth: "No, I made them myself."

"Really?" He sounded slightly awestruck. "Did you base it on their designs?"

"No, I've never heard of them."

Then he took out his phone and showed me a website for a clothes company based in New Zealand, which did have a few T-shirts similar to mine, but the rest of their merchandise was pretty mundane. There was nothing that looked as if it had once been a curtain, a tablecloth, or a pet blanket.

"Hmm, they're as loopy as you," Mrs. Billings said to me, looking at the website.

"I love their stuff," the man said. "But it costs an arm and a leg. They make them to order, and then I have to get them sent all the way over here."

I looked at the prices, and yes, some of them gave James's designer gear a run for its money.

I looked more closely. "I could make them," I said, looking at a page full of T-shirts.

He looked over my shoulder. "Which one?"

"All of them."

There was a moment's quiet in the kitchen while we both thought about what I'd just said. "Would you like me to make you one?" I asked.

"Really?"

I nodded. "What colors do you like?"

"Yellow and red are my favorites."

"I have yellow and red material," I said, and if I didn't, charity shop purchases on my bank statement went unremarked on by James. "I'll need to measure you up first, though."

I went to find a measuring tape while he boiled his kettle and Mrs. B stayed to watch in case he took a liberty and charged his phone as well.

"You making much progress down there?" she was asking when I got back.

"Well, it's only the first week," the man said. "But so far so good. The bones are coming in thick and fast, and we're cleaning and sorting them."

Mrs. B helped me measure him. I was nervous and my hands were rather shaky to start with. I'd never made clothes for someone else before, and I'd definitely never measured a man I'd only just met; I was glad it was only a T-shirt I'd offered to make. Mrs. Billings took to it like an old pro and soon we had arms, inner arms, shoulders, waist, and length.

By then the kettle had started to cool, so he gave it a quick reboil and prepared to return to the graveyard.

"I'll see you soon then, um, Lady Langley…love?"

"Daisy," I said. "My name's Daisy."

"Lovely name," he said. "I'm Artemis."

"Really?" I said.

"Yes, really. But you can call me Arty."

# CHAPTER TEN

"THERE'S BONES ALL OVER THE VILLAGE," MRS. BILLINGS SAID, arriving in the kitchen a few days later. Since the discovery in the graveyard, she had upped her hours and was here most days. She was enjoying being the go-between for the village gossips and Langley Hall, although she hadn't consulted her employer—me—about whether or not all this overtime was required, and I wasn't seeing a lot in the way of extra productivity. What's more, I was running short of knickknacks to put out for her and needed an urgent restock at the charity and souvenir shops.

"Brought these for you." Mrs. B dropped a handful of probably-finger bones on the table. "They washed up on the playing fields. Next door's boys brought them round, knowing I was coming up here."

"Thank you. Do you think the table's the best place for them?" I asked, stepping away, slightly disgusted.

"Where else?" she asked me, looking at the floor, and she had a point. "Still no word from Doug Newman," she said. "Jo's beside herself. She doesn't know what to tell the kids. It would help if she could just have some answers. I'd swing for him if I saw him now."

The story moved on a stage a few days later.

"They've found a body," Mrs. Billings said as we sat ourselves down for our morning tea, which I was finding less enjoyable now that it was a daily occurrence. I'd started ordering boring Rich Tea biscuits in an effort to hurry her along. So far it hadn't worked. For a moment, I thought she was talking about more bones and I didn't react to her comment. Then, the difference between what might be referred to as a bone and what we would call a body registered. "And?" I asked her, all agog to hear which one it was.

"They think it's Lennie Green," she said. "Poor, poor man."

Even though it had only ever been a matter of time, my heart stopped and my face froze.

"It were all over the village this morning. They haven't said officially it was him, but they're saying his family have been informed, so same difference."

"It could be someone from somewhere else," I suggested, but why was I suggesting it? Trying to put other ideas into Mrs. B's head wasn't going to change the outcome of the identification. Although it wasn't over until the results were announced: It *could* be someone else. Mr. Newman, for example.

"Couple of kids out playing found him, down by the river. Poor mites." Mrs. Billings shuddered. "They'll have nightmares the rest of their lives."

Yes, as I could confirm, he was in a pretty gruesome condition. Probably only held together by his clothes.

"Oh, Lennie, Lennie Green." Mrs. Billings was slipping into lament mode. "Dread to think what happened to him, to turn up like that, all these weeks after he went missing. Shall I put the radio on? There'll be a bulletin soon."

But I'd heard enough. I took a big gulp of my tea and scalded my mouth.

"You alright, Lady Langley, love?" Mrs. B asked. "You look like you've swallowed a wasp."

---

"Has anyone said anything to suggest they think there is any connection between Lennie and our old bones?" James asked me when I told him. "Have they found Doug Newman yet?"

"I've only spoken to Mrs. Billings," I said. "She didn't say anything about a connection, to us or to Mr. Newman." It was far from a final word on the matter, but no news was good news.

"Maybe they won't," James said and he looked hopeful, the hopeful look of an intelligent man following a logical thought through to a logical conclusion. "Compared to those old bones, Lennie is a pretty fresh kill. Why would they link them together?"

That was a very good point. I flushed with hope myself, but that hope was still tinged with concern about the body of Mr. Newman, which surely could only be days, if not mere hours, away from rising from the depths and traumatizing more children. The rumor of debts and an escape, which I hoped I had started and trusted Mrs. Billings to spread around the village, would not outlast that discovery.

---

I stitched Arty's new T-shirt together, a dazzling mix of reds, with a recurring sunshine yellow running through. It took me a day and a half. Sewing a patchwork T-shirt was something I could do in my sleep; it only took as long as that because of the unfamiliar measurements. But I waited before I delivered it. I didn't want him to think I had nothing better to do.

In the meantime, the archaeologists turned out to be friendly. It really was like *Time Team*, and I started making trips down to their site, ostensibly to see if they needed any biscuits—which turned out to be absolutely *essential* on an archaeological dig—but really for their company. And to check they weren't examining anything Lennie-related that I'd failed to find before. I was glad now that I'd put his bag in the priest hole and not in the mausoleum with him, for the contents of that to be scattered all over the place would have been a disaster.

"What's the best thing you've ever dug up?" I asked a grizzled old veteran of the trenches, and he talked at length about skeletons through the ages.

"What would be your dream corpse?" I asked a student, and she talked of how she'd like to go to Egypt and see mummies in situ.

"We did a project on ancient Egypt at junior school," I told her. Of all the projects we had done, it was one of the most memorable; we'd had a model of a body, and we'd had a go at mummifying it. The student nodded along as I described to her what we'd done, then she gave me a bit more detail I could've done without.

I saw Arty leaning over a half-complete skeleton and I went to look. He didn't hear me approach—he had earbuds in and he jumped a mile in the air when I tapped on his shoulder. When he took them out I could hear Boney M blasting from them.

"Best band ever," he said, when he saw me looking at the buds. "They were my mum's favorite and they kind of seeped into my blood, or my DNA, or something."

I looked at the bones he was piecing together. "It's a bit like a jigsaw puzzle, isn't it?"

Arty's expression said "no" when I asked that question, but his words were "Quite like a jigsaw puzzle."

Then he straightened up, stretched, and accepted a Nice biscuit from me; Mrs. B didn't know I had them and was still being strictly rationed to Rich Tea. "It's funny, it wasn't really archaeology I wanted to do, but this seemed liked the best choice when it was time to decide. I like it, don't get me wrong, but I really wanted to work in antiques."

"So did I!" I told him. "I worked at the bric-a-brac shop in town when I left school. I loved it there. I was going to be trained on the antiques side, but it closed down and then…stuff happened."

"And now you're lady of the manor. You must have antiques everywhere you look," he said. "So things seem to have turned out alright."

Which made it sound as if I'd achieved something.

"What's the best item you have?" he asked me.

"A partial suit of armor from Elizabethan times," I said.

"I said the best, not the oldest."

"There's a Victorian carriage clock; it's very ornate," I tried again, but he still wasn't convinced.

"What is here that you think is beautiful and unique and could never be replaced?"

I bit my lip and thought again of the original family tree.

---

The body that was found by the river was, of course, formally identified as Lennie. The reporter stood by the riverbank he had washed up on. Behind him, the ground was bedecked with flowers, soft toys, and handwritten notes bewailing the loss. More pilgrims approached to lay a wreath as the reporter spoke. You would've thought Princess Di had died again.

The camera closed in on some of the notes, and I saw "We will never forget you. Eric and Brenda." Eric and Brenda Billings, I had no doubt. The camera shot changed and we saw crime scene tape close to the flowers.

"The investigation continues," the reporter finished his piece. He turned to look back at the river and nearly toppled in himself, so surprised was he to see the body of Mr. Newman as it rose from the depths, just a few meters from the tributes to Lennie. The camera operator was quick enough to shift the focus from the reporter to the river, making both of their careers.

# CHAPTER ELEVEN

"SO, IT WASN'T GAMBLING DEBTS," MRS. BILLINGS SAID TO ME OF Mr. Newman.

"Unless his loan shark chased him and shoved him in," I suggested, but Mrs. B didn't seem convinced and there wasn't much point pushing that theory anyway: It wasn't going to stand up to scrutiny.

"Poor, poor Doug," Mrs. B said. "And Jo and them kids. And Meg, especially Meg. She's not a young dog."

Mrs. Billings put the radio on; it was time for a bulletin. The report was long, but with little of note so far about either Lennie or Mr. Newman, just that the police were treating both deaths as "unexplained."

"And unexplainable." Mrs. B shook her head sadly and I realized that, from her point of view, there was a lot that was not known, such as, did they die together or at different times? There was nothing on the bulletins about the state of decomposition. How did they die?

Had Mr. Newman come across Lennie's body, or had he—could he have—been hiding him? That would be a good lead to get out there, with all the barns and outhouses around the farm. "They'll want to do a postmortem," she said.

"On whom?" I asked and she thought for a minute, before saying: "Both of them."

I wondered what that would bring to light. Would Lennie's cuts and bruises still be visible? Had he broken any bones in the collision? Would Mr. Newman be written off as an accidental drowning? Or would a spade mark in the middle of his face give the lie to that?

When I said, "Do you think there's anything in the kidnapping theory for Lennie Green?" Mrs. B didn't take the bait.

And so we carried on. All that Mrs. Billings and the local radio station could talk about was the bodies, but no one came to Langley Hall asking about them.

Mrs. Billings wore black for days, along with a remembrance poppy for some reason.

"If anyone hurt either Lennie Green or poor old Doug, I'll string them up myself," she said.

I wondered exactly what that entailed and what her chances of achieving it were, particularly if I fought against it, which I would. Maybe if she got Mr. B involved? Would he help?

"Have them police officers been back here?" she asked me. "The ones who came because you were at the same party?"

"No," I said. "Why would they?"

"Just wondered," she said, pulling biscuits, sugar, and milk from her bag and switching the kettle on. I was annoyed to see she had brought Bourbons, although I had been clear in ordering Rich Tea.

I watched carefully for any sign of what she was thinking. Mrs.

Billings wasn't an idiot. Not only was I sure she had Lennie's phone, but she'd been reading his memoir; it was unrealistic to think she knew nothing. I wondered if I was going to have to bump her off as well. She would certainly be easier to do away with than James, one good shove down the stairs should do it, and with the way she wielded the vacuum cleaner, it would be a simple thing to pass off as an accident.

Maybe that was the moral of this story: Think twice before you hide a body because you'll end up hiding more. But as I watched Mrs. B enjoying a Bourbon, her favorite, the idea of dispatching her made me feel sad.

I told myself she must be waiting for a simple explanation to emerge. After all, she'd known me all my life, she was friends with my mum, and James was from a respected village family—his mum was a *supervisor* at the SPAR and his dad was on the council for years. Surely, she wouldn't think that James and I had done what we actually did.

Or, maybe she was keeping quiet out of loyalty to my mum and the history we had. I didn't like to think about how far that loyalty may or may not stretch. If I took too long to act, circumstances could overtake me, then I'd have years in a prison cell to reflect on what I should have done. And looking on the bright side, if I did help her shuffle off this mortal coil, it would be an opportunity to hire a cleaner who actually cleaned.

But I still didn't want to, so I decided to monitor her for signs and hints about what she knew and what she was going to do.

---

After a decent gap, to make it look like I had other things to do, I delivered the T-shirt I had made for Arty.

"I love it!" he said. He tried it on there and then, as "Rivers of Babylon" serenaded us from his phone, jiggling to the music, and I must say, he did look good. He also looked good without a shirt at all. On the way back to the house, I tried to forget I'd had that thought.

"What do I owe you?" he asked.

But he owed me nothing; the cost of the materials was small, I still had plenty left over, and the pleasure of delivering it was payment enough. "Would you like another T-shirt?" I asked and he said he would.

Within a couple of weeks, there were two of us on the estate dressed like rag dolls. I branched out into waistcoats, shirts, and a couple of cravats, just in case he had a special occasion. I couldn't bring myself to offer to measure him for trousers; I felt the blood rushing through me at the mere thought of it and wondered if this was passion or a hot flush.

Thinking about Kaboolu, I started making small labels with "Daisy Daydream" written on them and sewing them into the clothes. I remembered my mum saying that one day people would envy us for what we could do with a needle and thread.

I wouldn't accept any money from Arty. The new project gave me some respite from worrying about the bodies and the police and what they may or may not be thinking. While I was sewing I imagined setting up an empire of Daisy Daydream clothes, like Kaboolu, but with branches all over the world.

Sometimes we got together on Arty's lunch break and looked through his copy of *Miller's Antiques Encyclopaedia*, a comprehensive guide that he kept in his car for when he went to flea markets at weekends. Then, I would go back to the house and fantasize about running away with Arty to run an antiques shop by the coast.

I began taking various items from the house down to show him, a few of the smaller items, the Victorian clock, some silver, pieces of jewelry. We looked them up and he put prices to them. It turned out some of them were very valuable, particularly the jewelry, but that wasn't a surprise to me.

Arty's passion for the pieces I brought him reminded me of how I had been.

"Look at the craftsmanship in this!" he said, opening a locket, and we wondered who the picture inside was of, if the answer was in Langley Hall somewhere.

"Think of the history this has seen!" he exclaimed of a doll. "Look at the life it's lived!" as he examined a crack in a butter dish. Then he gave me an estimate for it. It ended up being left for Mrs. B, but even she had her standards.

---

Not long after the discovery of the bodies, an invitation arrived through the post. There was to be a fundraiser in memory of Lennie to raise money for his good causes.

It was to be an auction, which was something I'd never been to, but when I showed it to James, he assured me it would be both expensive and dull.

"They'll be selling theater tickets with meet-the-cast backstage passes and weekends on luxury yachts, or hampers of stuff you would never use. They know someone who's big in a TV production company, so there might be a walk-on part on a TV show."

"But we're not going?" I asked, horrified, as James propped the invitation up on the mantelpiece. It was to be hosted by Margery again, and her husband, who I now learned was called Gordon.

"Why wouldn't we go? We always go to these things."

"It wouldn't be appropriate for us to go," I said. "Under the circumstances."

"Try looking at it from the point of view of someone who doesn't know the circumstances. Imagining you don't know we're responsible for Lennie's death—excuse me, *you're* responsible—I'll ask you again: Why wouldn't we go?"

"Because there's nothing in it for you."

And that, James conceded, was a fair point, but we had to go anyway because it would look suspicious for him to decline an invitation for the first time in recorded history.

---

"You're driving again," James said on the night of the fundraiser, "but be careful this time."

"I can't drive. I'll be too scared," I told him, the emotions of that night were starting to come back to me and I hoped desperately for something to happen to stop us going. I even thought seriously for a minute about burning Langley Hall down, with or without us in it.

"We can't do anything out of the ordinary," he reminded me. "Just take a few deep breaths before we set off."

And so, it was decided. In preparation, I let James's suit back out again and added a bit to the waistband of his trousers. If nothing else, it would be a distraction to see his bafflement when he realized he was going to need a belt.

When the night came I wanted to go in a loose yellow dress, with daisies embroidered around the hem, which was the last thing my mum and I had made together. Over the years I'd had to add some panels in, to let it out, but it was worth it because it took me back to happier days and reminded me that there had once been someone who was on my side. It helped me stay calm. But James wasn't keen.

"What in god's name are you wearing?" he said, when I appeared downstairs.

"What's wrong with it?"

"It looks like it was cobbled together from old rags."

Which it pretty much was. I shrugged.

"Go and get changed."

Instead, I put on the same gray silk dress I'd worn on the night of the accident, which had survived the hot wash surprisingly well. It was just a bit smaller now, but I had shrunk as well. The stress had put the snacks in the priest hole largely out of my mind. I accessorized with another tablecloth-scarf.

"It's not meant to be a reconstruction!" James yelped, hoisting up the trousers I'd adjusted.

So, I went back upstairs—"Grab me a belt while you're up there!"—and redonned the yellow dress I'd started out with. "We'd better get a move on" was all James said about it that time.

Feeling much happier in the cheerful yellow, I drove us, mishap-free, to Margery and Gordon's, where we parked once again in the avenue outside their house. This time James didn't complain, so in that way this whole episode had made a better man of him. We marched to the front door and, as before, it was opened for us by a gentleman in a suit. Inside, all the usual suspects were lined up with all the usual refreshments and stilted small talk.

"Drink?" a voice behind me asked and I turned to see Margery, once again, with a bottle of wine tucked under one arm and a bottle of water under the other. And James said it wasn't meant to be a reconstruction?

"Water, please," I said. "Sparkling." It was going to be easy to stick to this time.

"Help yourself to nibbles," Margery said, nodding to a buffet set out on tables along the wall below the windows. That was different.

At the buffet, guests were milling around, talking about what they thought had happened to Lennie.

"I bet he fell in the river, drunk," one man said. "I always knew it would end like that."

A few people sighed and nodded, while others tutted and said, "Steffan!"

"You know, I'd been worried about his state of mind for a while," a woman said, then she dropped her voice and I had to turn round to see her tapping her head and mouthing the words "losing it."

"I think he was involved in something," her friend replied. "He was always consorting with those criminals."

"Reformed criminals," another reminded her.

A hush fell upon the gossips as the door opened and a young man, followed by an older woman, appeared. Anthony Green, son of Lennie Green, I remembered from the TV caption. I hadn't seen the woman, but I'd hazard a guess she was Lennie's wife. I looked at James, but he was choosing a whiskey with not a care in the world.

"James, look," I said, nudging him in the ribs. "It's Lennie's family."

"Yeah, I saw," he said.

"Aren't we going to say something to them?"

"Such as?"

I didn't know, but it didn't seem right to say nothing. I stepped forward and James pulled me back. "Don't go anywhere near them," he whispered.

"Shouldn't we even say sorry for their loss?"

"And our part in it? Stay away. Here…" And in a break from tradition, he handed me a plate from the buffet table and started piling food onto it.

But I only had time to eat two mini steak pies before we were all being ushered to our seats. The chatter in the room quietened down as Margery made her wobbly way—heels and alcohol-intake both high—onto the stage.

"Ladies and gentlemen," she said. "Thank you for coming on this most somber, but celebratory, night and thank you to Moira and Anthony for taking the time." I looked to see where they were and found them in the front row. James squeezed my arm hard, which I think meant don't look at them.

Margery continued. "If you haven't had a chance to browse the catalog we sent out, there are copies on your seats, but before we get to that, let me draw your attention to the inserts, which weren't in the original. I'm proud to announce this evening that we will be auctioning off a number of services by young people who have benefited from Lennie's charities."

And we were treated to a performance by insert number one, a band called The Rogues, made up of formerly unschoolable schoolboys Lennie had helped. They were offering their services for events, and after a set that was notable mostly for its volume, they were auctioned off to play at someone's thirtieth birthday party for £8,000. That set the night up nicely as a money-for-old-rope occasion.

Someone paid £15,000 for the theater meet and greet; £25,000 bought someone a coaching session with a football player I'd never heard of; and a weekend at a vineyard in France went for £30,000.

The bidding was interspersed with friends of Lennie's getting up on the stage to tell anecdotes about him, some short and sweet, some long and rambling. We all laughed politely, although for most of them you'd needed to be there.

Throughout it all, I kept trying to look at Anthony and Moira, and James kept squeezing my arm when he saw my head move, and it made for a very long evening, until my interest was piqued by the opportunity to go behind the scenes at *The Great British Sewing Bee*.

But James held my hands firmly on my lap while the bidding was taking place. It went for £35,000, which you'd think would be small change to a billionaire, and I would have been great for the show. Maybe I would apply to be a contestant.

With that thought, I cheered myself up as we waited for lot seventeen, the use of a Ferrari for a day, that James was planning to bid on. Then Margery got back up on the stage.

"Next up is item number two in your insert," she said. "I'd like to introduce you to a young man who made some mistakes in his early days. Indeed, he came to Lennie's notice when he was in a Young Offenders Institution, but there's no need to hold on to your wallets, ladies and gentlemen, our next lot is a leopard who really did change his spots. I give you..."

Music played, the song was "Daddy Cool," and onto the stage strode...

"Arty!" I squeaked. And lo and behold, there on stage was Arty, dressed in very tight-fitting jeans and one of the T-shirts I'd made him.

"What the hell is he wearing?" James said.

"In Young Offenders Arty learned an array of handyman tasks before being accepted to an archaeology course," Margery told us, and that remarkable change in circumstances got him a loud round of applause. "Now, as a thank-you for all Lennie's support, he's here to offer a day's work as an odd jobs man. Or he can give you an expert opinion on any skeletons you might have in your closet!"

James tutted as the other guests rolled in the aisle, but I didn't care: Arty, my muse, my inspiration, was up there on the stage! His eyes wandered over the audience as the bidding started. He cast his gaze toward our part of the room and I smiled, anticipating his smile in return, but he missed me. As his gaze came back my way, I thrust my left arm in the air and waved to him.

"Two thousand pounds with the lady in the unique yellow dress," the auctioneer said. James pulled my arm down. Arty smiled at me.

"Sit still!" James said, as someone else raised the bid to £2,500.

But no! If I couldn't have the *Sewing Bee*, I *would* have Arty. My limbs were turning to jelly as he danced around the stage.

"Three thousand pounds anywhere?" the auctioneer asked, and I put my right arm in the air. That one was harder for James to reach, but he got me in the end. The betting went up to £4,000, then five, then six. At £10,000 it started going up in two thousand increments and that was when I wriggled an arm free of James.

"Twelve thousand pounds to the lady in yellow."

James yanked my arm down hard.

"Come on, Dixon, let her have a bit of fun. You can afford it," said a voice behind us, and they were the magic words; James hated to be seen to be miserly. I won Arty for a trifling £18,000.

"Don't leave him on his own in the house," James said. "We don't know what he was in prison for."

James chose not to bid on the Ferrari after that; instead we left with a set of luxury bath products that could probably be bought for less than £100 on the high street, but in the hands of the auctioneer went for £2,000. As James lifted his arm to make the bid, his sleeve dropped down and I noticed for the first time he was wearing a different watch. It looked a far cry from the luxury item that, he was fond of telling people, cost nearly two hundred grand. It looked more like something you could get for a tenner on Amazon with free delivery.

"What happened to your watch?" I asked him as we got into the car.

He glanced at his wrist and pulled the sleeve down as far as it would go. "The Rolex was a liability," he said. "Makes me a sitting duck for muggers. It's like the Wild West in Bristol these days."

Having watched the regional news several times a day, every day, since the accident, there wasn't much I didn't know about local affairs and if Bristol had become a hotbed of violence, I think I would have heard. But I didn't argue with him.

# CHAPTER TWELVE

WE HAD RUN OUT OF CHIPS AND THE GROCERY ORDER WASN'T DUE for two days. It was coming up to rush hour and I'd spend ages stuck in traffic if I went to the supermarket in town, so I decided to take one of my rare trips into the village to buy some at the SPAR.

On the way I had to drive past the village hall, and what a sight it was to see. An enormous cardboard thermometer stood beside the main door, showing the progress of the church bell fund. The cardboard mercury was well on its way up the scale, only £25,000 left to raise, which was quite a progression from the quarter mark it had hovered at for as long as I could remember.

Bunting was strung everywhere, there were a couple of stalls on the driveway, one selling homemade ice lollies, the other an opportunity to give to another good cause, beaver repopulation this time. By the main door was a cardboard sign with an arrow, pointing to the interior, and the words "More Inside!" I remembered what Mrs. B had said about a raffle and a disco.

As I sat there, Mrs. Chambers from the small shop rode up on her bike, half a rib cage sticking out of the basket on the front. She gave me a cheerful wave when she saw me and rang her bell.

Being an outcast, I tended to stay away from social gatherings in the village, but this was too intriguing and Mrs. Chambers's greeting was encouraging. As long as I spent plenty of money in there, I should be tolerated, so I parked up and nipped over to the ATM. Before I entered the building, I stopped to give twenty pounds each to the bell fund and the beavers—a beaver dam in the right place might have stopped the mausoleum collapsing.

Inside the village hall, the table where the bones were collected was center stage and was manned by one of the archaeologists. It should have been a simple trestle table with a large, plain cardboard box on it, but under the leadership of Mrs. Faulkner from the newsagent's, the table had been adorned with bunting in pastel shades, and the box was covered with floral design paper. Alongside was an exhibition celebrating the skeletal invasion, including a display showing where some of the bones had been found. Most were in the flower beds and water features of the gardens nearest the river, those that had been flooded, although there was a skull and crossbones found on the roundabout in the playground, just a few hundred yards from where we stood. That may not have been how they had washed up.

Music played from a system on the stage, and around the rest of the room were the farm shop and tea stalls, the raffle, a separate raffle, a Guess the Weight of the Melon competition, various craft stalls from various villagers: crocheted doilies, macramé plant hangers, jewelry made from kits bought online, dried flowers glued onto bookmarks. Mrs. Dowden, whom I had once worked with at the SPAR, presided over a display of wooden plaques with names etched onto them. There was one for most residents of the village, forename and surname, making it hard to say no to making a purchase.

My name had been overlooked, but feeling the weight of their expectant stares, I bought a few with general platitudes on them: "There's no place like home" and "Love conquers all," along with a few more cautionary notes, "What goes around comes around," "Familiarity breeds contempt," and "As you sow, so shall you reap." They could go in the drawer full of knickknacks I kept for Mrs. B; eventually, I might even take one out to see if she would steal it.

Although the jamboree had been going on for some time now, it seemed Upper Ifflians never tired of a fete and the room was busy with people browsing and trying their luck. I had a wobble when I saw Jo Newman, deep in tea and sympathy with the vicar. Meg was lying on the floor beside her, head on her front paws, eyes cast down. She looked like a dog without hope. I wanted to leave, to get far from the evidence of the devastation we had caused.

Then Mrs. Thorpe from the tea stall shouted: "Daisy!"

I turned, wondering what vitriol was heading my way. But no, I was quite the celebrity. I was greeted as the bringer of the bones and, subsequently, all the gaiety I saw before me. I was stood by the bone table to have my photo taken, by myself, with the archaeologist, with the stallholders, empty-handed, and holding a couple of bones.

"There was a minibus came from Great Beadington to have a look-see," Mrs. Thorpe told me. "They've heard about the bones and they're jealous."

Mrs. Thrussell nodded. "They've never had anything like it. And they won't do; they don't have a stately home."

Mrs. Faulkner joined in. "I had to chase one of them Great Beadingtonites out, she was trying to take a vertebra." There were gasps, although no one could verify Mrs. Faulkner's story and Mrs. Thorpe said she'd made it up.

"It was one of the Morten boys," she said. The Mortens were not a well-respected family. "And he tried to take a skull, not a vertebra. Who would want a vertebra that wasn't their own?"

"Don't you worry, Daisy," Mrs. Dowden said, patting me on the shoulder. "We'll make sure all those bones get back to you."

I was sat down for refreshments, and a village teenager, who was hoping to become a journalist, was summoned to interview me.

"How did you feel when you realized all the bones had been washed away?" he asked me, and I had to consider my answer carefully because once the initial horror had worn off, my first thoughts were of Lennie and what had become of his body.

"I was mortified," I said. "I know now that it's just the usual ravages of time that caused it, but when I first saw them, I felt somehow responsible."

He nodded somberly. "Do you know how many bodies were affected?"

Including or excluding Lennie's? "No," I said. "I don't know."

"How long will it take to get them collected and put together again?"

I referred that one to the archaeologist, who answered with, "How long's a piece of string?" James wouldn't be pleased to hear that.

Then he asked me a few questions about life in Langley Hall, which I answered with, "It's loads of fun," "It's a lot of work," and "The time just flies."

"Next time you come, you'll be able to read what he writes," Mrs. Dowden said as we finished the interview. "Now, do you need any more of these?" She was brandishing her etchings again. "You must have a lot of rooms needing plaques up in that big house."

I bought "The best things in life are free" from her, thinking I could give it to James for his birthday. He'd hate it. Then I went around the craft stalls and bought samples from every one. Maybe James wouldn't think my homemade clothes were so bad when he saw these.

I was about to leave when there was a kerfuffle at the door and in came another journalist, one whose words would be published in *The Western Bugle Online*, not just the *Upper Iffley Pages*. It was Emma Beddoe, the reporter I had met on the day I went to Great Beadington.

Emma looked around the room, smiling, looking hopeful. Her bright-pink hair was tied back, she was wearing combats and an orange T-shirt that still didn't go with her gaudy tresses, with a rucksack slung over her shoulder and camera on a strap around her neck.

"Hi," she said to Mrs. Faulkner, who was the first person to make eye contact with her. "I'm from *The Western Bugle Online*. I heard you had a do going on down here. I thought I'd check it out."

*The Western Bugle!* It caused quite a stir and Emma was given much the same welcome as I had been treated to only an hour earlier. I could hear Mrs. Faulkner telling her about the coach trip from Great Beadington and the woman who had—allegedly—tried to steal a vertebra.

"Goodness!" Emma said.

I moved toward the door, but as I neared it:

"Hi! Wait!"

I should have ignored it and pretended I thought she was talking to someone else, but the volume of her voice made me look round. "We've met before, haven't we?" she said.

For a moment I wondered how she'd known, my hair had been hidden under my cap when we'd met and the cap had obscured my face. Then I realized she was looking at my T-shirt; it was the same one I was wearing on the day we met. My heart sank. It wasn't even one of my most distinctive ones, although apparently it was distinctive enough.

"I like your skirt," she said. It was a patchwork arrangement, made from countless leftover scraps that would otherwise have been thrown out.

"This is Daisy," Mrs. Faulkner told her. "From Langley Hall."

"Langley Hall," Emma said, and suddenly all her attention was on me. "Do you live there?"

"Yes, that's her ladyship," Mrs. Faulkner said. "Married to the village billionaire."

Emma's eyes widened. "You must have had a shock when that tomb-thing came down."

"The mausoleum," I said. "Yes."

"How many bodies washed out?" she asked.

"I don't know."

"What did you think when you first saw it?"

At that the women around her started to protest because these were the same questions I'd been asked by the local teenager and it didn't seem fair that she'd get her words printed in *The Western Bugle Online* and read all over the district, and beyond, when his would not go past the bounds of Upper Iffley—Great Beadington, if he was lucky. So, I was allowed to leave and Emma was dragged toward the stalls, but now she knew who I was and where I lived, and I suspected that might be the reason she went so docilely toward Guess the Weight of the Melon.

"Do you think there is any connection to the finding of Lennie Green?" she called out as I hurried away, but I pretended not to hear, even when she shouted, "Or Doug Newman?"

---

It turned out Emma Beddoe wasn't the only person to have connected the ancient bones to the body of Lennie Green. The next morning Mrs. Billings took a break from vacuuming our bedroom to tell me, "Old Bill's poking around in the graveyard."

"What's that?" I said, trying to sound nonchalant. "I'm very busy." I looked around for something I might be busy with; I chose to clear out a cupboard.

Mrs. Billings came hobbling through. "I said Old Bill's on the premises. What do they want now?"

"I don't know." I was already struggling to keep my voice level.

"Don't you want to come and see?" Mrs. Billings asked and I supposed most people would want to see, so I followed her to the bedroom, bouncing with nerves, adrenaline telling me to just *run*. I kept myself stationary as Mrs. B put her glasses on for a better look.

"Aren't they supposed to ask before they go searching through your property? Like they came and introduced themselves before," Mrs. Billings said as we watched five or six of them, small figures in the distance, often hidden by the trees, but unmistakable in their uniforms, and the car they had parked on the grass. The archaeologists sat in a line along the hedgerow by the road, watching as the police examined the ground.

"I don't think I can stop them," I said.

Mrs. B said, "Aren't you going to go down and speak to them?"

"I usually leave that sort of thing to James." I realized I ought to phone him. Wouldn't any innocent woman let her husband know if the police started to search their property, allegedly without cause or warning?

I stared as hard as I could at the graveyard and I thought I could make out Arty, sitting amongst the gaggle of bone experts. What did he think? Was he wondering what I had done? What James had done? Or did he think the police had taken leave of their senses?

"Just ask them what they're doing. And why. Hold on…" And Mrs. B took her phone out of her overall pocket and called Mr. B. A moment later he strode across the grounds toward the graveyard, there he stood speaking to the police officers before turning around and heading back. We made our way down to meet him.

"You heard they found Lennie Green's body?" he said to me and I nodded. "Well, they reckon it came from here. Same as all those bones they've been collecting up."

I gasped and that, at least, was genuine. Mr. B scratched his head while Mrs. B said, "Never!"

"That's what I said," Mr. B agreed. "Lennie Green was a man in his prime." That was debatable. "Them bones are ancient; what would they all be doing together?"

Presumably he hadn't made the connection with the collapsed mausoleum in the corner. They looked at each other, then at me.

"Are you alright, Lady Langley, love?" Mrs. B said.

I nodded feebly. "What else did they say?" I asked.

"Nothing else," Mr. B said. "What else would they say?"

"I think I'd better give James a ring," I said.

I had to ring five times before James answered, but when he did, he took the news more stoically than I expected. He told me to go down and ask them if they wanted him to come home, but the thought of going down there and looking their official faces in the eye sent me all a-fluster. So off Mr. Billings went again and came back with the news that, no, they didn't want him to come home, but they would want to speak to him later.

"And you, Lady Langley," he said.

So we left them to it. Mr. Billings was looking tired by then, so I agreed that mowing the lawn could wait until next week.

"It's a young man's game is mowing," Mr. Billings said.

"Not long now, Eric, and we'll be folk of leisure," Mrs. Billings said to him. "Like Lady Langley here." They looked at each other, smiled, and nodded. Their nest egg.

The police came and went that day without speaking to us, other than to answer Mr. B's questions. Consequently, James and I were agog to watch the local news that evening. And there it was:

"Police search stately home as Lennie Green investigation continues!"

"That's not what happened!" I shouted. They made it sound as if they'd come into the house and ransacked it. Then we saw the reporter in the road that passed the hall, police tape, police cars, police signs—all the paraphernalia—behind him. We hadn't been able to see the reporters from the house.

"This road has been blocked off," he said. Yes, that was obvious. "While the police carry out investigations believed to be linked to the death of Lennie Green." And on he went, saying so much without saying anything of use: *Why* did they believe that? That was what we wanted to know, along with how Mr. and Mrs. Billings got home if that road was blocked off? They must have had to go all the way round, through Great Beadington. They would have been caught up in the traffic from town. It would have taken them ages. I wondered if they'd been late for Silver Surfers.

Then, Arty, wearing one of the cravats I'd made. Artemis Rainbow, the caption bearing his name said. I'd never thought to ask him his surname, but it was every bit as good as his first name.

"They seem like a nice family," he said. "Well, I only met the lady of the manor, but she was always happy to boil a kettle for us, hand out a biscuit, or stop for a chat, and she's a genius with a needle and thread."

James looked at me, an eyebrow raised.

Arty continued. "That said, we don't know this is about them, it's easy to get access to the area. We opened the gate and drove through. So did the police. And so could anyone else who wanted to, there's no padlock on there."

"Three cheers for Artemis Rainbow," James said. "That will be our line of defense. After all, anyone can walk through there."

"Does anyone else have keys to the mausoleum?" I asked him, seeing a flaw in the defense.

"The mausoleum is lying in pieces all over the ground; no one needs a key," he said. "And no one's said his body was in there. They could've dug a hole and buried him but not dug it deep enough or dug it too close to the river. Or given up with digging and just dropped him in the water."

That made sense. I was starting to believe it myself, but the reporter had more to say:

"Daisy Dixon, formerly Daisy Langley, married to the billionaire owner of Langley Hall, was previously the perpetrator of a mass poisoning..."

"Oooh!" James said and he laughed. Even with all that was going on, he gave a little laugh.

"That makes me sound like Lucrezia Borgia," I said, master poisoner of sixteenth-century Rome. "That's not what it was." And I felt a little pang that Arty was probably watching this. If he'd heard that, would he still want to accept biscuits and T-shirts from me?

# CHAPTER THIRTEEN

THE NEXT MORNING, I LISTENED THROUGH THE WALL AS JAMES rose, showered, and dressed. I lay in bed, staring at the ceiling, wondering what I would do when I got up and how I was going to get to the end of the day, knowing what had happened in the graveyard the day before and what must surely be to come.

"I'll phone the police when I get to the office," James said as he prepared to leave. "I'll see if I can get the lie of the land and decide where to take it from there. Are you going to loaf around in bed all day?"

I shook my head. "It's only just gone six."

He sighed theatrically, said something about "the best part of the day," and left. The sound of the front door slamming as he exited the house was the best part of the day, after the sound of the car moving off the drive. I stood up, yanked the bedstead forward slightly, and made another mark on the wall before setting forth to wander aimlessly around the house.

I watched the breakfast news; house prices were down and cases of syphilis were up. Then I went to get dressed, a sleeveless top made from one of James's old shirts and a simple skirt made from a curtain, something I could have knocked together by age twelve.

Mrs. Billings would soon be arriving for her self-authorized overtime, but as yet, no word from James about what had been discussed with the police, and no sight of the police themselves. I put out a decorative plate for Mrs. B to pinch and hurried downstairs, just as she appeared in the old kitchen.

---

"It were murder," Mrs. Billings said, draping her raincoat over a chair.

"What was?" I asked, hoping she was going to say the journey home after the police had blocked the road, but she didn't.

"Lennie Green."

"Murder? Who said that?" I clutched the table to steady myself, while thinking that actually, it wasn't murder, it was an accident, a *complete* accident. But that would be beside the point if the police had decided it was murder.

"All over the village," she said. "It's all they're talking about." And she burst into tears.

I didn't know what to do. I'd never seen her cry before; I didn't think I'd ever seen anyone of her generation cry. I looked around for tissues. There were none, but we had kitchen roll. It was gratefully received.

I had a hundred questions, but I didn't know which ones were appropriate to ask: Who said it was murder? Who *exactly*? Was it a shameless gossip or someone connected to the investigation? How could they tell? Surely he was a lump of mush by the time they found him. Do they have any suspects? Who? If not, why not and when will they have suspects? And who will those suspects be? Did Mrs. Billings actually know him and, if not, why was she so upset?

I tentatively started with a very good question. "Couldn't he have just fallen in the water?"

Mrs. Billings looked at me, thinking. "Wouldn't the police have said so, if he'd just fallen in?"

"Maybe it didn't occur to them that someone would say it was murder. Maybe that's so far-fetched they didn't think anyone would think for a minute it was murder."

She frowned. "No smoke without fire." And she returned to her tears.

I dared another question. "But who said it?"

"Mary Bishop," Mrs. B said.

And I breathed again. Mary Bishop, the ancient matriarch of the amateur dramatics society, so old it was believed she did her training in the theaters of ancient Greece, was as sticky a beak as you could find in this village, and an absolute fantasist to boot. The claim was probably baseless.

"Did you know Lennie Green, Mrs. Billings?" I asked next.

She shook her head. "Not as such, but when you've grown up with someone on the TV and the radio, you feel like you know them. And with him being local. I met him one time. He came over to The Two Ts teashop and he signed a napkin for me. 'To Brenda,' he wrote…" and she trailed off there.

"He'll be a big loss," I said, wondering how I'd come so far in life only having the vaguest idea who he was.

"He will. It will never be the same." She clutched her kitchen roll and gazed into the distance. "To think, he'll never be on another Christmas special."

"Never, but they'll have repeats."

"That would be too sad. I couldn't watch him back in happier days."

I stared at the table top. We sat in a silence I wanted to break. I wanted to move, to put the kettle on and go back to normal, but I didn't dare to. I also wanted to ask what they were saying about Mr. Newman, but I was wary of drawing attention to the matter. I wondered if we were observing an unofficial two minutes silence and if it would be broken soon and we would go back to our lives.

And to my relief, that was exactly what happened. Mrs. B sniffed, stood, threw the kitchen roll in the bin, washed her hands, and put the kettle on.

"Did I tell you," she said, putting our drinks on the table, "the book club has a stall in the village hall now, selling off all their old books, but one of them was a library book. Mrs. Harris went spare when she saw it." Mrs. Harris ran the mobile library and I was fond of her because once, when I was a young girl, she gave me copies of *The History of Langley Hall* and *The Ghosts of Langley Hall*. They were old copies the library was discarding and selling for a pound, but she gave them to me for free. That is why I am such an expert on the matter, although James and I had added one, or possibly two, ghosts to the house since it was published.

Mrs. Harris was less generous with the book club. "She took the book back and took all the money they'd made as a fine," Mrs. B said. "Now the book club is trying to find out who brought it, and they're going to be booted out. Bringing their club into disrepute."

"How exciting!" Never let it be said that village life was dull. It almost took my mind off Lennie, Mr. N, and the activity in our graveyard, until Mrs. B ate a final biscuit, rose from her seat saying, "Anyway, Lady Langley, love, better show willing," and shuffled her way out toward our living quarters. I was left with my thoughts and my worries.

I waited, so as not to embarrass us both by overtaking her on the stairs and being sat watching *Monk* when she arrived, gasping for breath. After enough time had elapsed, I washed the mugs in the sink and headed for the stairs, but as I reached the entrance hall, there was a knock on the door.

I froze. Apart from Mrs. Billings, there were no cleaners in that day. There were no deliveries expected. It was rare, although not unheard of, to get door-to-door traders. But there was one cohort of visitors I wouldn't be surprised to see. My fingers fumbling the catch, I answered the door.

It was two detectives. The man introduced himself as DC Parker. He was slightly chubby, with pale skin, blue eyes, and the most amazing red hair that stood up straight from his head, as if he'd had an electric shock. A woman in a suit stood next to him. She was introduced to me as DS Khan. She didn't smile; in the weeks ahead I'd wonder if she could smile or if her unnaturally thin lips precluded it in some way. She had a dark complexion, long, straight hair, very deep-set eyes, and a beaky nose.

"Daisy Dixon," DC Parker said, "we'd like you to accompany us to the station."

"Why?" I asked.

"We'll discuss that with you when we get there."

I felt panic rising and I dug my heels in. "Why can't you tell me now?"

"Are you refusing? We could arrest you."

That was the phrase that changed my mind. "Can I let my cleaning lady know where I'm going?" I asked. "She'll be worried." They rolled their eyes but let me speak to her, following me upstairs as I made my way.

"Better get a solicitor," Mrs. Billings advised as I whispered the news to her. She looked grimly over my shoulder at them.

"But won't that make me look guilty?" I said, remembering to add: "I haven't done anything. And I haven't been arrested." Yet.

"Doesn't matter," she said. "Always get a solicitor."

I stood up straight and pulled my shoulders back. "I'd like a solicitor, please," I said to the detectives.

DS Khan spoke for the first time. "We'll sort that out at the station." They really were keen to get there; it must've been nearly time for their break.

When we arrived, I phoned James about the solicitor. Then I sat for hours in a cold, uncomfortable cell that smelled of bleach overlaying something I chose not to think about, while I waited for the solicitor James appointed to finish with all his more important clients.

Finally:

"Hello, I'm Tarquin, Tarquin Noble." A man, aged around forty, held his hand out. He looked slightly frazzled; his tie was askew and his hair was so untidy, I wondered briefly if we were related. "I'm your solicitor," he said.

"Do you know why you're here, Daisy?" DC Parker asked me as we all sat in the interview room.

"No."

"Really? After all that was going on at your property yesterday? We'd like to ask you about Lennie Green."

Beside me, my solicitor reached for his briefcase to take out a notepad. As the briefcase swung open, glitter scattered across us and over the table. "Sorry," he said. "Kids got into it. They think this is hilarious."

Instinctively, I started to wipe it off the table, but I transferred most of it onto myself, and for the rest of that day, everything I touched shimmered afterward.

"Lennie Green," DC Parker repeated, getting back to the point. "Tell us about him."

"I didn't know him. Don't know him."

"You don't have to know someone to run them over. The majority of victims and perpetrators in these incidents are strangers to each other."

My heart dropped to my feet and, I think, further. *How did they know?*

"I didn't run him over," I said, telling myself it wasn't quite a lie. "Run over" suggested to me that the wheels went over him, when that wasn't exactly how it was. "I don't know what happened to him."

"That's not what your husband said."

# CHAPTER FOURTEEN

"WHAT DID JAMES SAY?" I ASKED, MY VOICE HIGH AS I FELT MYSELF starting to panic. James had helped me dispose of the body. James had got rid of the car. It was all his idea. After that, James couldn't have said I ran Lennie over because James was implicated. And what had he said about Mr. Newman?

"You tell us," said DS Khan.

"Well, I wasn't there, I don't know what he said to you," I pointed out, trying to buy myself thinking time. It worked. I had a revelation. A recalling, actually—finally all those hours watching crime dramas had paid off—I remembered an episode of *The Bill* in which the police lied to get the culprit to confess. This must be what they were doing now. Maybe DS Khan had even seen the same episode.

I smiled. "I don't believe he said anything to you," I said. "Apart from maybe 'what were you doing in our graveyard yesterday?'" I folded my arms and sat back, victorious.

And I was victorious. They tried, for quite some time, with different angles, different questions, different allegations, insistent that James had thrown me under a bus, but I had them licked. I stuck to my story: I only met Lennie once, at the party, I didn't see him afterward. Although, really, that was what caused the problem: I didn't see him.

I told it the first time, I told it a second time, I told it a third time. I told it over and over and over. I could have told it in my sleep. I kept it simple. I didn't add any embellishments or introduce any other characters who might have tied me up in knots at a later date. I was something of a natural at this. And every time DS Khan said, "That's not what James said," or "James says you know something about it," I told her she was lying. She didn't seem to like that much and she stuck to her story as well, until I started to wonder if she really was telling the truth.

What had James said? Was he being interviewed too? He'd said he was going to phone them when he got to work, but he'd seemed free as a bird when I called him about a solicitor. It had been midmorning before the police arrived at Langley Hall—was that long enough for them to have interviewed James first? Had he had to wait for his brief? Was it this same one? Was James also covered in glitter?

And if they had interviewed James, had he told them everything straightaway? That wouldn't take long but didn't sound at all like the James I'd come to know and want to murder.

On the balance of probabilities, Khan was lying, but I didn't feel that in my heart.

Next, Khan leaned forward, looked at her laptop, and tapped a few keys. She turned the screen to face us. "Can you explain why you were driving like a nun on your departure from the party, Daisy?"

And Tarquin and I watched CCTV footage of me driving the car away from Margery's house, doing about five miles per hour in a thirty zone.

For a moment, I felt panic begin, but I was getting good at this now and after a couple of seconds, I calmed myself down and thought clearly. Should I ask for a few minutes with my solicitor, or would that assure them that they were onto something? Should I just own up to having had a drink? After all, I was borderline for the drink drive limit and sailing close to the wind was not evidence of a hit-and-run, and they couldn't breathalyze me now. Should I just say "no comment," or would that, again, convince them that they were right? Then I had a better idea.

"I was wearing stilettos," I said. "They're not the best thing for driving in. I should have taken more sensible shoes. The heel got caught and I couldn't control the pedals properly. I was going to stop and sort it out, but then it came free, so I just carried on."

"There you go, simple as that," Tarquin said, his work done for him.

We went through three comfort breaks, four small, bitter coffees, and one stale sandwich that I couldn't finish. My eyes began to droop, my solicitor seemed to be counting the tiles on the ceiling, and once, when I called DS Khan a liar, I swear I saw DC Parker snigger.

Then Khan changed the subject. "We've had the postmortem results for Douglas—Doug—Newman today. Drowning."

That sent a new shot of adrenaline rushing through me. Due to the relative recentness of the incident, I hadn't given so much thought to what I would say about him, but drowning as a cause of death sounded hopeful, accidental.

"Is there anything you'd like to tell us?" Khan asked.

I shook my head, promising myself I'd say no more than that, and Tarquin said, "He probably lost his footing and fell in. He might have had a drink or hit his head. Why are you asking my client about it?"

"Because as well as water in his lungs, he had a number of blows to the head, made by a blunt object."

I wondered what James had said about that, but I didn't want to poke the hornet's nest. Tarquin did that for me.

"What did Mr. Dixon tell you?"

"We haven't asked him yet," Parker said. "We've only just had the results. Daisy, do you want to go first?"

I shook my head again. "I don't know anything about it. If James says differently, he's lying."

And on we went for a little while, in the same vein as with Lennie, until Tarquin said that we weren't achieving anything, that I was obviously tired, and that sleep deprivation was a form of torture. DS Khan conceded the point and ended the session. I was allowed to leave.

My first instinct, as DC Parker saw us off the premises, was to get away as quickly as I could without saying another word. Then I found I had another instinct. I paused at the door and said:

"Ask James about his falling out with Mr. Newman."

"Ask him what?" Parker said.

I frowned; they weren't meant to ask me more questions after that, but I rose to the challenge.

"There was bad blood between James and Mr. Newman," I said.

Then I left, as fast as my legs would carry me without actually running, my solicitor hot on my heels. I felt slightly shaken by my own daring with the information about Mr. N, and I wanted to get away before they hauled me back for more questions.

"That's quite some nerve you have," Tarquin said as we walked out into the twilight. "Anyone would think you were a hardened criminal." That seemed like something of a backhanded compliment, but it hadn't been hard-nosed coolness, it had been blind panic.

Then he gave me his business card; he thought we were going to be meeting again. Before we parted, he apologized once more about the glitter. "My kids are out of control," he said.

---

James was waiting for me when I got back. I would have found it more comforting to have arrived home to Mrs. Billings, but her shift was over hours ago and James had bought fish and chips, even though it wasn't a Friday, and he got me a decent-sized portion for once.

He was surprised at how sparkly I was but not at the fact that I'd been interviewed by the police. "Stands to reason," he said. "They have a body; we have a graveyard."

I put my fish and chips in the microwave and thought that it was probably for the best that James was here and Mrs. B wasn't because, once again, I was thinking that a problem shared is a problem halved and was feeling the urge to unburden myself to her, which I surely would have regretted the next morning.

"What did the police want to know?" James asked me.

"I told them…" And I repeated the story I had told the police for what I hoped would be the last time. "They tried a really dodgy tactic, though," I said and turned to look at him. "They kept saying that you said I ran Lennie over."

He didn't look surprised at that.

---

I found myself preoccupied the next day with thoughts of the police, what James might have told them, and why and how he could have done it without implicating himself.

The most optimistic scenario I could come up with was that James was a very intelligent man, maybe he hadn't said anything incriminating, but he already knew the police lied to trick you into confessing and that was why he wasn't surprised. Maybe it was exactly what he was expecting. I was pretty sure he didn't know that from watching TV, but there must be loads of other ways someone could come by that information. Maybe one of his clients was a CID officer, maybe one was a solicitor. Maybe even the same solicitor who had sat silently in the interview room with me for hours and hours on end. Maybe, maybe, maybe…

If I wanted to stay on this side of a prison door, the first thing to do would be to get a new solicitor, one with no connections to my husband. I googled "Legal Aid," hoping it would point me in the right direction. What I found was a quagmire of vagaries, but a running theme seemed to be that they would take into account my income—zero—along with that of my spouse—zillions. If I wanted a solicitor who was independent of James, and I very much did, I would have to pay for it myself. I had about £400 in the account James paid my allowance into. That might get me an hour or two with a decent solicitor, but I'd probably be better off using it to flee the country. I wondered how far I'd get.

I searched on the name Tarquin Noble. I hadn't forgotten that I should be careful about my search history, but it seemed a reasonable thing to google the person to whom I was entrusting my freedom, especially since I had had no say in that matter.

I found him to be a respectable lawyer in a reputable practice.

That didn't tell me much, although I wasn't expecting him to post up there that he would help you get your wife sent down for your own crimes, should the need occur. For more useful information, I looked for him on social media.

I logged on to my Facebook, Twitter, and Instagram accounts, which I had opened years ago but rarely used, having no friends to add, and searched. I couldn't remember my passwords and it took me nearly half an hour to get into them all, but in the end, I was there.

I hadn't expected that name to be as common as it was, although the areas most densely populated with Tarquin Nobles seemed to be Texas and North Carolina, in the United States. It felt safe to rule them out. Following those eliminations, I spent some time scrolling through the Tarquin Nobles who had declared themselves to be in the UK, turning up nothing useful over and over again until I'd forgotten what I was looking for.

I scrolled on through "people you may know." Mrs. Billings, dressed up for something, with a big smile and a glass of wine, Mr. Billings, wearing cricket whites, a bat in his hand. Then a parade of people from the village, the Chambers, the Faulkners, Mrs. Thorpe and Mrs. Thrussell and a separate page for The Two Ts teashop, with pictures of their mismatched tea sets and lopsided cakes. Their pages had photos of them all together at village events and nights in the King's Head. May Day, the flower festival, the cricket league, the pub quiz. All those lives being lived, while I was up here counting out the days of mine.

I had a little look for Arty, but he didn't seem to be on there, so I left it and returned to the subject of James and the police interview.

I wondered if he'd done one of those deals you see on American shows? Where you get a shorter sentence in return for dropping someone else in it. Did they do that here? I wanted to google it, but I didn't dare. Yet, if he'd done one of those deals, surely they'd have done more yesterday than listen to me repeat the same story over and over again. And James wouldn't want any sentence at all; he wouldn't settle for a short one. I wasn't confident of much that morning, but I was sure James wouldn't agree to that.

As I skipped through my whodunits, unable to stick with any of them to the end, I couldn't shift the leaden feeling in my heart. Even as I told myself it's probably normal to feel down after being accused by the police of killing someone, however much they might struggle to prove it, I couldn't fend off a growing sense of doom.

I went outside, thinking fresh air might do me good. I picked a few berries from a gooseberry bush and, on autopilot, scanned the rest of the garden for things you could forage, but it was only June. Then I went back indoors. I tried to sew a hem on a new dress I was making, but I couldn't get it right, no matter how many times I stitched and unpicked it.

By the end of the afternoon I had come to no realizations or conclusions about James, but I'd begun to feel glad I'd thrown in my little tip about the bad blood with Mr. Newman. I'd given myself a small scare in doing so: I wasn't used to standing up to James, but in the cold light of day, I thought I was right not to take what he had thrown at me lying down. Whatever it was he had thrown at me.

James came home in a normal mood that evening, but he had hardly started his Turkey Dinosaurs, Potato Smiles, and peas when his phone rang.

"It's the police," he said, sounding intrigued. Optimistic even. He answered it and listened for a minute. Then moved out of my earshot. I tried to eavesdrop, but from where he was standing he could see me, so I couldn't move closer. When he came back, his mood had turned black.

"After everything I've done for you," he said, before stomping off to his office, slamming every door on the way. He didn't elaborate, but I was pretty confident he was talking about what I had told the police about Mr. Newman. I ate his Potato Smiles.

He was in a foul mood for the rest of evening and into the next morning, until it was even more of a relief than usual to see him leave. I didn't risk hiding any of his possessions that day, but I felt a little thrill of pleasure that what I had done had had such an effect.

The atmosphere was still frosty when we turned on the TV that night.

Lennie's funeral was item number three on the local news, and it gave me quite a turn to hear it. I would have liked to have gone myself, but it wasn't advertised beforehand, so I didn't know it had happened. Maybe it was for the best. The police often expect the killer to go to the funeral, assuming the killer knows it is taking place.

It was held in St. Margaret's Church, Great Beadington, the news anchor told us, and we were shown footage of the mourners entering the church, the great and good of Somerset and a few from London, all well-cut clothes and elaborate hats.

Moira, his wife, whom I recognized from the fundraiser, followed the coffin, along with Anthony, Lennie's son. Behind them were others, who I guessed to be other children/nephews/nieces/grandchildren. Among the dearly beloved, we were told, were beneficiaries of his philanthropy, and one young man stopped to tell the reporter all about it.

"I wouldn't be here today if it hadn't been for Lennie," he said, shaking his head theatrically, enjoying his moment. The truth of it was that he wouldn't be there that day if it hadn't been for *me*, none of them would. It was my careless driving that brought us all to this.

Then they showed us snippets from the service, a eulogy from the pulpit, the congregation singing "The Lord's My Shepherd," and the pallbearers carrying the coffin out. I thought back over all I had seen of Lennie in YouTube videos over the recent weeks. I remembered our meeting at the party. I thought of Mr. Newman and the cruel twists of fate, and I found myself welling up.

"Oh, for god's sake," James said, as he caught me wiping a tear away. And I hated him.

Maybe I should have been grateful for James's help on the night of the accident. But I wasn't. I wasn't grateful that he didn't let me call 999. I wasn't grateful that he made me hide Lennie in the mausoleum. And I wasn't grateful for what happened with Mr. Newman.

Moreover, I wasn't grateful for having my food constantly monitored; I wasn't grateful for comments about my weight; I wasn't grateful for the tasks he set me; I wasn't grateful for £250 a month, which had seemed like a fortune when my needs were not much more than needle and thread, but I now realized kept me stuck here, with no way of supporting myself anywhere else for more than a few days.

And I certainly wasn't grateful for the investment into his cryptocurrency, which had been sold to me as a get-rich-quick scheme and had morphed into a retirement plan and then the pot of gold at the end of the rainbow.

# CHAPTER FIFTEEN

"IT'S DOUG NEWMAN'S FUNERAL NEXT FRIDAY," MRS. BILLINGS SAID to me, taking off her coat and hauling biscuits out of her bag. "Are you going?"

As much as I'd wanted to go to Lennie's funeral, I felt repulsed by the idea of going to Mr. Newman's. Maybe it was because I'd already seen Jo Newman, accepting sympathy at the Bone Bonanza, and Meg looking like her world had ended, and I knew the havoc we had wreaked. But Mrs. B continued.

"I think you should. I know Doug and Lord Langley had their ups and downs, but the Newmans have been linked to this hall for generations and they're good village people. Lord Ashbury went to old Mr. Newman's funeral. Wouldn't be right not to pay your respects."

"I'll speak to James," I said.

And so it was that, on the Friday of that week, we donned black outfits—I'd had to buy mine especially, not having had anything in black. I'd spent £3,000 in the shop, then finished it off with a flower made from a stripey tea towel—and made our way down to the village church.

"Just keep your mouth shut," James said. "Unless anyone speaks to you. We'll go to the service and have a couple of sandwiches at the reception, then we'll make tracks."

In the pews, I looked around to see who was there. All of the village, it seemed, but the faces I was really looking for were those of Parker and Khan, here to see if they could spot the perpetrator amongst the mourners. I couldn't see them in the rows to our left, I couldn't see them in the rows to our right, I couldn't see them in the rows behind, and I couldn't see them in the rows in front.

Then, just as the organist began and it was all about to start, the main door opened once more and Parker and Khan snuck in. It was standing room only by then, so they stayed at the back, watching us all as the coffin was carried down the aisle, followed by the family, including Meg, who sat beside it for the whole service.

I slumped into my seat, hoping not to be seen, and once the service was over, I shuffled along in the middle of the congregation, keeping my head lowered, as we made our way out to the graveside, where Meg gave a loud howl as the coffin was lowered into the ground. I covered my ears. Everyone covered their ears.

"Piercing, isn't it?" said Khan's voice beside me as the howl died down.

"I love dogs," I said, although I didn't really have strong feelings about them. If I did I'd probably have owned one; I had the time and the space. I preferred donkeys.

Khan didn't say anything else. She just nodded at James, then she and Parker headed over to the King's Head for the buffet.

There, she chitchatted with everyone, as if she were part of the community. I assumed the whole performance was specifically to menace me. In defiance of both her and James, I turned my attention to the food and piled my paper plate up until it nearly folded back on itself with sandwiches and sausage rolls and prawns and mini scones and crisps.

"Looks like you haven't been fed for a week, Lady Langley, love," Mrs. Billings said, although she knew that not to be the case. "Not eating for two, are you?"

"Yes, me and James," I said. He was standing by the bar with just a whiskey and—I did a double take—DS Khan. Mrs. B gave a little chuckle and moved on as I stood watching James and the detective, trying to guess what they were saying.

"Thank you for coming." I jumped as Jo Newman appeared by my elbow, Meg standing next to her. "I know things were a bit strained toward the end."

"That's OK," I said. The proximity to her made my guilt surface and the hand holding my plate started to wobble. "All water under the bridge." I had a flashback to the day we had floated Lennie's body under the bridge, down the river, and into the path of Mr. N, and I shook a bit more. "In a manner of speaking," I said and Jo nodded vaguely.

She took a deep breath. "You know, we'd still like to keep the farm on; this doesn't change that. The boys are nearly ready to start running it themselves, and we've got Pete and Greg while they get on their feet." The boys were the older adult children from Mr. N's first marriage, who had been trained from childhood to one day run the farm. Pete and Greg were the farm foreman and manager. "It'd be a tragedy to cover all that good farmland with warehouses."

I did a slow nod up and down. I agreed, but business was business, according to James, and the warehouse people had made a higher bid.

"Doug had life assurance," Jo said. "We might be able to match the other offer." I nodded again. One of the younger children was calling for her, so she left it there before I had the chance to tell her that James made all the financial decisions. All the decisions, in fact, including where to hide the bodies. My views were irrelevant.

A moment later I was wishing she'd stayed to chat as DS Khan approached and said, "Moving service, wasn't it?"

In truth, apart from the harrowing sight of Meg, it had been pretty dull, but maybe Meg was what she had meant, so I nodded.

"We didn't know if we'd see you and Mr. Dixon here," she said. "With you not being on best terms with the deceased."

"What did James say about Mr. Newman?" I asked them, remembering what I'd said at the end of my police interview and feeling hopeful for a moment that they were hot on the trail of a vendetta between James and Mr. N and that I was to be treated as an innocent bystander.

"What do you think he said?" DS Khan asked. I heard myself sigh, but I rallied and humored her. "That he wanted to kick the Newmans off the farm and sell it for warehouses," I said.

She nodded, so I assumed that was what he said.

"When did that happen?" DC Parker asked.

"I can't remember," I said. "It was going to and fro for a while. I wasn't really involved." Khan stared at me; she made me nervous and that made me pile more crisps on my plate. It was so full they started falling off, but she was still staring at me, so I carried on. "What do you think happened? Suicide?" I asked eventually, crisps raining down onto the carpet.

"What? He battered himself around the head, and when that didn't work, he drowned himself? We don't think it was suicide," DS Khan told me. "We're between accident and foul play. Your husband's just been saying you have quite a temper when you're riled. He said you're known for it in the village."

"Not really," I said. "That's not the first thing people would say about me." Wondering what was the first thing and not liking the ideas that popped into my head: recluse, peculiar, impulsive maybe. Poisoner.

Khan looked at me, blinking, but not speaking, goading me into saying something.

"When do you think it happened?" I asked. "If you think he was attacked, don't you want our alibis? The reason I ask is that it's just come back to me that, around that time, James started taking evening strolls through the fields, which is something he never did before. Then the strolls stopped, just as suddenly as they'd started. I thought at the time it was strange, James suddenly going out for walks he never used to take, then stopping."

"People begin health kicks that only last a few days all the time," Khan said, and she walked away, leaving me wondering why James's word always seemed to carry so much more weight than mine. Or was she the other way round with him?

I watched as James finished his whiskey and clapped some peasants on the back. Then he took my plate from me—"How much?"—put it on the end of the table and led the way out. I grabbed a slice of Victoria sponge as I went.

---

The novelty of the archaeologists wore off and Mrs. Billings went back to her usual days, Monday and Thursday. It was a relief. I realized I had liked it better when no one came here most of the time, and I was just the hermit of Langley Hall. So, I was less than pleased when, on a Monday morning, there was a knock at the door more than half an hour before the Billingses were due.

I was upstairs and my car was in the garage, so no one could tell whether I was in or not, but the window was open, so I could hear whoever it was, as well as spy on them.

I peered down from behind the curtain. A young woman was standing outside the house. She was wearing combats, with a yellow T-shirt that was just the wrong shade for her pink hair; I felt my retinas start to burn. Once again, she had a camera around her neck: Emma Beddoe.

I ignored her. She knocked again. I ignored her again. I was still wearing pajamas, so I went to get washed and dressed to take my mind off it all, while I waited for Emma to give up and go away. But when I came back, wearing a dress fashioned from two ponchos, it was to the sound of tires on gravel and Emma asking Mr. and Mrs. Billings if Lady Langley was in.

"Should be, love," I heard Mrs. Billings say. "Follow us round."

I watched as Emma trailed their van to the back of the house and headed down to meet my fate.

"Morning," I said to them all as I opened the back door and Mrs. B walked in. "Come in," I said to Emma. "Come one, come all." What else could I say? I was going to invite Mr. B as well, but he was already off to his shed.

I took three cups from the mug tree, a *Poirot*, a *Death in Paradise*, and a *Midsomer Murders*, and set the kettle to boil, with extra water for our guest. I looked at Emma, feeling a headache coming on as she settled herself down.

Meanwhile, Mrs. Billings stared hard at our new companion until she told her, “My name’s Emma Beddoe; I work for *The Western Bugle Online*,” and handed her a business card.

Mrs. B looked at it for a long time. “Have you come to do one of those ‘day in the life of the rich and famous’ articles?” she asked her.

Emma looked surprised and I expect I did as well: She would have to be a very good writer indeed to make a day in my life interesting enough for a *Western Bugle* article. Until recently, anyway, but I didn’t want to discuss that.

“I came to see if you wanted to talk about Lennie Green,” she said. “We’re doing a feature on him.”

“Oh yes,” Mrs. Billings said, and she began to tell Emma of how she’d been a lifelong fan, she’d had posters of him when she was a teenager, she’d watched all his TV shows. She told her about the encounter in The Two Ts teashop. As she spoke, I tried to sidle away, but Emma turned to me every time I moved and I understood, for the first time, what the phrase “pinned me down with her stare” really meant.

“Goodness, you must be devastated,” Emma said, as Mrs. Billings paused for breath. She turned to me. “And how are you feeling, Lady Langley? Or can I call you Daisy?”

“Oh, she didn’t even know who he was!” Mrs. Billings said. “She were at a party with him the night before, and she didn’t recognize his name on the radio the next day.”

“You were at a party with him just before he went missing?” Emma asked me, her eyes wide. “And now the police are digging on your estate?”

It did sound bad when you put it like that.

“Talk about coincidence!” Mrs. Billings said.

"Alright if I record this?" Emma said, putting her phone on the table. "Did you know Doug Newman?"

"Everybody knows everybody round here," Mrs. B said. "He was one of the tenant farmers on this estate." Emma looked at me and I nodded.

"We don't have much to do with them," I said. "They pay their rent, we don't get involved with the farming."

"But you've had all that argy-bargy with the Newmans about the warehouse people," Mrs. Billings said, and Emma's eyebrows shot up.

"I wouldn't call it argy-bargy," I said. "We were in discussion about it. It's a private matter."

"Not down the King's Head, it's not," Mrs. B said, and I looked for something to brain her with.

"Do you have any theories about what might have happened to Lennie Green?" Emma asked me.

"None."

"Even though the police are digging on your property?"

"Nope." I was starting to relax; this was going to be no different to the police interview. In fact, it was going to be easier, with no concern that Emma was going to put me in a cell at the end.

"You want to look on *Whatever Happened to Lennie Green?*" Mrs. Billings said. "It's a little internet group we've got going in the village. Loads of ideas there. We're all on it at Silver Surfers."

I nearly fell off my chair! Mrs. Billings was going from here to a group dedicated to gossiping about Lennie Green and, no doubt, what was going on at Langley Hall. I recovered myself enough to lean in, as she took her phone from her bag and called up the forum.

Everyone was there: the Billingses, the Faulkners, the Chamberses, the Thrussells, the Thorpes, the vicar, Mary Bishop, who was a founding member, Mrs. Dobson from the primary school, people from the new estate, and a few suspected Great Beadingtonites. There were a fair number who used aliases as well.

"They're the ones that say the most scandalous things," Mrs. Billings told us. "Look, you can see who's in here when you log on." And she showed us a list of names along the side, with green dots by them to show they were there as well.

The forum was full of speculation about what had happened to Lennie, some vague and obvious: "He came to a bad end." Some specific, but inaccurate: "He was chopped up into tiny pieces and thrown to the fishes." The replies to that one pointed out that a) he was found in one piece; b) so far, only Mary Bishop had mentioned foul play; and c) the plural of "fish" is "fish." Then the original poster said that, actually, "fishes" is correct if it's more than one type and the thread descended into a row about which fish—or fishes—could be found in the river here.

It got back on track soon after, though, with an allegation that Lennie was a drug kingpin and James was his minion. It was an interesting idea, but judging by Lennie's house, in comparison to James's, unlikely.

They should track down where his phone went, an anonymous poster wrote and my heart started racing. Did they know something, or was that just the only intelligent comment we'd seen? No one goes anywhere without their phone these days.

We scrolled for a few minutes longer, until Emma announced she had to get going and thank you for the tea, she'd see herself out. A few minutes later, there was a new member on the forum, AllEars. I put away the plain digestives we'd palmed off on Emma and brought out the Jaffa Cakes. Now that Mrs. B was back to her normal hours, I'd reinstated the decent biscuits—or cakes, in this case.

"I think she liked you," Mrs. Billings said, helping herself to a couple. "It'll be interesting to see her article."

"Won't it just?" I set up an alert on my phone for *The Western Bugle Online*.

Then, we put the radio on and listened to an interview about the much-longed-for Little Beadington bypass, followed by Duran Duran, then Lady Gaga, then the national news headlines, followed by the local news, in which the local corpses, once more, were the hot topic.

This time they were talking to some kind of river specialist who was saying he could work out exactly where they had gone into the water. That would be very interesting to see, but I hoped he was wrong.

"It would be a good idea if the police set up a stall at the craft fair, asking for information," Mrs. B said. "They could put it next to the partisan beer tent; people tell the truth when they've had a few." I think she meant the artisan beer tent.

We finished our Jaffa Cakes and Mrs. Billings rose to begin her work. Between Emma and the river specialist, it had been quite a difficult morning and I was feeling a bit shaky; as I took the mugs to the sink, I knocked mine against the worktop and it broke.

"Oh," I said. My nice *Midsomer Murders* mug, with "What would Barnaby do?" written on it.

Mrs. Billings looked around. "Accidents happen with you, don't they," she said, and she shuffled off toward the hall. I was left wondering what was meant by that. Was it a warning? A threat? Or just a comment? I hoped, once more, that Mrs. B wasn't going to become another loose end I had to tidy up. Not that she didn't deserve it after her performance with Emma.

# CHAPTER SIXTEEN

THE POLICE EVENTUALLY FINISHED POKING AROUND IN THE GRAVEyard and the archaeology resumed. It warmed my cockles to see Arty making his way across the garden, kettle in hand. When he arrived at the backdoor, I was ready with a couple of T-shirts I'd made during the hiatus. Yet, I was nervous as I saw him approach. I didn't know if he'd feel differently about things now that the world was abuzz with gossip about what had or hadn't gone on here in regard to Lennie. I didn't know if he was coming in friendship or because he had no choice if he wanted to boil the kettle. He was wearing an ordinary T-shirt—was that a sign he wanted to disassociate himself from me? I shoved the new T-shirts I'd made for him into the microwave.

I took a deep breath as I answered the door. He jumped slightly, his hand raised to knock.

"Hi," I said. "Kettle?"

"Yes, please," he said and I stepped back to let him in. We stood in an awkward silence as he filled it with water and plugged it in.

"Getting on alright down there?" I asked.

"Getting back into our stride," he said. "After the"—he paused—"break."

It was quiet for a moment, then, "Did you see me on TV?" he asked. "I've never been interviewed by a journalist before. Luckily, I had one of those cravats you made, so I could dress for the occasion."

"That was lucky." I searched for something to say and found myself staring at his T-shirt, wondering again if there was a message in there.

He looked down, then back at me. "Everything else is in the wash," he said. "I should buy some more clothes. Or do the washing more often."

I took my chance. "Would this help?" I pinged open the microwave and held out the new tops. He took them off me and inspected them.

"For me? Wow! Yes, thanks."

"It kept me busy while we were all waiting for the police to finish."

"Yeah, did they find what they wanted?"

"I don't know what they wanted," I said, telling myself it wasn't a total lie. I only had a general idea.

"Well, they've gone now, so hey ho, we can all go back to normal. I wouldn't take any notice of the gossips: There's two sides to every story."

Which left me wondering what the gossips were saying and if Mrs. Billings could enlighten me. She probably could, but it's often best not to ask questions you won't like the answers to.

"Anyway, better get back to it. Will I see you down at the site soon?"

I nodded. "I'll bring biscuits."

"Lovely, we've missed them." He picked up the T-shirts. "Why were they in the microwave?"

"Keeps them fresh," I said.

"I didn't know that." And off he went, leaving me with the promise of biscuits and more chats and the knowledge that he hadn't been scared off. I sang myself a few lines of "Rasputin" and did a little dance. I was disappointed only that he hadn't changed into one of the T-shirts right there and then in the kitchen.

---

Following Emma's visit, I kept an eye on the forum, which expanded its scope and began calling itself *Whatever Happened to Lennie Green and Doug Newman?* You had to join to be able to read the comments, so I put myself up there as LooseEnds. I looked along the list Mrs. Billings had shown us, revealing who was in the forum. AllEars was there, along with NoseyParker, who was either an innocent bystander or had the worst pseudonym in the world.

Most of the chat was similar to the theory about Lennie having been chopped up:

Are they sure the body's really him?

Mafia hit.

Hit-and-run.

My heart stood still. Who wrote that and how did they know?

The next person said he would have been in the road, not the river, if it had been a hit-and-run and their attention was diverted away, but it left me feeling uneasy.

Then Emma, a.k.a., AllEars, steered around it and asked:

Did anyone here know Lennie Green?

You'd need to ask in Great Beadington, we're all Upper Iffley here, one of the pseudonyms said and the chat went quiet for a while, maybe sensing an outsider.

What about Doug Newman?

Oh yes, he was Upper Lfflian through and through, Mrs. Faulkner wrote. His family's farmed that land for generations, and Doug's granddad and great-great-uncle are both on the war memorial.

What do you think happened to him?

Well, he was found in the water, wasn't he?

I mean, how do you think he got there? Do you think there's a serial killer in Upper Iffley?

I gasped, and if I gasped, knowing what I knew, I could be sure other residents around the village were gasping too.

We had a series of burglaries back in 2006, Mrs. Chambers wrote. They broke into our shop, the post office, and the pub, but that's the biggest crime wave Upper Iffley's ever seen. It's not the kind of place you get a serial killer.

Anyway, you need three murders to make it a serial killer, Mary Bishop wrote.

That gave me pause for thought. If James and I bumped another one off, maybe the police would go looking somewhere else for a serial killer. Or even better, James could be the third victim. After that, the spree could come to an end. But it was quite a risk; it had all the makings of a plan that could backfire badly.

The idea caused a real stir on the forum, with everyone advising each other to be home before dark and check their doors were locked to avoid becoming the third body.

Then someone calling themselves BigDreams wrote, I don't think it's very helpful to be speculating like that. You'll only cause upset for the victim's families and anyone who is a bit nervous. We'll all be jumping out of our skin whenever we see a spade.

A spade? Mrs. Faulkner said.

Or anything you could batter someone with, BigDreams wrote. A hammer, a poker, a frying pan. We'll never look at household items in the same way.

We never will, Mrs. Chambers agreed.

So Emma went back to her earlier line of questioning: Does anyone actually know what goes on in Langley Hall? I mean has anyone visited there recently? Does anyone speak to the owners?

Evidence-based analysis was not de rigueur on *Whatever Happened to Lennie Green and Doug Newman?* The participants were usually happy to spout whatever came into their heads, but still, it was a while before Mrs. Chambers wrote:

You'd best ask Brenda Billings about that. She's up there every week, poking about.

To which Mrs. Billings replied, Don't know what you mean by "poking about." I'm up there giving the place a good clean and polish. Nothing more and nothing less.

I've seen the things on your mantelpiece, Brenda. And I've seen some of your charitable donations.

What are you saying, Betty? Mrs. Thrussell asked Mrs. Chambers.

If you're making allegations, you'd better have evidence, Mr. Billings said.

That's right, Mrs. Thorpe chimed in. Brenda'll have you for libel.

Or Eric and Terry can have a straightener outside the King's Head, Mr. Faulkner suggested.

Terry was Mr. Chambers, and disputes in Upper Iffley were generally decided by a fight outside the pub, a straightener. In this case it would be Messrs. Billings and Chambers on behalf of their wives. Once done, the matter would be considered settled, and regardless of the outcome, nothing more would be said. It was an interesting local spectacle, but Emma was not tempted by straighteners.

How does James Dixon make his money? she asked.

Everyone knew that and if she didn't, she'd clearly not done her homework. There was a chorus of "cryptocurrency!"

Why does he live here and not in London? she asked.

Views were more mixed on this, ranging from:

Why would you live in London when you could live here? Exactly.

And, He fell in love.

Followed by, No, he didn't, they hadn't met when he moved back.

To, He fell in love with Langley Hall. Who wouldn't?

Emma moved on. Why do you never see him in magazines and news columns, hobnobbing with celebrities?

That stumped them, until, eventually, BigDreams spoke up again. Not everyone is an extrovert and seeks the limelight, some people just quietly get on with it and don't look for public acclaim.

That level of modesty didn't sound much like James to me, the person who wrote that couldn't have known him, but it was enough of an answer for Emma and she went on to her next question.

Has anyone invested in his business? Would you recommend it?

Oh yes, Mrs. Faulkner was the first to pipe up. We moved our savings there when he showed us the graphs.

Us as well, Mrs. Chambers said.

And me, said Mary Bishop.

We weren't sure at first, said Mrs. Thrussell. But in the end, the Dixons are a village family and you trust someone you know. There was an emphatic series of "yeses" and "absolutelys" to this.

We're going to be the richest village in England in a few years, Mrs. Thorpe said.

Has anyone ever tried to withdraw a crypto coin? Emma asked.

Well, that just goes to show what you know, Mary Bishop said. You're not supposed to withdraw them for ages.

Think of it more like a retirement plan, Mrs. Faulkner said, which was exactly what James had said to me when I'd asked for my money back.

It's more like growing an oak tree than watercress, Mary Bishop continued, but did Mary Bishop have time left to grow an oak tree? Rumor had it that her sixteenth-century cottage had been built around her.

Aren't some of you ready to start treating yourselves? Won't you be wanting to spend that money soon? Emma was putting it politely, but it would not have been unreasonable for the Chambers to have rung up their till for the last time several years ago, and the Faulkners were senior to the Billingses. If they had all invested around the same time that I had, and it seemed fair to think that they had, whose retirement should we be thinking of?

Who are you anyway? You don't seem to know much about the village, Mrs. Faulkner asked.

Emma ignored the question and went back to her earlier theme.

You see entrepreneurs like Sir Alan Sugar and Deborah Meaden here, there, and everywhere, they're more than just business tycoons, they're celebrities. Why not James Dixon? she asked. He's an inspiration to us all, shouldn't he be flaunted?

They remained stumped, but I wasn't. The reason James lived out in the sticks and kept a low profile was because his business was a Ponzi scheme.

# CHAPTER SEVENTEEN

I'D FOUND OUT ABOUT SIX YEARS BEFORE, WHEN I'D ASKED FOR MY money back and received the usual platitudes about the value being low and leaving it to grow.

"But you said it would grow in months," I told him.

"I said it could do," he said. "But we've had adverse economic conditions, so it's taking longer."

Usually when he started talking about economics and market factors and accounting equations and so on, I admitted defeat. For years, I'd had no doubt James was right and I was too embarrassed to say I'd signed up for it without properly understanding it. When he sold the investment to me, I'd assured him I'd grasped everything he said and I was happy with the T's & C's.

But now, I had accepted that there would be no children, and the limits James had put on my life were becoming intolerable. This time, I couldn't just nod along with what he said. I admitted to myself that

I had made a mistake in investing, and I wanted to know how I could have misunderstood it so badly.

I started by googling his website, clicking on every tab to try to find something to give me a clue.

When James had first pitched the cryptocurrency to me, he'd opened up his laptop and showed me his website. The cryptocurrency was called Ingot, and its logo was a gold nugget. The website featured a picture of a big, shiny office block on the home page and a video of him, walking through the corridors, talking about the wonder of cryptocurrency.

He showed me a tab called "How it works," which mostly featured graphs, with their lines going up and up and up, sometimes literally off the scale. Then he showed me another page explaining the graphs—the writing was small and the paragraphs were long, and I gave up at the word "derivatives" in the first section.

"I'd be really sad for your mum if you missed this opportunity, and the inheritance she left for your future went to waste," James said, making me feel guilty. Then he said, "It's only ignorance that stops people from investing." Which made me feel stupid.

Now, years later, nothing had changed on the website, the graphs all looked exactly the same, only the years along the bottom were different, to make it look as if it was current. After everything James had said to me about adverse market conditions and a difficult economy, shouldn't that graph go down sometimes?

I made a note of the address and headed out to Bristol to visit the office. I'd asked to visit it before, and James had always said, yes, of course, but there was always a reason why it wasn't a good time. Now I wasn't going to wait to be invited; I was going to go along and see what he was doing all day.

The building I found wasn't as bright and shiny as the one on the website. In fact, it looked a bit run down, but it was a commercial building, with a list of the businesses it housed by the door. I looked for Ingot, but I couldn't see it.

I went inside, where a receptionist asked if she could help me.

"I'm looking for Ingot," I said, and she looked at me blankly. "The cryptocurrency business. This is its address."

She typed something into her computer and shook her head. "Has it changed its name? All the firms here are on the list by the front door."

"I don't think so," I said.

"Do you have a person's name? I can see if we have an email address for them."

I gave her James's name and she typed in James Dixon, but nothing came up. Then she tried Dickson, in case it had been misspelled, and she tried Dickinson and Dickenson and Dicks and even Dix, but James wasn't there.

An older man came out from the back room. "You looking for the cryptocurrency bloke?" he asked and I nodded, a bit of hope springing in my heart. "He moved out, more than a year ago, took all his staff and all his stuff and went. Don't think he could afford the place anymore. He was never here anyway, always at the gym or the golf course or something. I don't know where they moved to, didn't leave a forwarding address. He's got five grand of my money so let me know if you find him."

I hadn't known James played golf. I left with a sense of an unhappy epiphany dawning.

I continued to poke around on the website, hoping to find something I'd overlooked that would give me answers. In the end, I found them while poking around in the TV guide.

I came across a drama about a man called Bernie Madoff who ran something called a Ponzi scheme and conned people out of around $20 billion. I was watching it with half an eye at first, but I jumped to attention when I saw Mr. Madoff dazzling an elderly couple with tales of unimaginable wealth. He was telling them they could double, triple, quadruple their money in a matter of weeks, when really they couldn't.

I told James about it that night. "It sounds like your cryptocurrency," I said.

James smiled. "It's nothing like my cryptocurrency. It was before the days of cryptocurrency. That man was just a common thief. Everybody knows that."

I didn't. I hadn't heard of him before. I watched on and it did sound like James's business, except, of course, as James had said, there was no cryptocurrency then. Money was just money, so those people should have known that if it seemed too good to be true, it was too good to be true.

Later, it all started to go wrong. People stopped giving him money, while other people, who had given him money, started asking for it back. More and more was going out and less and less was going in and even I, who had only just scraped a C in GCSE maths, could see the way that was going.

The next day, when James had gone to work, I opened up my laptop and typed "Ponzi scheme" into the search bar. The description was thus:

Guaranteed returns with no risk.

Yes, that matched what James had told me.

Investment strategies that are "too complicated" to explain.

"It is pretty complicated," James had said when he told me about it. "Most people don't really get it. That's what I'm here for." And he had fudged and fuddled from there on.

The list continued:

Official documentation is hidden from investors.

That went some way to setting my mind at ease because I had a certificate, somewhere. I wasn't sure where I'd put it. Next:

Investors find it hard to withdraw their funds.

That was true, although James said it would be a different story in years ahead.

In years ahead. Years before, he'd said I'd double my money within weeks. He'd said I only had to leave it in longer if I wanted to triple or quadruple it, or more. He said.

I didn't say anything else about it to James after that, but I was sure by then that I would never get the money from my mum's house back.

I didn't know what to do. If I went to the police, it would be blown open and out of my control. If I waited, things could get worse. But they could get better. James could tap into a new vein of investment and the whole thing could right itself. He could turn it around and make it legitimate. At that time I still didn't believe James was nothing but a fraud—I thought the business must be fundamentally sound, but circumstances must have caused him to take a temporary detour. I believed that this could still be put right, with no one any the wiser and that that was what James would do. So I did nothing.

And for a while everything seemed to be on an even keel. Our lifestyle didn't change, and James seemed unconcerned. I told myself that, after all, I hadn't seen concrete evidence of a problem and which was more likely: I'd jumped to conclusions or my super talented, very clever husband, whom no one had a bad thing to say about, was a successful businessman? People did come from humble backgrounds to great success. I told myself that over and over again until I believed it, and life went on exactly as before.

Then, just a couple of years before the incident with Lennie Green, there was the first sale.

James used to own a yacht. It was a luxury one; it cost millions and could sleep ten, plus crew. It had everything you could find in an average house on board: a TV, a fridge-freezer, a washing machine. It had a swimming pool, and I don't mean the sea.

We used it once. There were just the two of us and six crew in our ten-berth boat, bobbing around off the south coast. It was too cold to go out on the deck and enjoy the sun, so we watched films in the lounge, which we could have done at home. After that it was left in the marina, costing a fortune and dwarfing all the other yachts. But James still liked to talk about "the yacht," as if we were hanging out there with celebs all the time.

He sold it. I asked him why and he said because we never used it, which seemed reasonable on the face of it, but knowing him like I did, I had my doubts. Next, he sold his Lamborghini. That was the first of the classic cars to go. He used to have twelve. One by one they were whittled down to six: the Rolls, the Bentley, the Porsche, the Jaguar, the MG, and the Mercedes. And, of course, the modern Audi for everyday use.

Now I realized why he hadn't divorced me; this marriage hadn't worked out any better for him than for me, but he couldn't end it because when the lawyers started poking into his finances, all would be revealed.

That was when the thought of killing him first crossed my mind. It was just an idle daydream at first. I pictured myself leaping out at him from behind a curtain, dressed as *The Scream*, brandishing a knife. But it made me realize how much I wouldn't mind if James was dead, and in fact, the more I thought about it, the more I thought I would prefer it. It wouldn't solve the Ponzi problem, but it would allow me to take some control over what happened next.

So I made the decision, in principle at least, to do away with him, but the plot got no further than that because I couldn't find a way.

I looked back at the forum, all the people in the village oblivious, thinking their futures were safe. I read back over the bit before, where Emma had been suggesting there was a serial killer at work and at what BigDreams had said about "jumping out of our skin whenever we see a spade." What did he know about a spade? The police hadn't said that, the papers hadn't said that, the radio station hadn't said that. Only James and I knew Mr. N had been battered with a spade.

BigDreams was James.

---

Encouraged by Arty's enthusiasm for the clothes I made, and by James's fury at them, while I mused over James's presence in the forum, I created summer dresses out of a huge collection of decorative handkerchiefs I found in a dusty cupboard. I made culottes from a selection of tote bags. I repurposed a 1960s hippy smock I saw in a charity shop window into a skirt and matching handbag. They were comfortable and stylish, whether James thought so or not. I made a few of his thousand-pound ties into hairbands.

I took advantage of the Pets at Home sale and made a jacket out of dog and cat blankets, the lovely polka-dot patterns along the sleeves, and one of the more expensive furry blankets around the body.

It wasn't long before I had a whole new wardrobe: skirts, trousers, tops, day dresses, evening dresses, summer dresses, accessories. All made bespoke.

I found a Boney M top in the Cats Protection shop, with all four of the band members on it. It was too small for Arty to wear, so I cut the pictures into separate patches and sewed them into a new T-shirt for him.

Better still, James had a big networking event, which I was required to attend alongside him, and knowing how much he loved my dressmaking skills, I set to with the sewing machine.

I made an evening dress from old velour tracksuits and made sure we were running late when we left, so that he didn't have time to scrutinize my outfit beforehand. When we arrived at the venue and I took off my expensive, shop-bought coat to reveal the creation beneath it, his jaw nearly hit the floor, for all the wrong reasons.

"Did you make that yourself?" he hissed and I smiled what I hoped was a mysterious smile. Then I sailed off into the crowd, where, actually, my dress was greeted with:

"What a unique dress."

"Is it custom made?"

"Is this velvet?" followed by, "Oh, no."

"Very sustainable."

And "How thrifty." "Thrifty" being to James as kryptonite is to Superman.

"Do you recognize this?" I asked one evening, pulling at the lapels of the loose waistcoat I was wearing over a patchwork blouse. He shook his head. "Are you sure?" I asked. "Look carefully."

Then I told him it was made out of his own favorite green T-shirt. I didn't follow him as he ran off to look, because I knew what he would find: I spoke the truth.

# CHAPTER EIGHTEEN

ON MONDAY MORNING I WAITED FOR MRS. BILLINGS IN VAIN, standing by the kettle, teabags at the ready, expecting to hear the crunch of Mr. B's van on the gravel at any moment. When she was more than half an hour late, I went up to the top floor, looking out of the windows for any sign of her. There was none, but what I did see was a bright pink head bobbing around in the fields: Emma Beddoe, no doubt looking for something scandalous to put in her article. I didn't care, she wouldn't find anything there. Those fields were part of the east farm, tenanted by the Tate family, and I hadn't been near them for years. She was wearing a purple T-shirt, and it was as dire as all her other outfits.

Just as I was starting to worry about Mrs. B, my phone rang and I learned that there was, indeed, something to be worried about.

"Lady Langley, it's Eric Billings," the voice at the other end said. "Brenda and I won't be in today. I'm afraid there's been a bit of trouble."

"Is Mrs. B alright?" I asked.

"Oh yes. Well, she's not been taken poorly, if that's what you mean. The thing is, we had the police here this morning, wanting to ask her a few things. She's gone down to the station. I'm going to go down and wait for her."

The phone! They'd tracked it back to her. To us. Then I remembered all the kleptomania; maybe it had caught up with her. Decades of stealing must have racked up quite a long list of crimes. But the phone seemed more likely.

"I'll get James to get her a solicitor," I said, remembering her own advice to me. "Tell her not to say anything until they get there." It may well be an untrustworthy solicitor that he sent, but this affected both of us, so James would probably tell him to do a decent job.

"Well, she's there now. I can't really tell her anything," Mr. B said.

"I'll tell him it's urgent."

The news had put me into such a dither, my fingers fumbled as I tried to call James; we needed a solicitor fast, before that chatterbox overcame her nerves and started talking. I wondered again if I should have polished Mrs. B off when I had the chance. Had I hesitated too long and sealed my fate?

"What now?" James said, as he answered the phone.

The solicitor was soon sorted after that, and I made myself a cup of tea.

---

Mrs. B was back at work on Thursday.

"Lord James got me a state-of-the-art solicitor," she said proudly, dunking her custard cream into her tea. "I'll have to thank him for that."

"What did they ask you?"

Mrs. B looked pensive. She took another biscuit and dunked for so long that some of it broke off and sank to the bottom of the cup, and I gagged slightly.

"I'm not allowed to divulge information about an ongoing inquiry," she said in the end.

"You told them that?"

"No, of course not. That's what I'm telling you. I'm not allowed to talk about it." She took a long slurp of her tea, then she asked me, "Where did you find that bag? That brown bag that I found downstairs? You said it was Lord James's, but I don't think it was."

I took a custard cream myself and dunked it for as long as I dared, but not for as long as Mrs. B because, when biscuits break off into my tea, the memory of the sludge it creates at the bottom stays with me for hours.

"I thought it was James's bag," I said in the end. "He has one just like it, but you probably haven't seen it because he takes it with him to work."

I waited to see if she was going to tell me anything else.

"Have you still got it?" she asked, and it took me three gulps of tea to decide whether to say yes or no.

"I don't think so," I said. "I haven't seen it since."

Mrs. B picked up her duster and polish and headed for the stairs. Did she know about Lennie or not? Did she know it was his bag? I thought so. But did she know I knew it was his bag? I didn't know. And what about the phone? Had she taken the phone? What had she done with it? Had she told the police? Again, I didn't know. I wanted to scream. The one thing I did know was that there was probably no point in killing her now; presumably she had already done her worst. I found that was quite a weight off my mind.

My next question was, who was that knocking on the door? My first guess turned out to be correct: It was Parker and Khan again.

This time, they wanted to ask me all about my fragile mental health. There was no need for us to go to the station this time, so presumably they wanted to poke their noses around the house. I offered to give them the tour, but they said they didn't need the tour. All they needed to know at that moment was, did I want my solicitor present? I phoned Tarquin, and he arrived half an hour later.

"James told us you've had some psychological issues," DS Khan said, leaning forward and speaking quietly to try to make herself sound sympathetic.

"Not really," I said, and when Tarquin gave me the side-eye, I wondered why I'd said that. I corrected myself. "Not at all."

"He said you were in quite a state when he first met you."

"My mother had recently died. I was upset. Isn't that normal?"

"It is normal, yes, but he said you'd had a complete breakdown."

"I hadn't."

"He said the house was in a state of chaos. Most of the appliances were broken, the housework was never done. There had been a fire; he thinks you may have set it yourself."

"No, I didn't!"

"He said you were clearly not coping and wondered if he should phone social services."

I had to take a minute at that. He was going to phone social services? I wasn't a child.

"I didn't have the money to replace things and I was working long hours, trying to make ends meet, so I got behind with the housework. It was a long time ago. What's it got to do with now?"

"James says he decided not to get outside agencies involved because you seemed to turn a corner when you met him, but you never quite recovered and you've deteriorated since. He says you shut yourself away in the house, never seeing anyone except him."

"I see Mrs. Billings."

"The cleaner?"

"Some weeks I see Mr. Billings."

"He says that you're keeping some kind of tally on the bedroom wall and that lately you have been wearing increasingly bizarre outfits…"

Everyone took a moment to appreciate the dungarees I was wearing that day, handmade from a selection of old jackets. Their silent appraisal and the withering description James must have given them stung.

"I don't shut myself in the house," I said. "I go into the village sometimes. I went to the Bone Bonanza."

"Wearing those clothes."

"It was just a T-shirt I'd modified slightly on that day. And a skirt."

"What does this have to do with your investigation?" Tarquin asked, speaking up for the first time. "I assume that's why you're here."

"We're wondering if Daisy is really in a fit state to drive these days, and if she was in a fit state to drive on the night of the accident," DS Khan said. "These things can be taken into account at sentencing." For better or for worse, I suspected.

"I'm fit to drive and I'm fit to be left in charge of a sewing machine," I said. "I did not run Lennie Green over. If you think anyone in this house is mad, think of James." And I told them about the family tree—ten children—and the cheap coat of arms, made in Nevada, and the titles he had bought. I told them all about it.

DC Parker smiled. "It's nice to set up a family heirloom."

"Ten children!" I repeated, but he ignored me.

"That is a lot," Tarquin agreed. "I'm exhausted with three." But Parker ignored him as well.

They wrapped the interview up there, but as they got ready to leave, Khan said, "Is it OK if I use the toilet? Do you have one downstairs?"

Of course we did. I pointed her in the right direction and a minute later she returned, her hands in gloves, asking Parker for an evidence bag. She was carrying Lennie's wallet! It was wrapped in plastic, which was dripping wet.

She looked at me. "Do you know whose this is?" she asked. I shook my head. "When we check this for fingerprints, we're not going to find yours, are we?"

I stared back. Of course they were going to find my fingerprints.

"Yes," I said. "You will. I found it when I was walking out in the fields. I didn't look inside. I just brought it back here and James said he'd drop it into the SPAR on his way to work and they could put it in their lost property locker." Lost property was an unofficial service offered by most of the local businesses in the village. "He must have forgotten. Where did you find it?"

"In the cistern in your downstairs toilet. James said he'd been having some trouble flushing it and when he looked in the cistern, he found out why. He didn't say anything about you finding it in a field."

James never used that bathroom. I stared at the wallet. Yes, they were going to find my fingerprints, but they were also going to find James's. He been through everything in it. Then I remembered the wine I had drunk and the times I had been out of the room that night. And at the end of the evening, he got me to put the wallet and address book in the case with the keys for the classic cars. Had he been planning this even back then?

I shrugged. "Nothing to do with me," I said.

And she said, "Nothing to worry about then." She smiled. Then she arranged for me to nip into Tippington police station to have my fingerprints taken, for comparison.

I thought I'd held my nerve, but as they left, I felt *very* shaken. I looked at Tarquin, but his expression wasn't giving anything away. Had my husband and my solicitor cooked this up between them, I wondered? Tarquin hadn't said much during the interview and now that I thought about it, the side-eye he gave me might have been a look of victory at my mistake. I wished his face would move to give me an idea of what he was thinking. It's hard knowing who to trust when you don't know whether or not your solicitor is corrupt.

I watched him walking to his car with a sign on his back saying "kick me." It must have been there all day because I hadn't stuck it on him, and for all their faults, I didn't think Parker or Khan had either. It was hard to reconcile a hapless father with a corrupt solicitor.

Then I went to the key case and unlocked it. One good thing about thc accident and following incident was that, in the aftermath, James seemed to have forgotten about his plan to install cameras in the house to monitor me, so I still had unfettered access to the priest hole. The address book was still in the key case. I took it and hid it in the priest hole.

# CHAPTER NINETEEN

"WHEN DID ANYONE LAST VACUUM UNDER HERE?" JAMES ASKED. HE was looking under the coffee table for a shoe I'd hidden from him.

"Mrs. Billings's days are Monday and Thursday," I said.

"But when did anyone last clean under the coffee table? There's loads of dust. And here and here." He forgot about the shoe and took himself on a dust inspection, running his finger over surfaces that neither Mrs. Billings nor I could reach without standing on something.

"She's more of a cleaner than a polisher," I said.

"I'm paying her to do both, aren't I? When was this last done?" He was peering behind the stereo.

"She's nearly seventy. You can't expect her to get behind there."

"I'm paying her to do a job. If she can't do it, I can't pay her for it." He stood up and looked at me. "Why am I paying her anyway? What do you do all day?"

I couldn't lose Mrs. Billings! "We need her," I said.

"Things need to improve around here if we're keeping her on," he said. "Tell her that, and tell her it's her final warning."

When Mrs. B arrived that morning I told her nothing of the sort. Instead, I waited until she'd been and gone, then I did her usual route, finishing the bits she'd missed. After that I did all the dusting James had found to do that morning. I wasn't used to the effort; I was exhausted. I had to message James and ask him to bring a takeaway.

"We have food in the house," he replied. That sounded more like my mum, back in the days of scrimping and saving, than my husband, who would gladly pay an extra grand just because he could.

James phoned again a couple of hours later. "What's all this money you've been giving Brenda Billings?" he asked. He must have been going through the joint account, which I had access to, so that I could do day-to-day errands for him. I'd been hoping that amongst all the outgoings, a few extra pounds for the Billingses wouldn't be noticed.

"She's been doing some overtime," I said.

"What's she been doing?"

"She's been sprucing up some of the top floor rooms," I said.

"That's not part of her remit. And what's she done anyway? Did she clean them, or did she just wave a duster at them?"

"She's a trusted employee, I don't go checking up on her."

"Well, you should do. No more overtime and make sure she does a proper job. Did you tell her what I said earlier?"

I told him I had, of course I did.

---

James wasn't always as bad as he seems. Or at least, he didn't always seem as bad as he was.

I never really had any thoughts about him when I was growing up. He was a few years older than me and even without that age gap, school had a very hierarchical structure and we would have been leagues apart.

He wore Levis and designer T-shirts. Or so he said, but he was the reason we in the lower-school years thought Levi was spelled Levy until we were about sixteen.

Before I had even started my GCSEs, he set off for Oxford University, to much hullabaloo, and returned, years later, to much of the same, as Upper Iffley's first cryptocurrency millionaire. Or billionaire—rumors varied. In fact, he was one of the earliest cryptocurrency tycoons altogether; James was always one of the first with technology.

He came back at a time when I was rather down on my luck. About a year before, my mum had been feeling tired, then she started to lose weight. She had a few aches and pains and was feeling generally unwell. So she took herself off to the doctor, expecting to come back with vitamin supplements or tablets for anemia, but after some to-ing and fro-ing she came back with stage four pancreatic cancer. She went straight into palliative care.

When Mrs. Billings heard the news she came running round, with casseroles and cleaning services, which she did for free, and she did a pretty good job back then. My mum and Mrs. B had once been friends. A few years before, circumstances had conspired to put a distance between them, but she said she would be there whenever my mum needed something for however long that was. She and Mr. B would cancel their bank holiday weekend away if need be.

But when that weekend came, my mum was feeling better. She got up unassisted and we sat in the lounge, with the late summer sun shining in through the window, and sewed. I made a sketch for a new dress we would make.

When Mrs. Billings called in on her morning visit, we told her things were looking up and it would be a good idea for her and Mr. B to go away. We'd be fine, we said, as we waved them off.

That's how it is with cancer sometimes, one last good day. My mum collapsed the following afternoon, and I had to call an ambulance. At the hospital, I sat with her alone as the doctors and the nurses made her comfortable and I waited and I waited and I waited. At first waiting for a miracle, then, understanding it wouldn't come, I waited for the end. Finally, she passed. At the age of twenty-six I had not one living relative in the world.

They gave me the death certificate because they said I would need it, but I didn't know what to do with it. When I was growing up my mum usually framed my certificates and put them on the wall. Was I supposed do that?

I found out over the following weeks. Mrs. B took me round to the undertaker, where she talked them into giving me a cost-price funeral. Then she took me to the bank to get my mum's accounts closed down. She helped me deal with the transfer of property. The house became mine, and so did the bills.

The bills, the bills! They never stopped coming. When Mum's estate was settled, I owned the house I lived in and inherited just under a thousand pounds, which she must have saved hard for. I did the last sensible thing I ever did and used the money to pay off my car loan. Then I got a part-time job at the village SPAR, stacking shelves, with the promise of more hours and more varied duties to come. It didn't pay enough to maintain a house like mine, even without a mortgage. I was forever begging for more shifts.

Mrs. Billings's help was gradually withdrawn, and I was left to my own devices.

I turned my attention to the housework. I had never realized how much my mum, and then Mrs. Billings, did, but now I learned that dust doesn't dust itself, washing doesn't wash itself, and food certainly doesn't cook itself. My life became a never-ending cycle of working, cleaning, working, cleaning, working, cleaning, but none of it was ever enough.

And it seemed that all the furniture in the house had just been holding on until my mum died. Within a week of the funeral one of the legs on my bed collapsed. Getting it repaired or replaced was an unaffordable luxury, so after a couple of weeks, I reluctantly moved into my mum's room, the spare room being packed to the roof with stuff.

Then the TV developed a blemish on the screen. It was a red patch, right in the middle, and it made it look as if everyone on everything I watched had rosacea.

I found the number for an electrics repair company and asked if they could fix it, but they laughed.

"How old's the TV, love?" We'd had it for at least ten years. "May as well get a new one, be more than it's worth to fix it." And I heard him muttering the word "frugal" as he hung up, as if that were a bad thing. A new TV was also outside my budget, so I got used to it as it was.

The house used to be a nice place to go home to; it used to be cheerful and warm. Now, as winter drew in, it was cold and dark when I arrived home. I couldn't afford to run the heating for more than an hour a day; in January my lips went blue. It was always untidy.

Tidiness and I had been at loggerheads ever since I was small. My possessions lived where they were dropped. My mum was the opposite and under her command, matters stayed fairly controlled; as soon as she departed, my things ran free. CDs separated from their cases and roamed around the house; books leaped off the shelves and into precarious piles in every room; childhood toys cavorted across the landing; laundry tumbled out of the basket on its way to the machine and again on its way to the clotheshorse .

Before she left, Mrs. Billings had started boxing up some of my mother's things. She said I might find it helped, not to have them everywhere I looked, and she would help with getting rid of them when I was ready. I didn't think there was going to be a time when I was ready; instead, I went in the opposite direction and unpacked them all.

I took out the clothes my mum had made and started wearing them. I took out items in my own wardrobe that we'd made together and started wearing them as well. The connection to her made me feel less lonely. I left them lying around, as if I was goading her spirit to say, "Daisy, tidy that up right now."

I would've been embarrassed for anyone to see the house, but I didn't have it in me to make a change. Yet, change was on its way.

---

At that time I was too preoccupied to notice when word spread that James Dixon was returning to Upper Iffley.

I heard dribs and drabs as I was standing in queues in the local shops, people wondering where he would live: in a rustic cottage on the road to Tippington? In one of the thatched abodes, like mine, clustered around the village green? In one of the sympathetically designed new builds on the outskirts? Or would he, perhaps, build his own? He could be on *Grand Designs*. We could all tune in to find out where he sourced his marble from, how much it had cost him, and what he hadn't got proper planning permission for. Then, in a satisfying end to the evening, we could message each other: "Did you see it? Omg, it's hideous!" Not that anyone in the village ever messaged me.

However, James had other ideas. For years Langley Hall had sat empty and unloved, until one day a rumor began to circulate that the hall had been sold. To a Hollywood star? To a member of the royal family? To a Mafia boss? No one knew…

Then James's mother made the big announcement at the May Day celebrations: James had only gone and bought it! Outright—no mortgage! She told everyone who passed.

"Exciting news!" she said to me, as I lurked behind the Maypole. "He wants to throw a ball. Between you and me, I think my James is ready to settle down. I think he's throwing it with a view to finding his wife."

"Enchanting," I said. We could all head up there in time-limited pumpkin carriages and glass slippers. Most of my outfits were made of rags, so I would have to think hard about how I would magic one of them into a ball gown.

Mrs. Dixon nodded. "He'll be needing a few waiting staff for the night; I could put in a word for you. You'd have to smarten yourself up a bit."

If only she'd known the twist fate was about to take.

Yet, aside from that, I didn't give it another thought. I was still trying to find my feet, living on my own, and I was struggling in every way. Not only had I had issues with the bed and the TV, but I'd found myself short of an oven, following an incident with a forgotten frying pan and a sleepy head.

"Three cheers for the smoke alarm," the Fire Brigade said as they left. "It saved your life." But I wondered if death might not have been a mercy.

The curtains were ruined, but the kitchen window faced the back garden, so I could manage without them. However, the walls were charred, the sink half-melted, and the cooker was unusable. Something inside it had died and not one function worked, no cooktop, no grill, no oven.

The price of an oven was the stuff dreams were made of, and I failed to qualify for a credit arrangement.

So, I microwaved everything I could, turning everything I ate into a three-course meal: veg course, potato course, meat course, and started saving for a new cooker at the rate of a pound or two a week. I reckoned I could have one in about a year, factoring in overtime at Christmas and the fact that I didn't have to buy anyone presents anymore.

But living on my own was hard, and one night I needed company more than I needed an oven. I changed into a skirt made from silk camisoles and took my life savings, £12 by then, down to the King's Head for karaoke night.

I was nervous as I approached; I was not liked in the village. In fact, I was shunned. I'd even noticed that there were people who wouldn't buy from a shelf in the SPAR if they knew I'd stacked it. But I couldn't spend another night on my own in the house, so I had to try. I walked to the front door and pushed it open.

Inside, I knew everyone. Ted from the garage was there, with his lank hair, his overalls, and his beer belly; Mr. and Mrs. Faulkner from the newsagent's, the sartorial opposite of Ted; Betty Chambers from the small shop and her associate from Great Beadington; the bellringers, having a drink after bellringing practice. Samantha Gibson and Euan Saunders, not yet married at that time, were at a table in the middle of the room. When I saw them I nearly did an about-turn, but they saved me the trouble by downing their drinks and "hummphing" out, Samantha barging my shoulder as she did so.

"What are you having, Daisy?" Mick, the landlord, asked me.

"Pineapple Breezer, please." I handed my money over and took a glug. Now I was committed to my plan, but no one shuffled up so that I could go and sit with them. I began to ask myself what I'd expected.

Still, once I had the taste for them, the Bacardi Breezers went down well and I began to relax. I drank three and ordered a fourth, but as Mick put the open bottle down in front of me, disaster struck: I was short by 50p.

"Well, you've got a problem then," Mick said, his hand still outstretched for the money I didn't have. "What are you going to do?" The room fell silent and everyone stared at me.

"What do people normally do when this happens?" I asked.

"Normally one of their friends coughs up for them."

I bit my lip and began scrolling through my memories for a friend.

Then there was a commotion at the door. The Dixons had arrived, Mr. Dixon, wearing the same clothes he always wore, Mrs. Dixon flaunting an expensive pair of earrings and a new coat. I didn't like Mrs. Dixon and I was pleased a few months later when James bought them a villa in Spain and off they jetted. Behind them came James, sporting a very heavy-looking watch, that I was soon to learn cost nearly two hundred grand, Louis Vuitton jeans, and a Dolce & Gabbana T-shirt. We'd all heard of James's incredible wealth, but this was the first display of it that we'd seen.

"What's happening?" James asked, looking around.

"Daisy here is about to perform a magic trick and make 50p appear from thin air," Mick said, nodding at the open bottle.

"Daisy ordered a drink and she hasn't got enough money to pay for it," Ted explained to James's puzzled face.

"Luckily, this is my round!" James said and handed a credit card to Mick. "Keep hold of that, the drinks are on me for the rest of the night."

On hearing that news, everyone flooded to the bar.

James turned to me. "Sorry to hear about your mum."

"Thanks," I said, but I wasn't there to think about that. In fact, I was specifically there not to think about it. I wanted to drink and I wanted to sing the songs of the Spice Girls and I wanted people to talk to me, but not about my mum. For some reason I said, "She looked like a corpse for days before she actually died," which wasn't even true and it sent James hurrying away, muttering something about catching me later.

The evening rolled on. I drank more Breezers. I had a turn on the karaoke. I had several turns. I did a duet with Ted. We sang, "You're the One That I Want." It was the best time I'd had since my mum's passing.

By the end of the night I was the only person left, drunkenly slurring out whatever came next on the machine as they closed up around me. I decided I would get a karaoke machine; I was working out which bills I wouldn't pay to save the money, and if this would be instead of an oven, or before it, or after it, as Vern, the karaoke man, packed his stuff up.

"One more song, Vern," I said. "I'll let you choose."

"'The Sound of Silence,'" he said, and pulled the plug.

"Don't you have a home to go to?" Mick asked as he collected the glasses.

"Well, yes and no." I had a house, but it didn't feel like a home anymore. Mick didn't stop to hear the details of that.

Then I had an idea. "Do you need any staff?" It would be nice to work in the King's Head and be there for karaoke every week.

"We've got everyone we need at the moment, thanks," Mick said. And I hadn't really expected anything else. "Door's over there." And with no other option, I went through it.

Outside, the fresh air hit me and I realized how drunk I was, but I could find my way home in my sleep, so it wasn't an issue. I took my keys out of my bag and held them between my fingers, just in case. Upper Iffley was a very safe place, but you can never be too careful. Then I stepped out off the pavement to the other side of the road, stood awkwardly on the curb, tripped, and dropped my keys down the drain.

"Noooo!" I lay on my stomach and peered down through the grid. I couldn't see anything and if I could, I wouldn't have been able to reach through the slats. Just like that, the best night since my mum had died had become the worst. I didn't even know back then what you were supposed to do if you dropped your keys down the drain. Previously, my mum would've let me in. And it was getting cold.

Headlights appeared and I scrambled to try to get up before the car was on top of me, but it saw me and stopped. The door opened.

"Are you alright?" a voice asked and when I looked up, James was standing in front of me.

"Yes," I said.

"Are you sure?"

"I dropped my keys."

"Oh, I thought you were being sick," he said. "You are quite drunk." I wasn't that bad. "I've got a car phone and a Yellow Pages in the limo," he said, gesturing at the long black car behind him, with a chauffeur standing beside it. "We can call an emergency locksmith."

So, I got into the car and used the only car phone I have ever used—it was already quite retro by then: Mobile phones were just starting to become common. Then we drove to my house and waited in the warmth of the car until the locksmith arrived and James settled up with him, which was slightly embarrassing, but he insisted and I didn't have the money anyway.

I didn't invite him in—I couldn't because of the mess—but as he was about to leave, James said, "Would you like to go out sometime?"

I wasn't expecting that!

"Yeah, OK." I managed to keep my voice calm. "When did you think?"

"Thursday maybe? Or Friday? If you're free."

Frankly, I could've done any evening except for the evenings I was on the late shift, but I made a show of thinking it over. "Thursday I could do," I said in the end. Why wait? Then I changed my mind: "Friday," I said. I wouldn't be paid until Friday; I was already thinking about what I would go without to pay for a round of drinks or whatever we were going to do.

"Great! I'll pick you up at eight." And once again, it became the best evening since my mum died.

That night I fell asleep thinking about James Dixon and how I'd never noticed before how attractive he was. His face was thin and his nose was quite sharp; I'd always thought of him as rather fox-like, but I realized now how lovely foxes were. His hair, I'd previously thought of as mud brown, but now I'd describe it as tawny; the shape of his lips I'd once considered as girly, now I saw they made him look sensitive.

---

On Friday afternoon I emptied out my wardrobe onto my bed and wondered what to wear. I had a mixture of shop-bought clothes and the homemade ones I was wearing more and more often. I wasn't sure whether Primark or Made by Daisy would go better with his designer gear.

In the end I chose the dress that my mum and I had made together for the one and only holiday we ever went on. It was our masterpiece; it was sleeveless and fitted, made from blue cotton, with satin sewn into the sleeves and skirt. We embroidered the dress with little daisies, for my name, and sewed tassels to the hem, using bookmark tassels left over from a jumble sale. It looked simple, but from design to completion, it had taken us weeks. It made me feel like my mum was with me, although I understand not everyone would want their mother with them on a date.

"Evening. You look...original," he said as I opened the front door, trying to wriggle out without him seeing the chaos inside. "Your carriage awaits."

The chauffeur stood by the car, and as we approached, he opened the rear door. "Hello," I said to him as I ducked my head to get in, and he ignored me.

"Do you always have a chauffeur?" I asked James as the door closed on us.

He shook his head. "It's a service you hire. I'm just trying it to see if I like it. I have him until midnight tonight."

"Then the limo turns into a pumpkin," I said.

He stared at me blankly for a moment, and we drove in silence out of the village.

"Where are we going?" I asked as we wound through country lanes; it wasn't the usual route into town. It came out sounding as if I thought I was being kidnapped. "There's no money for a ransom."

James smiled a more natural smile. "It's called Jacques's," James said. "It's just off Mary Magdalen Road."

"I've never heard of it." Mary Magdalen Road was not renowned for its nightlife.

"It's not really advertised to the mass market."

That sounded posh. I hoped I had enough money for a round. I would probably have to duck out before a second one, or forgo eating for the month.

But when we got there, my worries were for naught. It was colorful, it was cheerful, the smiles of the staff looked like real smiles. They brought us cocktails at a table below which was an aquarium, so we could look down and see neon tetras and something yellow I didn't know the name of. A sign on the wall told us the fish tanks were soundproof, to protect the fish, but asking us to please not knock on them.

"All on my tab," James said when he saw me scouring the drinks menu for prices. "So, what are you doing with yourself these days? Big career? Nonstop social life?"

"I'm in retail," I said. "It keeps me really busy. I'm thinking about taking on a sideline though." He waited for me to elaborate, and I waited for him to offer me some cleaning shifts at Langley Hall. When he didn't, I said, "Tell me about cryptocurrency."

"It's pretty straightforward, really. You mine for coins, put them in your wallet—your virtual wallet—and in a matter of months they double, triple, quadruple their value. Simple as that." It did sound easy. He continued, "Where I come in is that people don't understand it, so they don't trust it. Or they don't know how to mine for it, or which currency to invest in, or how to monitor it. It really could make everyone rich if they knew what they were doing. Instead, those that have vision, but not the expertise, invest in it through me. I cut through the confusion. Do you have anything you want to invest?"

"What's the minimum investment?"

"A thousand pounds."

"I'll think about it."

I was thinking about it. If I could get my hands on a thousand pounds, I could double, triple, quadruple my investment. Then maybe I could invest it again, double, triple, quadruple it and so on. It didn't take many multiples before I lost track of the fortune I could make, in the unlikely event I could get my hands on a thousand pounds.

"Are you planning to stay in your house?" James was asking. I nodded, he continued, "It's a big house. There's a lot of equity sitting there doing nothing. You could sell it and invest the proceeds."

"I'm using it for living in for the foreseeable future," I said. "I shouldn't think I could live in a crypto coin."

He smiled a charming smile. "I don't mean for you to risk your security. I was thinking, if you fancied living somewhere smaller one day, you could downsize and you could also have an investment for later. But don't do anything hasty."

"It's something to think about," I said, and that was true. I could sell the house, buy a modern flat, with a cooker, and run the heating all day every day with the money I would make from the cryptocurrency.

But my family had lived in that house for generations. It was full of my memories, and it was full of my possessions, which were threatening to make their way out of the front door and all over the garden. I needed every single one of them, and I didn't know how I'd fit them into a smaller abode. But I'd think it over.

And in fact, it was all I could think about while I was stacking shelves that week. Especially since my washing machine was sounding rattly, and I didn't relish the idea of doing my washing in the sink once a week.

I should save a grand and invest it in cryptocurrency. I'd failed to save up for a cooker, but if I kept to a strict regime, if I had no disasters, if I could get extra shifts, maybe I could save it within four years.

After that it would be just a few months to see my investment double, but I would leave it for longer. I would wait for it to be five thousand, ten thousand, twenty. In five or six years' time, I would never have to work again.

---

James invited me on another date.

We went to the local fun fair, which had rolled into town a few days before and was not a place I thought I'd be visiting myself. I wore a pair of secondhand jeans I'd embroidered around the hems and pockets, and a T-shirt made from patches of other T-shirts. James said that while the jeans were very individual, the T-shirt sounded a bit cannibalistic.

He bought a gazillion tokens, and we rode the rides until I felt queasy. Then we ate burgers from the burger van and went over the road for a drink, which did nothing to settle my stomach, but I made it through on high spirits. It was only the second time that year that I was having fun—if the truth be told, I'd found our first date quite stressful—even though the Waltzer seemed to have given me whiplash.

"What do you do in retail?" James asked me as we settled at a corner table with our drinks. I was caught off guard and my mood dropped.

"I'm involved in displaying the stock," I told him.

"Window displays? I remember you as being creative."

"Not quite." But I liked the idea that he thought I was creative, although I'm not. Or maybe I am; I'd been creative with microwave dishes after the oven burnt, and I made many of my own clothes. But those were from necessity. I didn't feel they qualified as creativity.

"Do you do the displays inside the shops, then?" he asked. Wasn't he going to let this go?

"Closer."

"Do you have to do a course for that?"

There was an induction day, then a few minutes watching a more experienced colleague putting packets of dried rice on a shelf and telling me to make sure the oldest stuff was at the front. "Not a long course," I said.

"Really? I thought it was quite involved."

"Look," I said, "I stack shelves in the SPAR. I worked at the bric-a-brac shop in Tippington and I loved it. I was going to go into antiques, Miss Bradbury said I had an eye for it, but it closed down. Then Mum died and I needed a job quickly and that is what I got. It won't be forever, I'll get another job in bric-a-brac sooner or later, or antiques, but for now, I'm working at the supermarket."

"Nothing wrong with that," James said. "My mother was at the SPAR for most of her working life."

I was so relieved I could have cried. It was easy to forget Mrs. Dixon had worked there with the way she swanned around like Lady Muck, although she was a supervisor, not a lowly shelf stacker.

"I'm sure things will get better," James said.

We finished our drinks and I couldn't face another after the way I'd been shaken around at the fairground, so I said, "Shall we go? I've got an early start—deliveries in the morning and much to put on the shelves."

He dropped me off at my house, but before I got out of the car… he kissed me!

---

We fell into a routine of regular messaging.

Good morning.

Really enjoyed last night.

Looking forward to next time.

Did you see Hollyoaks? OMG! (from me) and

Just watching Newsnight (from him).

Goodnight xx

xxx

xxxx

xxxxx

xxxxxx

xxxxxxx

xxxxxxxx

xxxxxxxxx

You win! Goodnight.

---

We met up more and more often, and I stopped being embarrassed that James always paid for everything.

Then one evening, as he dropped me off, he asked, "Aren't you going to invite me in?"

No, that was not part of my plan; I'd been daydreaming that he'd invite me to Langley Hall, rather than this way round. I'd even kept £10 tucked away in case he was going to charge me an entrance fee. I couldn't let him in to see the dead cooker, the burnt curtains, and the charring on the wall. He'd see the washing draped around the house, dripping wet, because I had made the decision to only use the machine for special occasions. He would see all my stuff taking over the house. He might look in the cupboards and find that they were nearly bare.

"Early start," I said.

"I thought you were on the late shift tomorrow?"

"I'm hoping to pick up some overtime. They said they'd phone me, I have to be ready."

He looked skeptical. "Just for five minutes?"

What were we going to do for five minutes? "Do you need the loo?" I asked, and I realized my mistake as he nodded.

"OK, then." I bit the bullet and led him up the garden path.

I unlocked the door, holding my breath, half expecting my possessions to be waiting, ready to tumble out and engulf us. We'd be found in the morning, buried under the avalanche. But nothing fell and James didn't bat an eyelid at the mountain of clothes heaped on the end of the banister, both mine and my mother's, or the shoes around the door and halfway along the hall, not all pairs, or the tower of post on the side table, or the childhood toys balanced on the radiator.

"Which way?" he asked. "For the toilet?"

"Up the stairs, straight ahead of you." There was also one downstairs, but the approach to that would've given him a view into the kitchen.

And off he went. As soon as I heard the bathroom door shut, I took my shoes off and hurried up after him to make sure all the doors up there were closed. I didn't want him peering inside to see the bombsite that was now my room or the spare bed with the broken frame. Then I tiptoed back down and did the same downstairs. I waited for him at the front door.

"Coffee?" he asked coming down the stairs, and my heart sank.

"This way," I said. I led him into the lounge, cleared a space for him to sit on one of the comfier parts of the sofa and went to make coffee, closing the door firmly as I left the room. I was poking around in the cupboard under the worktop when:

"Do you think I should buy a BMW?" James asked from behind me.

"Ow!" I jumped and banged my head on the cupboard doorframe. I turned as gracefully as I could. He was looking at the charred corpse of the cooker and the surrounding wall.

"I'm not going to keep the chauffeur service, I like driving. Have you had an accident?"

"Small one," I said.

"Does the oven still work?"

"I never used it anyway."

"I've got a plasterer doing some work at the moment," James said. "He's free tomorrow afternoon; he can soon have that wall ready for a lick of paint. Do you need any help with the drinks?"

We went into the front room. I put a CD on and we chatted until the music stopped, the lights went out, and I heard, from the kitchen, the hum of the fridge go silent.

"Fuse?" James asked. But no, my utilities were on a prepayment meter.

"There are candles somewhere," I said. "Or I can put it on emergency credit. My card's in my bag. If I can find it."

"Leave it," he said. "Who needs lights anyway? The sun will be up in the morning." And after all, there was nothing in the fridge, now that I'd used the last of the milk.

In the moonlight that shone through the window, I saw him put his mug on the floor, then he moved forward and did the same with mine. He took my hands and pulled me toward him. As we kissed, he put his arms around me and pulled me closer and down. And I followed, trying to pretend there wasn't a hairbrush digging into my back.

---

The next day, the plasterer came and plastered the wall. A few days later, once it had dried, a decorator came and refreshed my kitchen with a layer of magnolia paint. The day after that, a new cooker and sink arrived, with an electrician and a plumber to connect them up, and the old one was carted away. All paid for.

For the first time since my mum passed, I enjoyed being in the house. I felt accepted, I felt safe. I felt hope.

James and I began to meet whenever we could. We took walks through the countryside, we went for long lunches in neighboring villages—not Great Beadington—we took selfies at Stonehenge, we downed shots in the King's Head.

There was an incident with my car, and it ended up in a ditch. I had no insurance because I hadn't taken it for its mandatory annual roadworthiness check—double saving. Plus, I already had nine points on my license, the speedometer tended to stick, and I wasn't sure how I was going to explain it all to the authorities. I thought it was the end of driving for me, but when I told James he just laughed. He had my car taken away, and a few days later he was helping me choose a new one.

He told me I was worth the money, he told me I was priceless. He told me I was all he thought about all day. It had been a long time since anyone other than my mum thought about me at all.

One day, we were sitting on a bench beneath a tree when James suddenly "Eek!"-ed and leaped to his feet.

"What's wrong?" I asked, racing to help.

"It's a… It's a… It's a…" He held out his hand to show me a tiny money spider running across it. "I don't like spiders," he gibbered. "Can you get it off me?" And that was the moment I fell in love. At least I thought I did.

# CHAPTER TWENTY

TWENTY YEARS LATER, I KNEW ALL JAMES AND I REALLY HAD WAS A shared mania for founding a family line. How long it had taken me to work that out, I couldn't really say, but if I was being honest with myself, it hadn't taken twenty years. One year? Or two? Sooner than that? Maybe the moment he showed me his insane family tree. But I told myself that was what I'd wanted, so why was I complaining?

Regardless, eventually it dawned on me that, when James met me all those years ago, he didn't see someone he wanted to share his life with; he saw someone who was naive, isolated, and struggling. He saw someone he could control.

And he did: He took my money when he invested the funds from my house, then he took me to Langley Hall, away from the village, out of sight and out of mind. All I had left was Mrs. Billings, and I kept the worst of it from her.

Meanwhile, James constantly dangled the carrot of children and how much better life would be when I'd fulfilled my side of the bargain. And I waited for them to come.

Over the years, I became inured to the slights and the daily disappointments. I made myself believe that sewing and whodunits were all I needed, along with Langley Hall, my ancestral home. And I waited. Whenever I thought about making a change, I remembered the poverty I'd been living in when I met him, the misery of choosing between the utilities and food, and the constant fear of a new bill I couldn't pay. At least then I'd had a roof over my head; if I left now, I'd have nothing. I forgot that I'd ever had a choice, as I waited for something to change.

And when nothing changed, James took away everything else. He halved my allowance, he canceled my streaming subscriptions, he moved into his own bedroom. Finally, I understood that waiting would bring nothing but more waiting, until I realized I was waiting for the end of the Ponzi scheme.

Now something was going to change because James was trying to set me up for an accident that was his fault as much as—no, *more than*—mine, and a murder that was entirely down to him.

After all, if we'd done it my way, dialed 999 and shown remorse, maybe Lennie could have been saved and I could have a suspended sentence. If that. This could have been little more than a bad year. Lennie could be out of hospital, he could've put in a good word for me, and maybe I could have had even less than a suspended sentence.

Then, we would never have been by the river for James to attack Mr. Newman. Mr. N would still hate us and want to stop us selling the farm for warehouses, but he would be alive and well and we could fight that fight through nonviolent means. And with any luck, lose.

With thoughts of Lennie and Mr. Newman, I returned to the forum. Against my better judgment, I clicked into it.

All the usual suspects were there: most of the village, plus AllEars, still digging for gossip, and NoseyParker. James, as BigDreams, was doing his worst.

People think they know Daisy because she's lived in the village all her life, he wrote. But she's been shut away in Langley Hall for a long time, does anyone really know her? What does she do all day?

Isn't there a lot of work in running a big house like that? Mrs. Faulkner asked.

Yes and no, Mrs. Billings said. There would be, but she doesn't really do it. They live in a few rooms on the first and second floors. I look after all that area for them. The rest has gone to rack and ruin.

There was a pause. I had thought it was an open secret that Langley Hall wasn't what it once was, but it seemed to be news to some people.

They should be strung up! a pseudonym said. Beautiful house like that left to rot.

I fought the urge to explain that that was James more than it was me.

We should start a fund, Mrs. Chambers said.

We haven't finished collecting to replace the bell yet, Betty, the vicar said.

This seems more urgent, Mrs. Chambers said. We've been managing without the bell for seven hundred years.

BigDreams brought them back round to the original question. If she's not doing what she should be, what is she doing?

Doesn't she have a job? Mrs. Thorpe asked.

No. Why would she?

Does she paint? Mrs. Thrussell asked. Or play an instrument? Or garden? Something creative.

She sews, Mrs. Billings said. Good little seamstress, as good as Lorna.

There you go, then.

You can't sew all day every day, BigDreams said.

Actually, you can. But I didn't correct him on that.

What do you think she does? Mary Bishop asked BigDreams.

Well, I don't know, but I know their marriage has gone stale.

How would you know something like that? Mrs. Billings asked.

I think she's having an affair, BigDreams said, ignoring the question.

Who would she be having an affair with? Mrs. Faulkner asked. With an arse the size of hers?

Really! Is that relevant? I typed. Fatter women than me must have had loads of affairs. And men. But I didn't press Post. I deleted it and kept a dignified silence.

Wouldn't surprise me, Mrs. Thrussell said, but didn't elaborate on why.

I think there's more to it than just an affair, BigDreams said.

Such as? Mrs. Faulkner asked.

Well, it's not really for me to say, but it can't have escaped your notice the police were searching Langley Hall for quite some time.

The forum went quiet while they digested that. Then, Are you saying she had an affair with Lennie Green? AllEars was back.

That's not what I was thinking, but it could have been him.

What were you thinking?

There was a pause before BigDreams wrote. This has to stay between us all. I'm only putting this out because we're all from the village here. It has to be secret, let the police do their job and all that. Do you promise?

Promise.

Cross my heart.

Scout's honor.

I think she was having an affair and Lennie Green found out. I think the affair was with Doug Newman.

Never!

I don't believe it!

This will break Jo.

It will break Meg.

Meg won't care.

Meg probably knew. They should get Meg to sniff Lady Langley and see how she reacts.

I'm not sure she's keen on dogs, she'd probably react by saying "get off me," Mrs. Billings said.

How Meg reacts, to see if she recognizes Daisy.

It would work.

Doesn't Meg know Daisy anyway, just from being around here? Mrs. Thorpe asked.

I don't know that she does, Jo Newman replied. We hardly ever see Daisy out in the fields, and we don't tend to go up as far as Langley Hall ourselves.

That allayed any fears that the experiment would be compromised.

I think it's a very good idea, Mrs. Chambers said.

It's miraculous what dogs can do, Mrs. Thrussell replied.

BigDreams got the gossip back on track. I think Lennie was going to tell their spouses, so they killed him.

The forum fell silent and I fumed. I'd previously been wary of entering the fray, but now, disguised as LooseEnds, I made my first foray.

That theory has more holes than a box of Cheerios, I wrote. For a start, how did they know Lennie? He was from Great Beadington. And why would he care? Why would he tell anyone about it?

Yes, Mr. Chambers said. If they were having an affair, isn't it more likely that James Dixon found out and killed Doug Newman?

Thank you!

So, where does Lennie Green come into it? Mrs. Faulkner wrote.

Collateral damage.

But how? And why?

I waited a while to see what the response to that would be, but BigDreams seemed flummoxed. The forum went quiet and I logged off. I needed some aspersions of my own to cast.

---

If James was going to plant evidence to make me look guilty, he was going to find that two could play that game.

Clearly, I couldn't shove something into the plumbing and get the police round to find it as he had, that would unravel in seconds, but I had a secret weapon: Mrs. B. And so, before she arrived, I went to the priest hole and from Lennie's bag, I took the inhaler. I went to James's room, wiped my fingerprints from it, and left it on his bedside cabinet. James was not asthmatic, I didn't know if Mrs. B knew that, but I hoped the sight of a new medication would attract her curiosity anyway.

We went through the usual tea and biscuits routine and I learned from her that Archie Thorpe, son of Mrs. Thorpe from The Two Ts teashop, had a new job in America and would be leaving here within the next few weeks. Once we'd finished marveling over that, Mrs. B went to make a start on the cleaning and I put out a paperweight for her to take. Then I retreated to my sewing den and waited for her to go into James's room and make her discovery.

I waited, until…

"Toodle-oo, Lady Langley, love. I'll be off now," and I heard her making her way down the grand staircase. I'd expected her to come to alert me to the critical evidence I had planted; it wasn't like her to keep something like that to herself. Irked, I made my way out of my sewing room to see what I could see.

The first thing I saw was the paperweight, exactly where I had left it. I stared at it for a moment, then, with a sinking feeling, made my way to James's room.

The inhaler was gone, and the top of the cabinet was clear. Admittedly that had been the plan, but the presence of the paperweight and the lack of commentary on the finding convinced me that Mrs. B had taken the inhaler for all the wrong reasons. It wasn't definitive; she could be taking it straight to the police without telling me, and they could be sending it off for forensic tests later today. But in my heart, I knew the truth. Oh, that perfidious woman! I would kill her, if I hadn't already made the decision not to do that.

*Why would you steal someone else's inhaler?* For the first time, I googled kleptomania and learned that it is merely the compulsive urge to take things. It doesn't have to be valuable, it doesn't have to be of any use to the thief. It just has to be not theirs. That is why you would steal someone else's inhaler. I wondered if she'd taken the vertebra Mrs. Faulkner said Great Beadington had pilfered from the Bone Bonanza.

"Aaargh!" I shouted, and I threw the paperweight. It bounced off the wall and left a chip in the paint. That infuriated me even more, and I threw my phone across the room. It landed harmlessly on James's armchair and with it went my fury.

I sat down to think and after some time was able to console myself with the thought that this was just a trial run. It had gone badly, but I had other items to leave. Sooner or later something would be flagged as suspicious. Anyway, the inhaler didn't exactly scream "Lennie!" I would've been lucky if anyone had seen it and made the connection. On reflection, it was a poor choice. I put the paperweight away and went back to see what else was in his bag. I still had the sense that this was a realistic way forward.

---

And so it was. For Mrs. B's next visit, I set out the address book I had found in Lennie's pocket. I was hoping it had his own name and address in it, ideally under the heading "property of," but when I checked, that wasn't the case. Never mind, though, it surely wouldn't take the police too much poking about to find out whose it was.

This time, I left it sticking out from under James's bed. And soon…

"Lady Langley, love, come and look at this."

I went through and Mrs. Billings had the book in her hands. She was flicking through the pages. "Looks like Lord James has left this behind," she said. "Do you think he needs it? Should you give him a ring?"

"What is it?" I asked and she handed it over to me. I spent a minute looking at the names and addresses; they were all strangers. "This isn't James's," I said. "We don't know any of these people."

"Well, whose is it?" she said.

"I don't know, but why would he have someone else's address book? Where did you find it?"

And she told me she'd found it sticking out from under the bed.

"Maybe it's been left behind by the previous owners," she suggested.

"Lord Ashbury? This room's had a new carpet since then."

She looked thoughtful. "Whose, then? We should get it back to them; it looks important."

Mrs. Billings was of the same generation as Lennie, where the loss of an address book could equate to the loss of many of your contacts. And it was a generation where it was normal to hand lost property in at the local police station. So, five minutes later, the cleaning abandoned for the day, I drove us into Upper Iffley to the village police station, where young PC Wylie looked at us, bemused.

"It's only an address book," he said.

"That's someone's world," Mrs. Billings told him.

"It seems very strange," I said, "because we found it in my husband's bedroom at Langley Hall. It doesn't belong to him, but I can assure you that, aside from Mrs. Billings, no one but him has been in that room for a very long time."

They both looked at me as I realized what I had just told them about the state of my marriage.

"Don't you have a lot of ghosts in that place?" PC Wylie asked.

"They don't usually leave us address books. Mrs. Billings, tell him again how you found it."

She told him again.

"I just wonder why would someone else's address book be in James's room?" I said. "If we find out whose it is, I expect the rest will fall into place."

PC Wylie looked at me with a "why would anyone care?" expression on his face.

"It just makes me think of something the archaeologists on our estate said," I told him. "They said, 'your instinct is to focus on the big pieces, but the answers are often in the smaller things.'" They said nothing of the sort. Their pearls of wisdom generally revolved around how long to leave a teabag in a cup of tea. "I wouldn't want it to look like we were trying to hide anything. I'd prefer to hand it all over to the professionals, no matter how innocent it seems."

"And your colleagues from town have been digging around, looking for clues about Lennie Green," Mrs. Billings said, which was the way I wanted PC Wylie to be thinking, without wanting to have put it quite as bluntly as that. He acknowledged the point though and took the address book from us.

"Might give Tippington a ring," he said.

"Thank you. And to clarify, it was Mrs. Billings who found it, in James's room."

With that we made our way back to Langley Hall. As we turned into the drive I had a glimpse of a young woman standing in a field across the road, holding a camera. Gone was the pink hair, changed to green, but the orange T-shirt had made another appearance and it jarred as badly with the new shade as it had with the pink. I cursed under my breath and vowed that, if I saw her once more out in the open clashing like that, I was going to give her a color chart and I was going to stand over her until she had learned the lessons on it.

---

One of the frustrating things about planting evidence was that I could never really know what had been said to James by Parker and Khan.

I could only guess from his mood when he came home each evening. The night after we'd delivered the address book to the police station, he was in a bad one. I hoped it was due to contact from the constabulary and not just heavy traffic on the Tippington bypass.

My phone rang while I was mulling it over.

"Hello, Daisy?" the voice at the other end said. "This is Tarquin. We have a new development in your case."

"'My case'?" I said. "I didn't know I was a 'case.'"

"Well, you're the prime suspect in a hit-and-run killing, so, yes, I think I should keep your file open."

I had to sit down. It was quite a shock to hear it put so bluntly. "They don't really think that, do they? Based purely on something they said my husband said. Which I'm sure he didn't. Don't they have to go looking for evidence these days?"

"They have some new evidence. They've had Mr. Green's phone details and his phone was in or around your house on the night he went missing. They'd like you to go down to the station tomorrow morning to speak to them. Would you like me to meet you there?"

# CHAPTER TWENTY-ONE

"SOMEONE'S COMING FOR THE BENTLEY TODAY," JAMES SAID AS HE got dressed the following morning. "To pick it up. I'm selling it. We've done the paperwork; you only need to give him the key."

"Why?"

"How often do I drive it? It's just sitting there in the garage. It may as well go to someone who'll appreciate it."

As with the yacht, that didn't sound like a James kind of sentiment.

"Alright," I said. Did that mean he didn't know I wasn't going to be in? I had the police interview that morning, and I couldn't make promises about what time I would be home. "I have to go out this morning."

"Where?"

"To see my solicitor."

James half smiled. "OK," he said, uncharacteristically reasonable. "I'll put them off until tomorrow. Are you in tomorrow?"

"Yes," I said. Unless I was banged up. But the next day was a Mrs.

Billings day anyway, so there was no need to further delay the removal of the Bentley; she could hand over the keys if necessary.

---

Forewarned is forearmed and I made myself some sandwiches and a flask of coffee for this second outing to the cop shop. I'd been starving by the end of the last interview, and I find it hard to remember the lies I've told when I'm hungry. I thought about a few Mr. Kiplings to round them off with, but there weren't enough in the packet to share around four of us.

My solicitor—or should I call him James's solicitor?—was already there. He had a file with my name written on it and was using correction fluid to cover up a doodle.

"Kids?" I said.

"They're going to be in a lot of trouble," Tarquin replied, with a smile that said they weren't, although they should be. I felt a pang for children of mine who had never had the chance to make their presence felt through doodles.

DS Khan sat opposite us, tapping her fingers on the table. The whole gang was back, but hopefully this time not for so long.

"Morning, Daisy, thank you for coming, we just have a few more questions," DS Khan said, and I noticed for the first time how wonky her mouth was. "Shouldn't take up too much of your time," she added, trying to lull me into a false sense of security.

I nodded as if I were falling for it and we began. The first things they wanted to ask me were the same questions as last time, all over again. But the story I had told was so ingrained in my memory by then that I told it as before, word for word. Then:

"We've had information from Lennie's mobile provider, and it shows he was in or near your house on the night he went missing."

Even though I'd known this was coming, I felt flustered. But Tarquin stepped in. "It shows his phone was in the area that night," he said. "That's not proof Lennie was. Or that he was in my client's house or that he had any contact at all with my client."

That was more like it! I'd been struck in the past by how little he intervened. I thought James might have told him to do that.

"But it's a very high likelihood," DS Khan said. "There are only fields for miles around."

"Lots of public footpaths, though," I said, although Lennie Green hadn't looked like a man who walked many miles along country paths. "Are you asking James about this?" I asked them.

"We're asking you at the moment," Khan said. "Let us worry about who else we're asking."

Parker moved on. "That wallet we found belonged to Lennie Green. We had it tested for fingerprints. Yours were all over it."

"I told you, I found it in a field."

"But you also said that you gave it to Mr. Dixon and he said he'd hand it in to lost property."

"So?"

"Doesn't it seem strange that his fingerprints were nowhere to be found."

"Not if he wiped them off."

"You can't wipe off one set without wiping another."

Good point.

"I left it on the coffee table for him to pick up," I said. "I didn't see him pick it up, so I don't know what he did next or why he would avoid getting his fingerprints on it." Except I knew very well why he would do that. Under the table, I clenched my fists.

"There's nothing you've said that means the wallet wasn't found in exactly the way my client said it was," Tarquin said, and the detectives decided to move on.

"You handed in an address book to your local police station a few days ago. Can you tell us about it, please, Daisy," Parker said.

"It wasn't me handing it in, it was Mrs. Billings, I was just giving her a lift down there. She found it in James's bedroom. I told her it wasn't James's because all the people in it were strangers, and we decided the best thing would be to hand it in. You'd have to ask Mrs. B if you want to know any more."

"You know everyone Mr. Dixon knows, do you?" Parker asked.

"We've been married a long time. We know most of the same people." By that I meant we both knew everyone in Upper Iffley.

"Do you know all his business clients?"

"I've met most of them," I said, feeling a bit defensive. I'd been to a lot of networking dos, but it was probably fair to say James wheeled and dealed with a fair few I'd never even heard of.

"Did it occur to you that address book may just be a backup list for his clients in case the internet went down?"

I thought of the book and I thought of a million and one objections to that idea. "It was full of postal addresses," I said. "If the internet goes down for a couple of hours, he's not going to write to tell them that." Followed by, "There were blank spaces in it. James's client list would fill that book and a hundred more," and, "Have you checked the handwriting?"

To which Parker replied, "He likes to be prepared for a major internet collapse. It's just one of many books, which are confidential, for obvious reasons. We will check the handwriting, but it's so scrunched up in there, it's going to be hard to make a valid comparison."

Tarquin gave a little snort. "Don't they have magnifying glasses?" he asked. Parker ignored him.

Whatever they believed or didn't believe and could prove or could not prove, I realized the address book was not the bull's-eye I had imagined. It was not as good as planting Lennie's wallet on me.

---

All good things come to an end, and the next morning, Arty called in to tell me that they thought they had collected as many bones as they could and they were expecting to finish by the end of the week.

"They'll probably be finding little bones around the village for years to come, though," he added. Then, "We should set a date for my DIY day."

"We should," I agreed, although part of me wanted to keep it as something to look forward to in the future.

"It needs to be soon; my girlfriend and I are going traveling afterward. We decided just recently."

A girlfriend! I don't know if I kept the dismay off my face when he mentioned her. And not only that, but they were leaving and he would not be around the grounds or coming to the kitchen to boil up. He would not be in the area at all. There would be no chance of bumping into him on one of my rare outings to Upper Iffley or Tippington. He'd be hundreds, maybe thousands of miles away. With his girlfriend.

I'd known the day would come and in truth the archaeologists had been here longer than I had anticipated, but it felt like the end of a happy stage in my life, the end of a time when there were moments I could forget about James, Lennie, and Mr. Newman for a while. And the DIY day now had a use-by date.

"Could you come on a Wednesday?" I asked, picking a day almost at random. Almost. There would be no James and no Mrs. Billings on a Wednesday.

"Next Wednesday?"

I nodded.

"What do you want me to do here?" he asked. That was a good question and one that I hadn't given much thought to, but Arty didn't wait for an answer. "As soon as we have a final date for the end of the dig, I'll let you know, then we can go round and make a list."

Then, he said, "I've been wearing the clothes you made all over the place. My girlfriend loves them as well. We wondered if you could make her one like the first one you made me, the red and yellow one."

"Yes," I said. "There's loads of that material left. I'll have to measure her. When can she come round?" They could have matching his and hers, I thought, with chagrin.

We arranged a visit for the following week, on a Mrs. Billings day, in case I needed help with the measuring.

I spent the rest of the day in a depression I kept telling myself to come out of. After all, Arty was nearly two decades younger than me and I was a married woman. He'd never suggested anything other than what we were doing, and I'd never expected anything different. But it had been such a change from the time I spent with James.

There was more bad news when Mrs. Billings arrived.

"Polly Thrussell's boy's been let go from your place," Mrs. Billings said, as I poured the tea. "Have you got any positions here?"

After a minute I realized that "Polly Thrussell" was Mrs. Thrussell from the teashop, but I couldn't make head nor tail of the rest of it. "From my place?" I asked.

"Lord James's business," she said. "He's let them all go. All the ones that were left, most of them had their marching orders a while ago. Young Oliver Thrussell was working there."

"Oh dear," I said. "I don't think we're taking on here at the moment."

"She's going to be disappointed. I said there was always something needed doing."

After that, things felt slightly awkward, and it was a relief at the end of the morning to finally see Mrs. B climbing into Mr. B's van.

As they drove away the implications of what she'd said settled on me: He'd let all his office staff go. The Bentley was gone and the two-hundred-thousand-pound watch was gone. Whatever next?

---

James said nothing about the redundancies when he got home, nor did he mention the skirt I was wearing, made from hand towels and created especially to provoke him. He didn't even comment on the crispy shredded breaded duck I presented him with—a new find. He said nothing. Nothing at all.

So I asked him about the redundancies.

"I'm tightening up the ship," he said. "Getting rid of the dead-wood." Then he gave me a very strange look.

"But they were our wedding guests!" I said.

When James and I were ready to send out wedding invitations, we found that between us we had no friends and very little in the way of family to invite, but the church seated more than four hundred and the reception venue—Langley Hall—had room for significantly more.

So, James took out his BlackBerry and opened up his emails. "This is how you fill a church," he said and typed "save the date" in the subject line. Then he wrote:

> You are all warmly invited to the wedding of James William Dixon and Daisy "Daydream" Langley on Saturday, 17 May 2003, at 2 p.m., St. Anne's Church, Upper Iffley and to the reception and evening event afterward at Langley Hall. Overtime will be payable to each attendee from 1.30 p.m. until the *free* bar opens at 7 p.m. RSVP by 29 March 2003.

He pulled up contact groups from his address book, and invitations went out to the staff at James's office and the contractors who carried out building maintenance. Then we sent paper invitations, with the same offer, to Mrs. Dobson, who was my first primary school teacher, the Crawford family, whom I used to babysit for, and Mr. and Mrs. Billings. In that way we filled the church.

In the run-up to the wedding, James was too busy to get involved with the preparations, he just instructed me to make it the event of the year and kept topping up the account he'd opened for the expenses. I went to all the dress fittings by myself, and I didn't care. James offered the services of his mother, Mrs. Dixon senior, to accompany me, but strangely, we couldn't find a time that would suit, even though we both had all day every day.

Anyway, I could tell whether the dress looked nice or not without an audience. I could have done with a bit of advice on whether to buy some kind of headwear or not—I was still new to unimaginable wealth and I didn't know if it would be class or crass. In the end, I judged by the prices, assumed they were class, and bought a diamond-studded diadem. When I thought about it later, I realized nobody at the wedding was going to be able to naysay me. We were all pretty common.

I had a team to help me with everything else. I had a florist, an interior designer, a hair stylist, a makeup artist, the cake company, the caterers, a photographer, and we all really hit it off. In no time we were a little posse. We set up a messaging group, which was a new experience for me, called "Daisy's Big Day," and I found myself checking morning, noon, and night for their chatty little messages.

Your hair is going to look amazing, the stylist wrote. I can't wait to see it with the dress and makeup.

I'm really excited for the photos, the photographer said. The house is such a great venue.

Are you going to take a pic of the cake? the baker asked her.

Of course!

Get the dress in the sunlight. I'm weaving silver thread through it, the dressmaker posted.

It will look magical, the photographer replied.

We were all getting on so well, I wondered if we might keep in touch afterward, but the replies to my messages stopped coming after the event.

On the day, we paraded out of the manor grounds in horse-drawn coaches. We had issued fresh invitations to the evening do, and the free bar ensured a few people turned out into the street to see us on our way to the church. It was like being royalty; they waved, a few of them clapped, and I sat up straight and graciously waved to one side, then the next, which really was embarrassing and I wondered what my mum would say if she could see me. Probably: "Daisy, you don't have the cleavage for a dress like that."

The rest of it was a bit of a blur. I remember saying "I do," I remember the photographs, I remember being in the ballroom for what felt like a lifetime. Everything sparkled: the chandeliers, the tableware, the diadem, my dress, the champagne. It was quite hard on the eyes after a while; we should have had headache tablets out on the tables.

There were speeches from James's dad, from his longest-standing employee, who was getting triple time to double as his best man. A speech from Mrs. Dobson about my first year at school. She might have had a very good memory, or she could have made it all up. I didn't know any better.

The disco started with our first dance. James chose it. It was his one contribution to the wedding, and he chose the twist. It was the most uncomfortable two minutes of my life, until a few more people came to join us and we were able to blend into the crowd and from there to make our way to the edges of the room. The DJ moved on, song after song, everyone whirled by, everyone stopped to talk to me, as if they liked me. I felt myself flagging, until finally, he announced the last song. The bar closed, the music stopped, the lights came on, the DJ thanked everyone for coming and bid us a good night. People began to make their way to the door and into prearranged minibuses waiting outside.

My wedding day was over, but I had a bright future with the husband of my dreams. The rest of my life was beginning.

I realized for the first time that in all the excitement, we hadn't booked a honeymoon. We hadn't even discussed one! In fact, our relationship had been such a whirlwind, we'd never even been on holiday together. Not so much as a weekend in the Lakes.

James finished saying good-bye to one of the contractors and turned to me, grinning.

"I've got a surprise for you," he said, closing the front door on the guests. Maybe he'd arranged a honeymoon and he was going to whisk me off somewhere? But I hadn't packed! I hoped he hadn't done it for me and made a man's job of it—I didn't want to go on my dream holiday with just a week's worth of underwear and a spare T-shirt. And I hoped he knew I didn't have a passport.

He took me by the hand and pulled me toward the entrance hall. "I left instructions to set it up while we were at the wedding."

That didn't sound like plane tickets, not unless they were to be displayed very elaborately. I hurried after him, wondering what it could be. He'd had to ask them to "set it up" so presumably not jewelry—and anyway, he'd given me the ring of a lifetime that morning. Probably not flowers, that would be "arranging." Something musical? My ears were still ringing from the disco. I was stumped. Something made from Lego, perhaps?

The wait was nearly over. We were in the hall, standing before what had been the family tree of the lords of the manor.

Gone was that beautiful, centuries-old piece of art. In its place was a blank canvas, a brand-new family tree. I stepped closer. The only names were right at the top, the founding couple, James and Daisy. Below us a long, horizontal line, with short vertical lines protruding from it at intervals for the names and dates of children. I counted the tabs.

"Ten?" I said, turning to look at him. James was grinning like a maniac.

"There's room to add more if we need it."

"Ten?" I repeated. Maybe we should have discussed this before.

My eye was caught by a little doodle above our names: a shield shape, split into four, with red and yellow backgrounds, red then yellow in the top two, and yellow then red in the bottom. Each quarter had a little picture in it, but I couldn't make them out at that size. "What's that?"

"It's our coat of arms," he said.

"Since when did you have a coat of arms?"

"*Our* coat of arms," he said. "The Dixon coat of arms. We have this as well…"

He nipped into the nearest room and returned with an A5-size folder. He presented it to me. On the front, the coat of arms was reproduced again and now I could see that in the first red square was a picture of a large building, maybe a house, maybe a museum, I wasn't sure. Diagonally opposite, in the other red quarter was a dollar sign; that was pretty unambiguous. In the yellow squares were a flower and a rectangle with something sticking out of the top of it; it looked like an old-fashioned TV set.

James was standing by my shoulder, looking down at the folder. "The pictures represent us, our achievements and interests. I chose red for me because I like red, and yellow for you. You like yellow, don't you?"

I nodded. I preferred blue.

"It shows this house that I've bought and the money I've made: they didn't have a pound sign, but dollars are recognized all over the world. And to represent you, you have a daisy, for your name, and a TV. You like watching TV, don't you?"

Was that the only thing he could think of when he thought of me? With dread, I opened the folder. Inside were certificates proclaiming us Lord and Lady Iffley, although you won't find us in *Debrett's* and it was never mentioned again. I turned the folder over and on the back was the name and contact details of a company—Titles To Go—based in Nevada.

I turned to James. He was grinning as if all our Christmases had come at once, and I realized this wasn't a joke.

My heart sinking, I looked again at the family tree. Of course I wanted children; after all, I had a bloodline to continue. But ten? And I'd thought we might wait a while. I stepped closer and counted again. James misinterpreted it and began pulling me by my arm toward the door.

"Shall we make a start on tab number one?" he said.

At the time, I set aside my misgivings. I was confident things would settle down. I thought maybe James had meant it as a joke, and I hadn't responded as he expected. Either way, I was sure our vision for the future would fall into line. In every other way he was perfect.

---

Arty duly brought his girlfriend to the house to be measured. She was pretty and petite, and when I got to speak to her I found she was incredibly likable. Mrs. Billings thought so too, when they found out they were distantly related.

"That's what it's like round here, though," Arty said. "You can't go anywhere without meeting someone from your family tree." I kept quiet and thought about our empty tree in the hall and how James was the only person I was related to, which suddenly felt wrong, while hearing about all their relatives. But then again, I was from Langley Hall, which, really, trumped all of it.

I saw them off at the back door, where a pane of glass had fallen out of one of the panels in the top half. Mr. Billings had already covered it with newspaper.

---

By the end of the afternoon, the fact of Arty's imminent departure and the reality of his girlfriend had deflated me. I went to the priest hole and took out a multipack of Chipsticks. But I'd forgotten to keep an eye on the time.

"WHAT IS THAT YOU'RE EATING?" James's voice boomed across the great hall, making me jump out of my skin. I dropped Chipsticks all over my lap. I was still shaking as he noticed the priest hole that was open next to me. "What the hell is *that*?" he asked, striding up to see. He peered into it. "Did you cut a hole in the stairs?"

I stayed silent, looking at him. "*Well?*" he shouted.

"It's a priest hole," I whispered and I began to explain about the religious kettle of fish they'd found themselves in, in the sixteenth century, but he wasn't listening, he was too busy pulling out everything I had in there.

With every item—my Monster Munch, my Hobnobs, my Cadbury's Mini Rolls—he turned and stared at me with incredulity, until he got to Lennie's satchel. He tipped it out onto the floor and started going through the contents. He picked up the pages of the memoir and scanned them.

"This is his, isn't it? Lennie Green's. How long have you had it?" I stared at him, trying to think what the right answer would be. "How long!"

"I found it," I whimpered. "In the field. I knew we couldn't leave it there, so I brought it here."

"You didn't think to tell me? I was out there looking for it for days on end." He didn't expect a reply and he didn't ask me anything else. He just took the whole lot, bar one packet of Jaffa Cakes that he missed.

"You could hide a body in this," he said of the priest hole, before stomping off with my goods. Yes, James, I thought, as my heart rate returned to normal, that was rather the point of it. Which he would have known had he listened to my explanation.

He threw all the snacks in the bin, shoving them deep down into the depths of the waste. I don't know where he took the satchel. I didn't see it in the house again.

# CHAPTER TWENTY-TWO

IT HAD BEEN A WHILE SINCE I CHECKED IN ON THE FORUM. WHEN I did, I found Mrs. Billings regaling them all with the news that James and I had separate rooms, which she may well have told them before, and that apart from James, and her to clean, no one had been in my husband's bedroom for a very long time.

It was humiliating and it fed into the earlier theory I was having an affair. Subsequently, the idea of the Meg-test, whereby Mr. Newman's dog, Meg, would be brought to sniff me to see if she recognized me, was gaining support.

I didn't much care for that line of gossip. Jo Newman was only a couple of years older than me, and she bucked the trend at school by sometimes being quite kind. There had been occasions on which it was a relief to get onto the school bus and see her move her bag so that I could sit down and be sheltered for a little while by her popularity. She deserved better from me than an affair with her husband.

We'd all been surprised when she married Mr. N. He was widowed and already had sons who were well on their way to adulthood, so it was an age-gap relationship. But marry they did and Jo stepped into the role of farmer's wife, up with the lark and out in the fields. Rather her than me. And if I'm being honest, rather her than me for Mr. N as well.

However, I was starting to see the lie of the land in the forum, and the idea that James had killed Mr. N in a fit of jealous rage was gaining traction. Could I tolerate Jo Newman's animosity for the benefit of staying out of prison? It was a sacrifice I was sorry to make, but I thought I could do it.

I heard Daisy likes older men. I cringed as I wrote, but it worked and they began to dig in on their new favorite subject once more.

Probably because she didn't have a male role model when she was growing up, Mrs. Faulkner wrote. It's a common thing.

She made a pass at my dad once, Samantha Saunders said, and I gasped because that was an out-and-out lie. But it was greeted with No! and Really? and When? and Where? Samantha, however, didn't answer their questions. Because she couldn't. Unfortunately, her dad was now on the other side, so we would need a séance to clear my name.

Jo, you really should get over there with Meg, Mrs. Chambers wrote. That would settle things.

I don't know that I'd want to stir up trouble, Jo wrote.

But don't you want to know? said Samantha, who very much did want to stir up trouble. Jo didn't answer.

I'd want to know if it were me, Mrs. Thrussell said. And in this case, it could lead to a conviction.

The idea of justice for Mr. N helped to tip the scales in that direction.

The Meg-test wasn't the most scientific research I could think of, but it seemed to be the gold standard amongst the witchfinders of Upper Iffley. I gave them one final shove:

Dogs never forget a person, I said, and nothing more was needed; they were already on the scent.

They decided to come to the house as a group, with Meg, on Friday and catch me by surprise. They would ask if I could spare a bit of change for the church bell fund, seeing that the final target was nearly in sight. I added chicken to the shopping list and stitched some extra pockets into a patchwork dress.

Sure enough, Meg was all over me when I answered the door that Friday, pieces of chicken stuffed into every pocket. The squad were so astonished by the sight, they almost forgot their cover story and we were there for quite some time before they babbled it out. While I was out of view, fetching my purse, I took a piece of the chicken from a pocket; it seemed mean not to let Meg have some when she'd done such a good job for me.

"Alright if I give her this?" I asked, emptying what cash I had into their collection bucket and handing the chicken to Meg. There was a collective gasp and recoil. "What?" I asked. They continued to stare at me. I realized why. "Wait there," I said.

The chicken was chargrilled and packaged ready to eat. I fetched the packet and showed it to them. "I had no part in the preparation," I said, and they walked away, shaking their heads and muttering about an innocent animal.

As they went, I noticed that these days Meg was walking with her head held high, a spring in her step, and a wag in her tail. It looked like Meg was making her way through the bereavement process and was recovering from the loss of Mr. Newman.

---

Is Meg well? Mrs. Chambers posted on the forum a few hours later. No stomach upsets?

She's fine, but she loves Daisy more than she loves me! Jo Newman moaned.

And so did Doug, Mary Bishop said, but most people said that was uncalled for and I was just his bit on the side.

The verdict, however, was unanimous: Meg knew me very well indeed, Mr. Newman and I were having an affair, and the finger for his death was pointing more and more firmly at James. I looked at the list down the side to see if AllEars was listening in, but she was busy stirring trouble elsewhere. Never mind, she could pick it all up later. NoseyParker was there.

Do you think she still called him "Mr. Newman" when they were in flagrante? Samantha asked, but no one cared to speculate on that.

I could've done with some crisps, but of course, the priest hole was mine no more. I decided to keep the Jaffa Cakes he'd missed for another day.

# CHAPTER TWENTY-THREE

I SPENT THE WEEKEND BUOYED UP WITH HOPE THAT THE MEG-TEST was going to move things in my favor. When on Monday morning there was a knock at the door, I answered, my mind still on Meg and how easily they had fallen for it. The sight that met me wiped the smile off my face.

"Daisy Dixon," DS Khan said, not bothering with pleasantries. "I'm arresting you on suspicion of death by dangerous driving."

"Arresting?" I felt myself preparing for fight or flight. "Why?"

"We'll get to that down at the station. Please come this way."

I thought about resisting. Or about making a run for it. I looked around for the best way to escape, I should have rehearsed for this, but as DC Parker unhooked a pair of handcuffs from his belt, I just said, "Can I phone my solicitor?"

On a brighter note, I didn't have to wait long for Tarquin. He already seemed to have been primed and arrived at the police station not long after me. In no time at all we were back in that little room, ready to talk all things Lennie.

For the occasion, Tarquin was wearing a tie that had been chopped off a couple of inches below the knot. Another riotous success by his offspring.

"There're all like this," he said. "This was the longest one. No more pocket money for a while." But I was starting to think he should really get a grip. I would've done by now, if they were mine. In fact, it never would have got this far if they were mine.

DS Khan opened a folder. In front of her was some kind of report. She turned straight to a page with a diagram of a human body on it, parts shaded over, with lines linking the shading to notes around the edges.

"Do you know what this is, Daisy?" DS Khan asked and yes, actually, I did. I'd seen it on documentaries. It was a diagram used to show the injuries sustained by a victim. I answered her question. She asked another one. "This report relates to Lennie Green. Do you know what might have caused any of these injuries?"

Yes, of course. "No," I said.

She started to point to various bits of shading. "Every rib on his left-hand side was fractured, and the sixth rib pierced the lung."

That probably explained why his breathing had seemed labored.

She continued. "Mr. Green had extensive bruising across much of his torso, a broken radius and thumb—"

"Which one's the radius?" I asked.

She pointed to the lower arm and continued. "He had a contusion on his forehead"—I'd seen it done, on the dashcam video—"which may or may not have led to concussion or loss of consciousness." No, it didn't lead to loss of consciousness, I could have confirmed that for them. "All of these are injuries consistent with a collision with a road vehicle. A collision at quite a speed."

I was about to protest: I hadn't been driving fast, around thirty, but I remembered my official story and I nodded and looked at her, as if I were keen for the next part.

"The most interesting injury is this one," she said, pointing to the neck on the diagram.

"Whiplash?" I guessed.

"No, a broken hyoid."

"Oh, of course!" I'd forgotten that; it had been a clue in many a police drama.

They all looked at me in surprise. I realized why:

"Hang on a minute," I said. "That's for when someone is strangled."

After that the whole thing descended into mayhem, in my head at least. I didn't strangle Lennie! I never touched his neck. Strangling was the last thing he needed; I'd been trying to help him.

The two detectives were looking at me, waiting for clarity I couldn't give. I was so surprised, it took me a minute to realize that, if I hadn't killed him, someone else had done so, and done it deliberately. I turned to Tarquin, who looked equally dumbfounded.

"Are you saying he was killed by strangulation and not by the collision?" he asked.

"It certainly looks that way," DS Khan said.

I thought back to the moment I'd returned to the drawing room after looking for first aid supplies: James bending over Lennie, "checking for breath," he had said.

James jumping when he realized I was back in the room. The way Lennie's head hung so loosely.

"Do you think my client could strangle a grown man?" Tarquin asked.

"A grown man who was already seriously injured."

I could hardly hear them, my head was spinning, but I remembered a gem from a number of murder mysteries: "I believe it takes a long time to strangle someone," I said. "I don't have the patience."

James was a killer: a murderer. As well as a fraudster. I was just accident-prone. Tarquin was speaking again, but I was hardly hearing.

"And what are you suggesting she did with the body?" he asked them. "I think we're in agreement that Mr. Green didn't die where he was found."

"We agree the body was moved."

"Do you agree that even if my client could have strangled him, which a jury would find hard to believe, it would be impossible for her to move a man of his size for any distance? Look at her..."

They all looked at me, in a shirt that had started life as a Welsh flag.

"Look at her size, not at her clothes," Tarquin clarified, but instead we all looked at the stub of his tie.

"We think she had help."

I came back to attention at this. At last, we were getting to James and his part in it.

Khan continued. "Your husband tells us you are having an affair."

James had told them that? From what was on the forum, I'd thought James wanted to steer them away from that.

"An affair?" I repeated. "Who with?" With whom, I should have said.

"That's for you to tell us."

"I don't know. I never meet anyone I could be having an affair with." Although I thought wistfully of Arty. "Who does James think?"

"He doesn't know, but certain people in the village have said it might be Doug Newman," DS Khan said. "Can you shed any light on that?"

I shook my head to bring myself back into the real world. Khan was still talking. "Mr. Dixon said he'd suspected an affair for a long time. He said on the night of the accident he'd had a lot to drink and he passed out almost as soon as he got back to Langley Hall. So, he can't be a witness to what you did next, but he knows that when he fell asleep his Audi was in the garage and when he went to get it, to go to work the next morning, it was gone. A lot of people remember him driving a classic Rolls Royce that day."

Tarquin and I sat in silence.

"Did he report it as stolen?" Tarquin asked.

"Not straightaway, the garage hadn't been broken into, so he knew it wasn't thieves. He said he knew immediately that it was Daisy. He didn't want to get her into trouble for what he thought at the time was a domestic matter. Later, he helped her by falsely reporting it as stolen. Foolish of him, but the things we do for love. Then he heard the news reports."

DS Khan sat back, triumphant, while DC Parker picked up the narrative.

"So, Daisy, we believe that you and your unknown beau arranged a rendezvous once your husband was asleep that night. Somehow, what was probably initially an accident occurred and Mr. Green came to grief. Instead of helping him, for reasons best known to yourselves, you decided to finish him off. Then you took him back to your estate to dispose of the body."

I'd once heard that when you're telling a lie, you should try not to deviate too far from the truth, and it sounded as if James had heard that same advice. Well done.

"Is that what happened, Daisy?" Khan asked me. "Or is there anything you want to tell us?"

I looked at them, wondering what I might want to tell them. Parker spoke next.

"Because there's another death to take into account and a version of events that means it may have been six of one and half a dozen of the other."

"What?" Tarquin said.

"In a nutshell, we think Daisy was responsible for Mr. Green's death, but who killed Mr. Newman? That is a different question. Who might have had a motive? A lovers' tiff between him and Daisy or a crime of passion committed by someone else?"

This was my chance to tell a load more lies, to say that, yes, I was having a fling with Mr. N and point the finger at James.

"How well did you know Doug Newman, Daisy? Did he come up to Langley Hall often?"

I opened my mouth to say, yes, I was Mr. Newman's other woman. We met at Langley Hall when James was at work, we christened every room, as well as Mr. Billings's shed. We fantasized about running away, just us and Meg, we laughed at the ignorance of James and Jo. We were the Romeo and Juliet of Upper Iffley.

But I couldn't do it. I couldn't sit there and say I'd had an affair and make up scenarios in which we met and tell them about the things we did. For a start, how explicit would they want me to be?

"I don't know what happened to Mr. Newman," I said. "I don't know how he died."

DS Khan reached behind her for a clear plastic evidence bag. Inside the bag was a phone.

"Do you recognize this, Daisy?" she asked.

"No," I said, but I could make a good guess at what it was. Whose it was. Khan confirmed my suspicions, and more.

"It's Mr. Green's phone," she said. "Your husband gave it to us. He said he found it on your side of the lounge."

James had it. No wonder he wasn't worried when I said it was missing. And I thought Mrs. B had taken it. I'd plotted to kill her because of it. Now I remembered I'd lost my hairbrush that day. Was that what she'd pinched? James must've taken the phone at the same time as he killed Lennie.

Now it was Parker's turn to reach behind and bring out a much larger item in another clear bag. Lennie's satchel.

"Do you recognize this, Daisy?" he asked.

Out of habit, I shook my head, but I knew what they were going to say.

"Mr. Dixon gave it to us. He says you had it."

"No comment," I said, my answer of last resort.

"What's more, a witness says that a satchel, the contents of which point to it having been the property of Mr. Green, was seen at Langley Hall on the morning after his disappearance, but it never appeared again."

He made it sound as if it had been glimpsed making its own way through the copse. The witness must have been Mrs. Billings.

I was outwitted. I began to hyperventilate, and they fetched me a paper bag.

Once my breathing was back to normal, DS Khan said we should take a break. She and Parker left the room.

"I think they're going to charge you," Tarquin said somberly.

"But I didn't do it!" I said, and now I was telling the truth. I suspected Tarquin knew that as well. I just didn't know whose side he was on.

He smiled a rueful smile. "They were going to have to choose between you and James eventually," he said. "James got his story in first and they obviously think it's a better one. To be honest, repeating "I didn't do it!" isn't much of a story, more a refrain. Now we need to think about how we're going to approach this."

He recommended that from then on I continued with the "no comment" style of defense, which is harder to stick to than you'd think because they keep trying to pique your interest with little nuggets, like "you were seen talking to Lennie for a long time at the party." Which was not true, I only spoke to him for a few minutes and nobody saw, I wanted to tell them. But after some practice, I got the hang of it.

And it seemed to be going better until they left the room again, then returned to say:

"Daisy Dixon, I'm charging you with the death by dangerous driving of Lennie Green."

"Charging?!" I said. "But that's not how he died." They knew it wasn't how he died—they'd just told me—but I suppose details like that aren't important when you're stitching someone up.

"Charging," DS Khan said, and before I knew it I was in the cells again, looking forward to an overnight stay. The police didn't want to give me bail, so it was off to the magistrate's court in the morning.

So now it was serious. Or even more serious than it had been before because now, not only did we have a *murder* victim—another murder victim—there was a risk that we were about to have the corresponding prison sentence. Only with the wrong person serving it.

And that, I had no doubt, was going to come about through the collusion of my husband and my lawyer.

That lawyer was making out that I was lucky because they'd charged me with dangerous driving and not murder.

"I suspect that's because they don't know yet if it's you or your beau who strangled him, so they're not confident they'll make murder stick. Who is it anyway? The gentleman you're having an affair with? Was it Mr. Newman? If it's someone else, you shouldn't protect him, you know."

"It's no one. I'm not having an affair." Although I wondered again if I was wrong to protest; it could be my way out of this.

"Anyway, you'll almost certainly get bail," Tarquin said. "And if they keep it as death by dangerous driving, you'll get a much lesser sentence. You could be out in a few years. Best-case scenario, one or two. But they could up it to murder later in the process."

"Just get me bail, please," I said.

In the cell, I ate what I could of my tea—the chicken nuggets were not Waitrose nuggets—and tried to find patterns in the stains on the walls. I thought about what I was missing at home and felt homesick for the boring meals, the dramas I'd watched a hundred times, the heart-sink feeling when another tile fell off the roof. I even missed James's snippy comments and the time I would spend wishing him away.

I had a sleepless night, with the plastic mattress and thin blanket and the shouts of other captives on their way to and from other cells, but it was a time and a place to think. First I thought, inevitably, about how I was married to a fraudster and a double murderer, and also, how I no longer needed to find a way to continue Lennie's work because it hadn't been me who killed him. Instead, I would be going to prison for a crime I didn't commit, and Lennie had died in vain. What a waste. I moved on to the phone. It seemed reasonable to think that James had taken it at the same time he had killed Lennie, and from that it seemed fair to assume there had been something on there he didn't want anyone to see and that he'd removed whatever it was by now.

And the bag! The bag! I cursed myself for the lapse in concentration that let James find the priest hole and the bag.

Then I thought about Tarquin and I began to think a thought that had previously been reserved for James, and briefly Mrs. B: How could I kill my solicitor? It seemed fiendish to think of doing to death this young lawyer, with his mischievous, some might say delinquent, children, but if I'd only learned one thing from all of this, it was that it was dog-eat-dog in the world of covering up a crime.

My motive gave me pause for thought because the point of killing him was that, otherwise, I would go to prison for a killing that I hadn't done, but I would leave the philosophy for another day. If I left things to run their course, I would go to trial and James and Tarquin would conspire in making things as easy as possible for the prosecution.

I didn't know what would happen if Tarquin was no more. There was always the risk that the same firm might just send another corrupt lawyer, but at least they would have had a warning: They couldn't fit me up and still sleep safely in their beds.

I didn't want to do it, though. I didn't hate Tarquin like I hated James; in fact, I was rather warming to him. I would need to force myself to be businesslike about it and eliminate him as a clear and present danger. I would have to become hard-nosed and ruthless. But only for a day, then I had the rest of life in which to assuage my guilt.

I asked myself if I was really sure Tarquin was corrupt. He had said I shouldn't protect my alleged boyfriend, which would be good advice, if there was such a boyfriend. But that would be what anyone would say. It wasn't evidence of good intentions. I referred myself back to the hard-nosed, ruthless version of me: Did I want to spend years in prison mulling that over?

But what about Mrs. Billings? I had plotted to kill her based on a misunderstanding. What if this was the same? Yet, Mrs. B and Tarquin were very different propositions. Mrs. B lived a simple life, doing no one any harm, always thinking the best of people. Tarquin was trained in deception, and he was skilled at making a jury think one thing or another: The truth was something he constructed to suit his own needs. He could not be taken at face value. After all, Bernie Madoff probably seemed nice. People had believed him. I was sure Mr. Ponzi had seemed nice. James seemed nice, once upon a time.

I still didn't want to do it. Amongst all the turmoil, learning that I hadn't killed Lennie had brought a feeling of relief. It's hard to live for months with half your mind brooding on the fact that you're a killer, while the other half concentrates on how you're going to get away with it. And I'd always known I hadn't killed Mr. N. Now, I was reluctant to abandon the fact of my innocence and swap it, once more, for guilt. But it would be harder still to suffer the penalty for a crime that James had committed.

And that thought made me angry. I *could* do away with Tarquin, and I *could* live the rest of my life not caring. And when Tarquin was gone, I'd turn my attention to James once again.

Right there, in that tiny little cell, I believed I could do it. I didn't know who the next lawyer would be, but I would have made my point: Cross me at your own peril. I was not the feeble victim they thought I was—there was more to me than wacky clothes and whodunits.

I moved on to the question of how would I do it, and at first that seemed to be a quest as futile as killing James. Yet there was one difference between Tarquin and James: Tarquin was not from the village, and he didn't know that you should never, *ever* eat or drink anything I had prepared.

---

The next day was a Tuesday and I was off to the magistrate's court for a bail hearing, as nervous as you might expect.

"Chin up, this should just be a formality," Tarquin said as he arrived, wearing a new tie but with faded remnants of permanent marker all over his face. "Kids caught me sleeping on the job. Literally." He smiled and the lines stretched across his face.

Bail wasn't as easy as he made it sound. The prosecution started by saying I was a significant flight risk: I was made of money and could go anywhere in the world. I whispered to Tarquin, who whispered to our barrister that I didn't have a passport, and I wasn't made of money, I only had my allowance. That was two points to us.

Then the prosecution barrister talked about James at length, about his money and his reach in the business community. About how easy it would be for me to slip away…

I nodded dolefully as we told them that I wasn't well liked in the village, and I had no connections outside the area. In fact, I'd hardly ever been out of the county. That drew a raised eyebrow from the magistrate and a comment about narrow horizons.

In the end, Tarquin's children had done me proud. With a solicitor like that, the magistrate found it hard to take me seriously as a hardened criminal, which I wasn't anyway, and let me out on bail.

He finished with a warning for Tarquin, "If you appear before me again looking like that, Mr. Noble, I shall find you in contempt of court."

I arrived home to find that the Nevada-bought coat of arms James had had installed above the front door had fallen off and lay broken on the doorstep. Normally the crumblings and crackings of Langley Hall left me dismayed, but the sight of that atrocity lying in shards on the ground cheered me. I hoped it was an omen. I picked the pieces up and scattered them across the gravel of the drive.

But inside, I looked at the grand staircase, the steps that were once varnished and polished now dull and scuffed. I made my way toward them and up and up and up to the third floor, a place I had not been to since I collected the buckets the night after the storm that had washed Lennie's body away. I didn't know how seriously the situation had deteriorated since then.

There were nine bedrooms on that floor; of those nine, the ceilings of three were now collapsing in, with plaster on the floor and wooden beams visible through the gap. In another, the ceiling was sagging. I didn't go into that one, but as I stood looking, a tile fell from the roof, passing by the window on its way down.

My beautiful, beautiful Langley Hall—home of my ancestors, loved by generations—had been left to rot by a Ponzi fraudster.

The work needed to rescue it from this would be immense. It wouldn't be habitable. It might not be safe for me to be in now, but, having nowhere else to go, I made my way back down the stairs to the first-floor rooms we lived in. That night I lay in bed, listening to the creaks and moans of the house and wondering if they were the sounds of the building coming down and if that wouldn't be such a bad way to end it.

# CHAPTER TWENTY-FOUR

IN ALL THE TURMOIL, I'D SOMEHOW FORGOTTEN ABOUT ARTY AND I was caught by surprise when he knocked on the door at nine o'clock that Wednesday morning, dressed conservatively in a dark-gray T-shirt.

"I didn't want to risk spoiling the nice tops," he said when he saw me looking at him. "I've been storing them in the microwave to keep them fresh, like you said." He carried a toolbox in one hand and a packet of Tunnock's Caramel Wafers in the other, which was lucky because since James had discovered the priest hole, the only snacks I'd had were what I could eat while Mrs. Billings was here. "What do you want me to do?" Arty asked.

That was a good question and one that I still hadn't decided on. I looked around me. There was so much, he could hardly make a dent in a day. Could he fix the roof or the guttering? Probably not. Could he clean some of the unused rooms? Probably, but it seemed a waste if he had handyman skills. I still had the etched room plates I'd been forced to buy at the Bone Bonanza—maybe he could stick those to the doors. But I didn't want them put up and, should I change my mind, it seemed like something I could do myself.

All jobs were either too big or too small. I could probably find him something to do in the garden, although Mr. Billings would take that as an afront. Even more so if he knew we'd paid £18,000 for the privilege when Mr. B got £12.50 an hour. In the end I asked him to look at some minor restoration work.

"Can you do anything about this?" I asked, rattling a banister rail that was loose. He gave it a shake, then peered into the hole it sat in. He poked his finger into it, then took out a penknife and dug out a piece of cloth I had stuffed in years before, to try to steady it, his expression bemused.

"I had a go myself," I said. "Can you do something?"

"I should think so," he said.

"You have to be careful because it's old. We can't just patch it up with new stuff," I told him.

"It's OK, we can keep this railing."

I'd had a go at fixing a few things over the years, but my efforts had been feeble: I showed him cracked tiles that had come loose from the floor. I kept them in a drawer in a side table, along with bits and pieces I had tried to replace them with.

"I can make some improvements," he said. "But where they're broken or missing, I can't magic new ones in."

I showed him warped, creaky doors.

"Yeah, I can do something about that," he said.

I left him to it for an hour or so, happy that a tiny piece of Langley Hall's grandeur was going to be returned to it, regardless of the disaster upstairs. When I came back, with refreshments and biscuits, the rail in the banister was fixed in place and he was examining the tiles.

"You're a lifesaver," Arty said, reaching for a Tunnock's Caramel Wafer and settling himself down on the stairs.

"Mind if I join you?" I asked, taking a seat on the other side of the staircase.

We drank and munched in silence for a while, until Arty addressed the elephant in the room.

"Do you want to know what I was in trouble for?" he asked.

Of course I did.

"Do you remember when the cricket pavilion burnt down?"

Absolutely! It was the most heinous crime Upper Iffley had seen—the 2006 burglary spree notwithstanding—since Great Beadington stole our bell nearly seven hundred years before.

"That was me," he said. "No harm meant. I just liked to watch the flames, but it got a bit out of hand."

I was dumbstruck. For weeks after the pavilion was razed to the ground no one had talked of anything else. There was outrage throughout the village. Mr. Faulkner started a petition to bring back the death penalty and the police warned us not to take matters into our own hands. I remembered someone having been caught for it, but I didn't remember the name. Now I knew, the name was Rainbow, Artemis Rainbow.

"How long were you in prison for?" I asked.

"Two years."

It didn't seem like much, but he was a *young* offender.

"It wasn't all bad; it's where I met Freddie. He was the auctioneer at the fundraiser. He used to make replicas of antiques and sell them as real. Now he works at an auction house. Funny how life turns around. If you want anything else valuing when I'm gone, I can put you in touch. Or if you wanted to sell any."

"I'll bear it in mind," I said.

"When I got out of Young Offenders, it felt like tempers had hardly cooled, even though the pavilion was rebuilt."

"Well, the old one was a listed building," I said. "The new one's not much more than a portacabin."

"I see," Arty said. "Anyway, they have long memories around here. I felt like I was being punished all over again when I came back. I've wanted to leave ever since, but it never seemed possible until I met my girlfriend. Now we're off around the world and who knows when we'll return, or where in the country we'll go to when we do. I always fancied Scotland."

"It can be a bit like that around here," I said. We sat quietly for a minute. Apart from a brief consideration, after my mum died, it had never occurred to me to leave Upper Iffley. Now I wondered for the first time if a fresh start might have been the best thing, and if it might still be possible.

"These jobs won't take me all day," Arty said in the end. "Do you have anything else?"

I was about to say, not really, he could have an early dart, or—better—extra tea and biscuits, but then my eyes alighted on the helmet of the Elizabethan suit of armor, and I said, "Would you like to value some more antiques?"

So, Arty went to his car to fetch his encyclopedia and I fetched a notepad and pen and led the way upstairs.

"This is a real goldmine," he said, as we made our way through the upper rooms. "Is this real?" he was pointing at a vase.

"They're all real," I said. "I think." I'd never questioned it, but now I took it off the shelf and turned it upside down, looking for a telltale John Lewis sticker. There was no sticker. Instead, there was a marking on the base that sent Arty a bit funny.

"They're not alarmed?" he asked. I felt panicky for a moment and had to remind myself that he wasn't a thief.

Even so, I erred on the side of caution. "They're alarmed at night," I lied.

We worked for a while in silence, until Arty suggested a break.

"It's very quiet in here," he said. "Can we play some music?" He took his phone out of his pocket, but I could do better than that. A few minutes later, Boney M was booming out of James's expensive stereo speakers all across Langley Hall.

The rhythm got into our bones and there, with just Arty's company and any court trial a long way off, I was able to relax. When Arty started to move to the music, I joined in. I was surprised to see Arty was not a good dancer. He moved as if the floor had suddenly become electrified, which gave me a nervous moment, knowing the state of the wiring. But when I crouched down and touched it, there was no electricity. I suppose no one is good at everything.

I shuffled, then I swayed, I swung and I bopped, while he leaped around as if someone had set a fire underneath him. When we'd had enough of Boney M, we finished with a bit of Abba. I couldn't remember the last time I'd had fun like that. I looked up at the ceiling to check that the noise wasn't about to bring it down.

By then, time was marching on and Arty had to make tracks.

"Do you have time for one more antique?" I asked.

"Just one."

I showed him the figurine of a shepherdess with a lamb and a basket of flowers that Mrs. Billings had once taken and subsequently donated to a charity shop, the one I'd bought back for a fiver.

"Seventy to eighty grand in an auction," Arty said after a detailed examination and referring to his book. He put it carefully back down.

That was the end of the DIY day, and it had been an absolute pleasure: Arty's company, the antiques, the quiet absorption in what we were doing. Despite everything, for that one day I felt calm and contented. I'd been able to put all my troubles to the back of my mind and concentrate only on Arty and the antiques.

When he'd gone, he'd be gone forever. It would be a long time before he was back in the country, and it seemed unlikely our paths would cross again.

# CHAPTER TWENTY-FIVE

"I SAW LANCE AND PHILOMENA IN THE TEASHOP," MRS. BILLINGS said, as she arrived the next morning.

She looked at me, waiting for a response, and I tried to remember who Lance and Philomena were. Oh! Of course: Mr. and Mrs. Dixon senior, James's parents, who lived in Spain.

"Said they'd moved back," Mrs. B said. "They've sold up abroad and are living in their old house again. Kicked the tenants out; they weren't village folk anyway. Said it were too hot for them abroad—Lance and Philomena, not the tenants."

"It took them a long time to work that out," I said. They'd been there nearly twenty years. I wondered if it had been their or James's decision to sell.

Once Mrs. B had started her rounds, I sat through a terrible 1990s episode of *Columbo*, while I waited for her to do what she had to do and leave. Then, I headed out. It was time for me to put my plan for Tarquin into action. I took with me a pair of gardening gloves and a Tupperware in a small rucksack and walked across the fields to the woodland my mum and I had walked through, day in, day out, all those years ago.

Time was, I could've walked round and taken what I needed in less than half an hour, just like shopping at the supermarket, but with the passing of the years since I last visited, it took me a while to find what I was looking for. But find it I did.

The flowers were over, but the small, dark berries were still there for a few more weeks: deadly nightshade. I put the gloves on and picked a few off. I put them in the Tupperware and headed home.

Next, I phoned Tarquin and asked him to come over to discuss my case.

"Can you get into the office?" he asked.

Not unless I'm going to poison the whole firm, I thought, and that might not be a bad thing, but it would be harder to engineer, and I'd certainly need to go back for more berries.

"No transport, car's at the garage," I said.

"Can't you use one of James's? He has about twenty."

Was he mad? They were all classic cars. "James is out in the Audi. I'm not allowed to touch the old ones," I said. "And he only has a few now."

And Tarquin said fair enough, but could I wait until tomorrow? He'd call in midafternoon on his way back from another appointment.

"Great, I do have something I need to discuss with you," he said, before I hung up.

Scene set, I drove to the Waitrose on the outskirts of Tippington and bought the ingredients for a cake.

---

James was out late that night and I spent the evening watching TV, or rather in front of the TV, thinking about what I was going to do the next day and how I didn't have any actual evidence that Tarquin was corrupt.

Then I'd think about the consequences if I didn't. "They might up it to murder," Tarquin had said. Yes, if he got his way—James's way—they might well do that. I hardened: Sometimes you have to do what you have to do. Then I softened. He had three children and he always seemed so affable. Then I made myself harden again.

When I went to bed, I slept the sleep of someone who is about to roll the dice and hope for the least bad of numerous bad outcomes.

When James had left the next morning, I took the cake ingredients out of the cupboard and baked. It was so long since I'd made anything like that, it took me ages to weigh and mix, but in the end, I was quite pleased with what I'd done. I iced with lilac icing to try to hide the slight tinge of purple the nightshade berries had given it.

Sure enough, Tarquin was round that afternoon, ready to add another billable hour, and I was ready with a kettle and two mugs, one *Poirot* (his), one *Death in Paradise* (mine).

I showed him in, said "Tea?" and began pouring before he could answer.

"Sugar?" I asked.

"No, thank you," he said.

"Milk?"

"Yes, please."

"Cake?" I began to cut it with the fearlessness of the damned. "I call this one Tea and Terror."

"That's an unusual name for a cake. What can I do for you, Daisy?" Tarquin asked.

"Well, you can keep me out of prison," I said, laughing slightly hysterically and dropping the mug down harder than I meant to on the table. I put the slice of deadly cake next to it. "You know I didn't strangle Lennie."

He opened his briefcase and marbles cascaded from the pocket at the top. As I helped him gather them up, I felt a surge of guilt for the children who were not going to be laughing that night.

I looked at the cake, so far untouched, and thought about snatching it away. Then I was seized with inspiration.

"There's no money," I said.

He looked up, surprised.

"James's business is a scam. He's made his staff redundant, and he's been selling all his stuff."

"I don't know about that, but it's funny you should say because what I came to tell you is that unfortunately, I can't represent you anymore. James hasn't been paying his bills, and we've run out of patience with him. Plus, after the interview last week, we were thinking that this case is not what it seemed and you and your husband seem to be at loggerheads now."

*Now?* I thought.

"I understand you don't have funds of your own?"

I shook my head.

"You should be able to get a public defender, then."

He picked up his cake and raised it to his lips.

"Do you know what? I think I forgot to put sugar in that," I said, snatching the cake as it came within millimeters of his jaws. I dropped it into the bin.

Tarquin looked crestfallen, so I said, "Wait there," and checking he wasn't following, ran to the priest hole for the packet of Jaffa Cakes

James had missed. "You can have these." I tipped most of them into his hands, and he cheered up.

After he'd gone, I checked he hadn't taken a sneaky slice of the cake while I was at the priest hole. He hadn't. The reality of what I'd been about to do overcame me, and I had to sit down and eat the remaining Jaffas myself. As I sat there, my phone beeped. When I looked at it, it was for an article in the *Western Bulge Online*, the one Emma Beddoe had been working on all summer.

"**WHO LIVES IN A HOUSE LIKE THIS?**" the headline ran. "By Emma Beddoe, junior reporter, crime."

"From afar, Langley Hall, just outside the picturesque village of Upper Iffley, looks tranquil and idyllic, but draw closer and it's not long before you notice the crumbling battlements, cracked windowpanes, and overgrown flowerbeds."

I made a mental note to speak to Mr. Billings about the flowerbeds. "The dereliction outside, it seems, only speaks of a rot at the heart of Langley Hall, for presiding over it all is lady of the manor, Daisy Dixon, née Langley, otherwise known as the Upper Iffley Poisoner. I was invited in..."

Then she described the old kitchen as "on the shabby side of shabby chic" and the biscuits we gave her as "humdrum."

She said Mrs. B was "busy, lively, and youthful" and I was "nervous, guarded, and fidgety." I wondered if she'd got her notes mixed up. "Despite having all the money in the world, Daisy dresses as if she doesn't have a penny. Her outfits are always mismatched, and she has no eye for color."

I nearly had a fit when I read that. People in glass houses! I looked at the picture of Emma at the top of the page—it was only a headshot, so her readers couldn't see the hypocrisy in what she had said.

Then she got down to the nub of it.

"Despite welcoming me into her home"—that was one way of putting it—"Daisy was strangely reluctant to speculate on why the police might be digging up the graveyard attached to Langley Hall. We could tell ourselves that is because she has thought of reasons but knows they are wrong; we can tell ourselves she is uniquely unimaginative"—charming—"or we can tell ourselves it is because there is something she doesn't want us to know. My only facts are that James and Daisy Dixon were at the same party as Lennie Green on the night he vanished, and weeks later the police were digging on their property. And now Daisy has been linked romantically to Doug Newman, whose body was found in the river just days after Lennie Green's."

I looked at the date, the article had been written before the latest developments. I braced myself for an onslaught of veiled allegations and insinuations, but Emma had chosen to take a different path.

"Of course, speculation on this has been rife, but to really understand life at Langley Hall, you have to go back a few decades to what must have been a formative experience in Daisy's adolescence. I spoke to a number of residents about what happened all those years ago."

Oh, she'd really done the rounds. She'd spoken to most of the village, but to my surprise, most of what they said wasn't too bad.

"There's nothing more dangerous than someone with a little bit of knowledge," Mrs. Dobson said. "She thought she knew what she was doing."

"She brought a cake to the shop not long after her mum died. She wanted to see if we'd sell it," Mrs. Thorpe had told Emma. "We had to say no, but it was only because of health and safety rules. I think she thought it was because of the incident." Yes, I had thought that.

"Tragic accident," Mrs. Billings said, but I would have preferred it if she'd said nothing.

Beneath the comments, Emma had surmised, were the words of a tight-knit community protecting one of their own. Then she'd got down to the nitty-gritty and the testimony of BigDreams.

"She has a vengeful side," BigDreams told her. "She's coldhearted and ruthless when she wants something." And he went on to say I had been bullied at school, I had plotted my revenge for years, and when the time came I executed my plan.

---

I hated school. All through primary years, the words, "Daisy has fleas," followed me around. It was thought, at Upper Iffley Primary, that this was an inevitable consequence of being hard up.

At secondary school, they upped the ante. There, our primary was combined with other schools from the area, and there was a pressing need to inform the pupils from these other establishments that "Daisy buys her clothes at Barnardo's."

I was never brave enough to say to them, "No, my clothes are not from Barnardo's; they are your own clothes, resurrected. Or else they are your old curtains and tablecloths transformed."

But I tolerated it in the way I always had: Maisie Brookes would make a snide comment in the morning and find her maths homework was missing in the afternoon. Philip Whitaker would have a dig at me on a Monday and find the sleeves of his jumper sewn together on a Tuesday. Samantha Gibson, now Saunders, would throw a hockey ball at me on the playing field and find her towel had vanished when she came out of the shower.

In year eight, they stepped it up another gear and the issue of my unknown dad raised its head again, along with aspersions on my mother's character, which were then ascribed to me.

"Daisy has fleas" became "Daisy has STDs," and humping gestures were made as I walked past.

I knew I shouldn't care and that my Langley Hall ancestry more than made up for anything they could say, but it was hard to keep my spirits up with just the belief in a noble past and a better future.

---

I bided it until our GCSEs were upon us, at which time I begged my mum to let me either leave school or go to a sixth-form college in a town other than Tippington for A-levels. But she didn't want me ruining my chances by leaving school early, and she wouldn't be talked into the extra expense the bus fare beyond Tippington would incur. Not even when I offered to pay it myself with the money I made from waitressing in the King's Head.

"That money's for you to spend on nice things," she said. "Or save it."

Not going back to Tippington Comp would be a nice thing, but nothing would move her on this. She didn't know how bad the bullying was. I could never tell her what they were saying about her.

But before A-levels was the summer after our GCSEs, a long one with exams finished and no homework. I prepared to spend it picking up waitressing shifts, raiding the mobile library, and maybe the odd day out, although sadly not to Langley Hall, as that had long since been closed to visitors.

Then there was a knock at the door. My blood ran cold when I heard my mum answer it to an ultrapolite Samantha Gibson and her henchwoman, Lauren Fisher. A moment later, I was called through.

"Hi, Daisy," Samantha smiled. "We're all going camping to celebrate the end of our exams. We wondered if you'd like to come?"

I opened my mouth to say thank you, but frankly, I'd rather fry my own kidneys, and why were they inviting me, because I knew they didn't want my company. But my mum turned to me and said:

"That sounds like fun!"

"You only need about £40 to chip in for the campsite and food," Samantha continued. "We've got plenty of space in the tents. It's just four nights. We're going on Monday."

My mum had never been able to afford to send me on any of the overnight school trips—which I also hadn't wanted to go on—and on hearing how cheap this was, she was beside herself with excitement at being able to pay for me to go on holiday.

"Katie's coming," Lauren piped up. Katie Connelly was one of the few classmates who was never horrible to me and sometimes, in fact, quite nice.

"Brilliant," my mum said and that was the end of the discussion.

The weekend ruined with Monday hanging over me, I packed what I could, while my mum made a list and set about borrowing various odds and ends.

"Daisy's going camping," I heard her tell the neighbors. "First holiday on her own." Very nearly my first holiday altogether, in fact, preceded only by a week in Devon a few years before.

On Monday morning, off I went to meet the others, with a borrowed sleeping bag under my arm and a rucksack full of secondhand or homemade clothes on my back.

There were about twenty of us and six parents had agreed to drive us out to the campsite and pick us up again on the Friday. Into the cars we piled, and about an hour later, piled out again at a campsite not far from Weston-super-Mare. There, the parents helped us unpack and set up the tents, then they left us to our fates.

Surprisingly, it wasn't too bad. We sat out in the sun, and no one bothered me much. Two of the older-looking boys went into town and came back in a taxi with a couple of crates of Carlsberg, and later that evening I learned that I didn't like lager and that drunk people are very boring when you're sober.

The next morning, while the rest of them slept off the night before, I went for a walk through the nearby fields, looking with the eye of a forager as I went: gooseberries, horseradish, and then a huge field of mushrooms. I knelt down and inspected them; they were field mushrooms, I'd know them anywhere. I collected them up in my sun hat and took them back to camp.

The others weren't very keen when I first showed them what I had, so I took one, raw, rinsed it off and ate it, right there in front of them.

There were gasps and a whisper of "suicide," but they needn't have got their hopes up. I had one moment of hesitation, just before I swallowed it, wondering if I had somehow missed a telltale speckling of a death cap stem or the gills and skirt of an early destroying angel, but I hadn't. I knew I hadn't.

I swallowed it and the others stood in silence, waiting for me to collapse, clutching my throat, or my heart, or my stomach. I stared back at them.

"The poison from a mushroom takes hours to work," Maisie Brookes said in the end. She was top of the class at science and planning to become a doctor. "It has to get to your liver first. Nothing to see here."

With a palpable air of disappointment, they set to work getting breakfast—without mushrooms—ready. I looked for a pan for my fungal treats, but they said there was nothing to spare.

Then Katie stepped up and said she had eaten mushrooms picked by me or my mum and she would like some too. Katie's word, it seemed, was good enough and it turned out there was a frying pan available, after all, although in the end only Katie and I ate them.

The rest of the day passed peacefully, with just occasional glances over to see if either of us was about to bite the dust and, the following morning, I was woken by someone poking me in the eye to see if I was still alive. But yes, I was alive, so was Katie, and we were not just alive, but well.

I began foraging each morning for the bits and pieces you could find to eat in June, the others ate what I found, and it seemed that the week was going to pass peacefully. Suspiciously peacefully.

On the final evening, it began. Samantha asked us all, "Who wants to play Truth or Dare?"

I sighed. Who, in their right mind, would want to play Truth or Dare? It was a horrible game. Yet, predictably, I was in the minority on that one.

I offered to spend the time tidying up the camp, so that it was all shipshape and easy to pack up the next morning, but they wouldn't hear of it.

"Come and have some fun!" But one girl's fun is another girl's nightmare.

I tried saying that, simply, I didn't want to play, but Euan said, "Come on, we've brought you all this way; just join in, for god's sake." And that was the end of my fight. A few minutes later, I was part of a circle, ready for the first round of Truth or Dare. At least Katie was to my right, so I knew the questions wouldn't be too bad. As soon as Euan had finished handing out lagers, we began.

Samantha started by asking Lauren, "When's the last time you cried?"

"The last day of school," Lauren replied—for god's sake!—and turned to Maisie. "Have you ever stolen something?"

"No," Maisie said and turned to Philip Whitaker, on her left. "Would you sell your pet for a million pounds?"

"No," he said and turned to Euan. "Would you sell your brother for a million pounds?"

"Yes," Euan said and turned to Katie. "How would you rate your looks on a scale of one to ten?"

Slightly embarrassed, Katie gave herself a modest five and asked me, "Who would you choose to help you hide a body?"

Unwittingly, I got the answer wrong when I said, "You." Although I didn't exactly *choose* to hide a body with James. I turned to my left and asked Tyler Carson if he had ever cheated on a test. He hadn't, apparently.

Soon after that we had our first dare when Philip Whitaker was asked if anyone had ever walked in on him pleasuring himself. He chose a dare—why didn't he just lie?—and was sent to shout "Geronimo!" into the neighboring camp.

The next dare saw Lauren going to the campsite office to tell the site manager she loved him and soon after that, Katie had to swallow a teaspoonful of pepper.

We returned to truths, until Samantha announced that the game was boring, which it was, and we should mix it up a bit. She fetched an empty bottle and put it in the middle of the circle.

"We'll do it like Spin the Bottle," she said and spun. As it came to a stop, it pointed at me. The circle went quiet. Samantha smiled. "Daisy," she said. "Who's your dad?"

No one spoke. The summer breeze suddenly sounded loud in the trees; by my knee, an ant scaled a blade of grass.

"You have ten seconds to answer," Samantha said. "Or it will be a dare."

"Dare," I said.

Samantha and Lauren leaped to their feet. "What shall we tell her to do?" Lauren asked, but Samantha already had an answer.

"Do a striptease." Some of the others laughed, some of them groaned. I said nothing.

"Give her something else," Katie said. "She's not going to strip, is she?"

"You have to do the dare that is set," Euan said. "I'll get you some music." And he ran off into his tent.

For a moment, I thought about doing it. I thought about shrugging off my darned cardigan and throwing it to my left; undoing the buttons on my homemade top and hurling it to my right; unzipping my patched skirt and tossing it high in the air. Then I'd remove my Primark underwear and sling it at Samantha's face.

Instead, I turned and began to walk back to the tents.

"You have to do the dare!" I felt a weight on my back as Samantha jumped on me and started pulling at my clothes. Next came Lauren. I gave her a good kick and she backed away, but before I knew it, Euan was above me, saying:

"Come on, Daisy, be a sport."

In my peripheral vision, I could see everyone else standing, watching. Some covered their faces, but no one came to help.

I managed to punch Samantha hard. She swore and put her hand to her jaw, and I wriggled free. There was a moment when none of them had hold of me and it was enough. I stood and I ran.

"Go, Daisy!" I heard Katie shouting, and Samantha yelled at her to shut up.

I ran until it was too dark to run anymore and too dark for them to find me if they tried. They didn't try. I sat down under a tree and there I stayed until first light.

As the sun rose, I examined the scrapes and scratches on my arm and the torn seam of my top. Then I began to walk, but not back to the campsite, not straightaway. I walked away from it, across fields not yet explored. I would have to go back for the cars that were coming to take us home, but that wasn't until midmorning. At that moment, it was not long past dawn, and it was nearly midsummer.

As I walked, I crossed another field of mushrooms. I stopped and crouched down amongst them. Then I picked and picked and picked, taking off my cardigan and carrying them in it. There were no thoughts in my head; I just picked mushrooms. One, two, three, four, fifty, a hundred, more. My cardigan was bulging with them by the time I stopped.

I don't know how long it took me to get back to camp, but when I got there, most people were still in their tents; just a couple were up and they stared as I dropped the mushrooms by the stove. Then I marched to my tent, collected my washbag and fresh clothes, and headed for the shower block.

By the time I got back, the mushrooms were cooked, along with bacon and sausages, and the others were all stuffing their faces.

"There's plenty left," Samantha said when she saw me, as if nothing had happened. I ignored her and went into the tent.

Katie came in as I was putting Savlon on my cuts. "I'm sorry," she said and I shrugged. I would forgive her, I knew, but not right there and then. "Come and have some breakfast," she said.

"I'm not hungry."

---

There was an accident on the M5 that day. It was closer to midafternoon than midmorning when our lifts arrived, but finally the cars drove in procession along the A370 toward the reopened M5 and back to Upper Iffley.

We were nearly home when the first car had to stop. Maisie was the quickest to jump out and run for the verge, followed by nearly everyone else. Soon their bodies littered the embankment and ambulances were called. The hospital subsequently declared a major incident.

Seven people died. Of those who survived, nine required kidney transplants, Samantha and Euan included. Interesting fact: Upper Iffley has the highest number of kidney recipients, per capita, in all of Europe, if not the world.

---

I thought the inquiries and inquisitions would never end; I thought they would take up the rest of my life. Twice I was arrested and questioned under caution.

I answered their questions about how well I knew my mushrooms and could I have made a mistake? Could I have done? I could recognize a field mushroom as easily as my own face, but I was *very* upset at the time of picking.

Eventually, the last question was asked, the coroner made his report, conclusions were drawn, and I was found guilty of nothing more than a tragic, but honest, error of judgment.

My mum's friendship with Mrs. Billings became another casualty of the camp, and the rest of the village retreated with her.

Katie, a transplant recipient, didn't speak to me again and after A-levels she went to university in London. She rarely returns.

---

Emma ended that part of her article with a final anonymous voice. "There's always going to be some that remember it and think badly, but accidents happen and that Samantha Saunders is a nasty piece of work."

"And on that, most of the village agrees" was the last comment in the article.

So, they didn't all hate me for what happened, but I'd lived my life since then as a reaction to that misunderstanding. I'd rarely ventured into the village and when I did, I'd interpreted every interaction as hostile.

I thought back on it all over the years. When they'd said, "Is that all?" and "Anything else?" I'd thought they'd been wanting me to spend more money—to give as much as I could. That, or they wanted to make sure I didn't have a reason to come back. If they didn't smile, I thought it was because they didn't want to serve me.

Maybe, on reflection, they were merely the polite questions of shop assistants, and if they didn't smile, it was because they were busy, or harassed, or bored.

I remembered people browsing my shelves when I worked in the SPAR, then walking away. Could it be they just hadn't found what they wanted? I'd felt so guilty, I'd thought they were walking away from me. I never wanted to approach them because I was ashamed.

I went back through the piece. I wondered who had said what, but apart from the ones I thought I knew, I would only ever be able to guess.

I looked again at the comments from BigDreams: "She has a vengeful side," and, "She's coldhearted and ruthless."

On the worktop to my left, the poisoned cake sat in all its useless glory, waiting to be thrown in the bin. I stood up and walked away.

---

A couple of hours later, I heard James's dulcet tones shouting, "Who made this?"

I went to see what he was talking about and found him peering at the cake, the piece I had cut for Tarquin, assumed eaten from his point of view.

"Mrs. Billings," I said.

"What for?"

"The Bone Bonanza, but it's finished. It ended when the archaeologists left." I walked away from the kitchen, pretending to be uninterested.

"Have you eaten some?" He managed to make that sound like a threat, but I defended myself:

"Just a small piece. Mrs. Billings ate most of what's gone." I had cut Tarquin a sizable slice.

"Why is it purple?"

"Parma Violets," I said, hoping he'd not ask me how I got those crunchy little purple candies into a cake.

"Weird."

I waited, slightly nervous, for him to cut himself a slice, but he left the room and went to get changed. Disappointing. He came back a few minutes later but left again without even looking at it. He sat down and started scrolling through his phone. Then he turned on the TV and I heard the theme for the news.

"Why haven't you started tea?" he shouted.

"I lost track of time. I'll do it now." I turned the grill on high and took a packet of Alphabites out of the freezer, potato pieces shaped into letters. I arranged them carefully on the tray: "I know you strangled Lennie Green," and "I will beat you," I wrote.

I thought about asking him if he'd like a snack while he was waiting, for example, a piece of cake, but I didn't normally do that. I would have to be patient.

The Alphabites came askew as I was serving them out, crisp and brown and shimmering with menace; I hadn't really meant to present them to him that way. So James never saw the warning, he just shoveled them down his neck, along with fish fingers and mixed veg. James was particularly fond of fish fingers and if this was to be his last meal, I wanted it to be a good one. Afterward, he poured himself a glass of whiskey, which he didn't normally do, and my hopes began to fade. But the cake would still be edible the next day.

Then it happened! James finished his whiskey, stood with the glass in his hands, and made his way, not to the drinks cabinet, but to the kitchen. He returned with a slice of the cake.

He took a bite. He took another bite and looked thoughtfully at it. "It doesn't taste like Parma Violets. Not bad, though." He carried on eating and I watched him, hardly believing what I was seeing as he munched quietly until it was gone.

I sat, trying not to fidget, waiting to see what would happen. After a couple of hours, he went to get a glass of water because his mouth was dry. A little while after that, he went to get another, but he went all the way down to the old kitchen for it, which was a strange thing to do. He had to call me to remind him of the way back to the lounge. One of the symptoms of deadly nightshade poisoning is confusion, and it seemed to be hitting him hard.

"You seem a bit muddled," I said, but he shook his head and said it had been a long day.

The waiting was harder than I'd have imagined. It was too early to go to bed, so I went for a bath to pass a bit of time and to save me from having to sit in the room with him, looking normal, when I was not feeling normal.

"What the hell are you wearing?" he asked when I came back, his voice slightly slurred.

I didn't answer. He could see what I was wearing; it was a dressing gown I'd made from deceased soft toys, eyes, ears, and noses still attached. It was the last thing he said to me, and it was perfect for his final words.

A bit later, he seemed to be in some discomfort. His face was flushed and he kept putting his hand over his heart. He wriggled back in his chair and mumbled something nonsensical about an army of spiders. He looked quite upset.

"Why don't you go to bed," I said. "You don't look ever so well. A good night's sleep will probably sort it out." And he must have been feeling rough because he took my advice. I followed him to make sure he went the right way.

# CHAPTER TWENTY-SIX

IT TOOK ME SOME TIME TO GET TO SLEEP THAT NIGHT, BUT EVENTUally I nodded off and I dreamt of berries, mushrooms, and cakes.

I woke the next morning knowing the deadly nightshade would have done some work on James, but would it have done enough?

I listened for the sound of him getting up and going to work at the usual time, but the house was silent. By quarter to eight, it was beyond a late start. In all the years we'd been married, I'd never known James get up later than seven. I rose and went to his room.

I was glad I hadn't been there. Judging by the expression on his face, he had not gone gentle into that good night and I would not have liked to have heard what was going on. It might even have prompted me to call an ambulance. I thought of all my hopeless plotting and scheming, and in the end he did the job himself. I lifted his arm, rigor mortis hadn't set in, he was still quite warm, but I'd have to get a move on.

I went to the lounge to think and soon afterward went back to his room with his phone. I unlocked it with his fingerprint and began to scroll through. I started with his WhatsApp.

I scrolled down his many contacts until I found messages between him and Lennie going to and fro, often laced with expletives. The essence of them was much the same as the conversation I'd had with James when I asked for my money back:

Lennie wanted to make a withdrawal.

James said that was fine, but he'd be making a big loss.

Lennie said he only wanted a little bit.

And James said, yes "but it affects the baseline differential, which impacts the foundational basis of the investment and will impinge on the ultimate, optimum return potential."

That didn't make any sense to me and nor did it to Lennie, and I think that was the point. As Lennie said in his reply, Does that mean anything, or are they just random words you've chosen? GIVE ME MY MONEY BACK!

The messages went on, for days, until Lennie announced he was going to the police, unless James a) gave him the money he'd asked for, and b) made a substantial donation to his hospice appeal.

Right. Fine, James wrote back. As a gesture of goodwill, with no admission of liability, I shall make the payments. How much?

£50,000 to me and £500,000 for the hospice. So, Lennie really was a saint and James had paid nearly half of the money raised for the hospice on the night of the accident. That must have stuck in his craw.

There were no more messages for a while and I thought Lennie would exit stage left at that point, but in a final twist, there was one more WhatsApp message from him, sent on the morning of the party.

I'M STILL GOING TO THE POLICE, YOU CHARLATAN!

Was that the WhatsApp that sealed his fate? If so, the moral of Lennie's story was that blackmailers should stick to their side of the bargain. Although at that point, none of us knew I was going to run him over. That was just a lucky break from James's point of view. When it happened, he spotted his chance to get rid of Lennie and set me up to take the fall.

If the police had seen those messages between Lennie and James, it would surely have sent them in James's direction. It seemed fair to assume that was why James had taken the phone.

So, Lennie had also had trouble getting his money back from James. I had imagined that if I were cleverer or stronger or more assertive I would have persuaded James to return the funds I had invested. I thought that if I were the kind of person who understood phrases like "baseline differential" and "foundational basis," I would be able to talk him round. But no, not even a man as successful as Lennie could get blood out of the stone that was James without threatening him with the police, which was something I would not be well advised to do. Although judging by the way he'd been selling property and cutting costs—the Bentley, the redundancies, and, I was sure, his watch—some people had. I wondered what they'd had to do.

I looked through other apps and found a list of his clients. Most of the names I didn't recognize; they were wealthy people, and most of them had put in at least a million pounds. After a while, I found a copy of my own, then I found investments for a Gordon and Margery Fisk, a more modest £125,000 each. That must be Margery from the party and her husband.

Next, I found documents for the Faulkners, the Chamberses, Mary Bishop, the Thrussells, and the Thorpes. I found entries for most of the rest of the village. The amounts they'd invested mostly ranged from fifty to one hundred thousand.

Near the bottom I found one for a Mr. Lennie Green, £250,000.

And then, Eric and Brenda Billings for £20,000. Their nest egg.

I would have liked to have told Tarquin about what I'd found on James's phone, but he no longer had any interest in the matter. I wondered if it would put things in a different light with Parker and Khan, but I had a dead body to deal with now, and that made the new evidence something of a sideshow.

---

I opened James's Amazon account and went on a spending spree. I bought the basics you would need for a new life: clothes, shoes, toiletries, towels, bed linen, crockery, and pots and pans. Then I had them delivered to an address I picked at random, somewhere in Greater Manchester, and I addressed them to Mr. George Strange. I spared a thought for the poor soul who was about to receive it all, but at least, when James was declared missing, it would point the police away from the idea that he had died in his bed.

Next, I drove down to the SPAR, and as I arrived, I paused, opened the car door a sliver, and dropped James's phone on the ground, just outside the carpark. I went inside, bought a few things I had been known to buy before: chips, chicken nuggets, crisps, crisps, crisps, crisps, crisps, and more crisps, now that I was no longer restricted by James, plus chocolate. Then I left, taking care not to run over the phone as I drove away. I was trusting in the honesty of Upper Iffley shoppers to hand it in when they saw it. It was not a stunt you could pull in Great Beadington—they'd be off with it quicker than you could say "lost property."

I went back to Langley Hall to face the issue of the body. I'd previously shied away from killing him in the house because of the difficulties I'd encounter in moving him anywhere. Circumstances had overtaken me now, but that still didn't mean I was strong enough to carry him out of the house. I imagined getting him as far as the car, but not being able to get him off the ground and into the boot, then being found by the postman, a leafleteer, or a Jehovah's Witness.

And anyway, where would I take him? Digging a hole somewhere was too risky, and I'd already learned that floating him down the river was not a good way to go about it. I could've done with James's help; in fairness he would have had a cool head and some useful ideas.

I was left with dismemberment, which I had already rejected as being too gruesome, but it was starting to look like Hobson's choice.

I couldn't see myself cutting through joints and scattering limbs around the district, but I had an idea for a variation on the theme. A bit of searching on a vividly illustrated primary schools' educational website soon gave me all the information I needed.

You take the brain out through the nose. You have to stick a hook up through the nostril first and mush it all up. I went to my sewing box and took out the tools of abandoned projects: crochet hooks and knitting needles. I tried a crochet hook first, but it wasn't quite long enough and I had to get started with a knitting needle. It worked better than expected, though, and the mess could be cleared up with a few towels.

After that, I went out into the garden to reset. It was a gruesome job, and it wasn't going to get any nicer. After clearing my head, so to speak, I headed back in, passing through the kitchen, where the rest of the deadly nightshade cake was still on the worktop. I shoved it deep into the bottom of the bin.

I wandered through the house looking for something to put under the body. Eventually, I found a huge blue IKEA bag in a dark corner of Mr. Billings's shed. It must've been his own because most of our furniture was antique, and what wasn't was custom made. I hoped he wouldn't mind me borrowing it. If he knew what I was borrowing it for, he probably would.

Still, I couldn't really go on Amazon and put in an order for polyethylene sheeting. For a start, next-day delivery would not be soon enough. And I couldn't go to the shops and look for it myself. What if I met someone I knew?

"Ooh! That's a lot of polyethylene, Daisy!" they'd say. "Are you cutting up a body?"

So I took the IKEA bag upstairs, laid it on the floor, and pulled James down from the bed onto it. Next up was internal organs.

I cut his clothes off and he lay naked on the sheet. It was the first time for many moons I'd seen him like that. I hadn't missed it. My mind wandered to Arty, but I got a grip and focused on the task in hand. The instructions said to make a slit along his side, but that made no sense to me, he had ribs all the way along his side. I decided to do it along the front—after all, the instructions were a guide only. I'd already skipped step one, where I was supposed to wash him in either wine or water from the river Nile, and I would not be storing the organs in animal-shaped jars, which was step four.

I wasn't sure I could do it. I felt ill just at the idea of his insides spilling out, but it was a bit late for changing my mind. A dead body in the house would be hard to explain—a dead body with a missing brain even more so.

I fetched a carving knife, washing-up gloves, and a bucket. I wrapped a scarf around my mouth and nose, and I cut…

Oh! The blood! The instructions didn't say anything about blood. They'd seemed comprehensive and straightforward, but now that I was using them, I found they weren't fit for purpose. I wondered what other little surprises I might find along the way.

I needed to think quickly before it spilled off the IKEA bag and into the carpet; I could not have that. At least, having cut him along his front instead of his side, it wasn't flowing all over the place. That deviation from the instructions was to my credit.

I went upstairs to the old, old cupboards and brought down all the curtains, linen, lace, and vintage clothing I could find. I piled it around James. Then I tilted him sideways and the blood began to ooze out onto the materials, where it was soaked up.

It took ages. I filled the bath with cold water, as Mrs. Billings had advised me to do for blood back in the happy days when the only blood-stained cloth I had to hide was the rag I'd held against Lennie's head. Whenever a piece of material was sodden, I transferred it to the bath, to rinse, but it wasn't as simple as that—of course it wasn't. Every piece of material was so drenched with blood, it turned the water red as soon as I put it in and I had to rinse it over and over again.

As I worked I sang a song to myself that we'd sung when we'd done our school Egyptians project all those years ago. It was about a pharaoh called Ramesses. But after a while I needed to hear other voices, so I fetched the radio from the old kitchen and listened to the usual local station. They were having a phone-in; they wanted us to get in touch to let them know what we were doing that afternoon.

"See if you can surprise us!" the presenter said. I managed to resist the temptation.

All the cloth I used wouldn't fit in one bathtub. Soon the bathtubs in my own bathroom and both the guest baths were filled with bloody evidence. It felt like it would never end. I took a break to look up "how many pints of blood in a human body." The answer was eight to twelve. It seemed there should be a zero on the end of that. And all the way through it, I had to remember to stop, to message James and ask him, "What time will you be home?" and "Did you see my message?" and "Where are you?" to create a credible story when I reported him as missing.

I went through a cycle of resolve, determination, despair, and then, finally, relief, when the flow slowed. But there was no real relief. It was time to go back to the script and deal with the organs.

They were every bit as bad as I had imagined. In fact, they were worse than the blood because at least I had seen blood before. The washing-up gloves I was wearing made it harder because I kept losing my grip, but I didn't want to touch them with my bare hands. Eventually, with several fresh air breaks, it was done and I carried them, in the bucket, downstairs and out to the back garden. I couldn't leave them long, but I had a bit of time to decide whether to bury or burn. Meanwhile, I went back upstairs.

I surveyed the scene. The carpets had come out of it unscathed, which was cause for great celebration, but the IKEA bag was a mess. Furthermore, I had four baths full of blood-soaked cloths. And the smell was sickening. I opened every window.

I wondered what my mum would say if she could see me now. Probably, "Tidy this mess up at once, Daisy!" And that would be good advice.

I rinsed the soaking materials until I could carry them without blood dripping off them, then took the first load to the washing machine. I hauled the IKEA bag into the bath to rinse it off, until it was clean enough to carry downstairs. Outside, I finished it off with the hose.

I didn't need to eat—I didn't think I'd ever want to eat again—but I needed to rest for a few minutes and to think of blue skies, fresh meadows, sea air, anything other than what was upstairs. And I needed to get changed. My old clothes went into the bath to soak, although ultimately they would be thrown away.

The next step was to stuff James to recreate his shape, and truth to tell, he was looking a bit saggy around the middle. The instructions called for straw, sawdust, or rags, but the rags were all in the washing machine, or waiting to go in. As soon as the first load was done, I tumble dried it and took it back to the scene.

Every item was unrecognizable as to what it had originally been. They were all old, old pieces, many of them made before the days of modern machines, and the spin cycle had ruined them. Before, that would have saddened me. Now it was a tragedy I could not waste tears over. I began to stuff James full. I got a little bit carried away—he had something of a bulge by the time I'd finished—but I didn't want to take anything out, so I left him that way and went on to the next step, the salting.

For this, I needed natron and the purpose was to dry him out, but a quick look online made it clear I wasn't going to be able to get natron salt, so I went to the kitchen for a box of Saxa. I sprinkled him liberally and hoped it would work in the same way. I had to do it every day for forty days. I was going to need a lot of salt, and a new tally on my wall.

I wrapped James in a new sheet and dragged him down to the priest hole. He was lighter, without his brain and his insides, but still quite a weight to haul. Then I went back outside and fetched the IKEA bag in again to put underneath him; I wasn't sure what to expect in the way of mess in the days ahead.

I buried the entrails. I would have preferred burning to completely vanish them, but I wasn't sure how well a fire would catch, seeing that they were fresh, or what the smell would be like. I dug deep. I did not want any wildlife wandering by and digging it up. Strangely, it felt very final to dispose of them like that, even though they weren't of any use to James by then.

After all that, I spent the rest of the day feeling ill. I thought about tea and biscuits, but my stomach turned over. I couldn't foresee a time at which I was ever going to want to eat again, so in that way, James had found the simple behavioral change he was looking for that would lead to me losing weight.

---

"Chilly in here," Mrs. Billings commented when she arrived on Monday morning. I'd left every window in the house open since the mummification to try to expunge the smell. Along with the cleaning I did, it seemed to have worked. Mrs. B began taking biscuits out of her bag, but this time, I thought she was never going to stop, and I still didn't feel like eating.

"How many?" I asked her, reminding myself of James and giving myself a flashback.

"This is my redundancy payment," she said. "I'm not going to be able to work here anymore I'm afraid, Daisy. I'll do my week's notice, but after that I'm going to go and clean at the cricket club. They've been after me for ages."

Daisy? What happened to Lady Langley, love?

"Don't *I* give *you* a redundancy payment?" I asked. "I'm not making you redundant."

"A leaving present, then. My leaving present to you."

I still thought that went from me to her. "But why?" I asked. "Aren't you happy here?" I wondered what the cricket club were going to make of her light fingers, lackadaisical work ethic, and flextime.

"They're paying me 50p an hour more," she said.

"I'll pay you 50p an hour more. I'll pay you 60p an hour more."

She looked serious. "In honesty, Daisy, I've been hearing some things I don't like recently. Things about you and Doug Newman. I'm shocked, I won't lie, and your poor mum will be turning in her grave. I can't work here anymore, not in good conscience. It makes me sick to my stomach."

If that made her sick to her stomach, she should've been here yesterday. But then the sting of what she'd said kicked in: She was leaving because she was ashamed of me. I hadn't even done what she thought I had, but I couldn't put the record straight.

"Think of those kids," she continued. "You tried to wreck their home. Alright for you, up here with not a care in the world, no children to worry about, no one but yourself to please."

And that stung the most.

"I'll just do the season at the cricket club, then Eric and I are going to retire. The time has come."

"Your nest egg?" I asked.

"That's right," she said. "Speaking of which, we've been trying to get hold of Lord James, but he's not answering."

"I haven't seen him for a couple of days," I told her. "He hasn't replied to my messages. Do you think I should be worried?"

"Hmmm," Mrs. Billings said. "I'll put word out at Silver Surfers, see if anyone's seen him."

She did and they went to the forum and all their social media apps, but no one had any sightings to report. Meanwhile, in the priest hole, sprinkling James with table salt every day was making him look a bit crusty, and after a week I had to go over him with the vacuum cleaner nozzle to get the bits that had clumped together and the residue that fell to the bottom of the space. But it seemed to be working.

I sniffed the air every time I walked past, never sure if there was a slight smell or if my guilt was making me imagine it. Just in case, I sprayed a bit of his aftershave from time to time to keep any odor at bay. This was an all-or-nothing strategy, either it worked perfectly or it failed completely. So far it was working.

Meanwhile, I was wondering how long I should leave it before I reported James as missing. It was hard to know what kind of time lapse would make me look concerned without jumping the gun. James was a grown man in good health. If he wanted to ignore a message, he had every right to do so and often did.

Then the situation resolved itself. There was a knock on the door. I ignored it. There was another knock.

"Police!" a voice said. It was DS Khan. "Open up, we can see you."

Sniffing the air, I made my way down the grand staircase and opened the front door to the familiar sight of Parker and Khan. I stood there, barring their way inside.

"Do you want me to come down to the station?" I asked, unusually enthusiastic about it. "I don't have a solicitor, so we don't have to wait."

"We're looking for Mr. Dixon, actually," DS Khan said.

"What for?"

"We just want to ask him a few questions."

"What about?"

"Oh, the weather, the Little Beadington bypass, the church bell fund. What do you think?"

"I don't know where he is," I said. "I've been trying to get hold of him."

"We know. So have we, but he seems to have parted ways with his phone."

Three cheers for the honest folk of Upper Iffley! And if they had the phone, they had the messages from Lennie. I tried not to smile.

"What's happened to his office?" Parker asked.

"I don't know," I said. "What do you mean?"

"It's gone. He emptied out all the rooms he used and left without paying the rent."

"He did make the staff redundant," I said, remembering the tale of Oliver Thrussell. "I suppose then he didn't need the office, but he didn't say anything to me."

They gave me a look that said another interview was in the offing. They probably didn't realize exactly how separately James and I had been living, but for now they left me alone.

"If you see him or hear from him, please let us know," Khan said and with that, they left. Was it too much to hope, I wondered, that the tide was turning.

# CHAPTER TWENTY-SEVEN

JAMES WAS GONE, THERE WAS NO NEWS YET ABOUT MY IMPENDING trial, and of course, the police now knew a bit more about James and Lennie Green. Mrs. Billings's last shift was approaching.

She duly arrived on her final day and we went through our usual tea and biscuits routine, but for once, we had nothing to say. I'd thought we were friends, just as I'd thought I was more important to her than Jo Newman, innocent victim though Jo was. I knew it wasn't friendly of me to have considered killing Mrs. B, but I was sure now I would never have done that. And she didn't know about it anyway, so that hadn't influenced her decision. I felt the rejection sharply.

Eventually, tea drunk in somber silence, Mrs. B took out a duster, while I went to catch up with Miss Marple. Before I settled down, I set out the shepherdess she had once taken and given to a charity shop, the one Arty had valued at seventy to eighty thousand. I wrote down Arty's estimate, tucked the paper into the basket of flowers she carried, and put it in the usual spot for pocketing.

"That will be me done, then," Mrs. Billings said at the end of the morning, putting her coat on and picking up her bag. "Off to pastures new."

"Thank you for your help here," I said. "Altogether, I mean, not just the cleaning that we paid you for."

She nodded. "Well, I can't grumble about the biscuits…or the gifts." She gave me a wry smile and left. When I checked the lounge, the figurine was gone, replaced with the key to Langley Hall I had given her when I first moved in.

---

Parker and Khan came round again. This time they brought with them a team of forensic investigators, and they set about tearing the rooms we lived in apart.

"What's that smell?" Khan asked, as they made their way up the staircase. "Smells like teenage boys."

"No teenagers here," I said. "I can't smell anything."

They took away James's laptop and all his gadgets.

Then they took away me and spent an afternoon asking me what I knew about his business. I told them about my own investment and how I hadn't been able to get my money back and in the end, they explained to me, in as sympathetic a manner as they could muster, that the business was a fraud and I would probably never see my money again. I did my best to look shocked.

They asked me if James had any connections to Greater Manchester, so they must have discovered the Amazon purchases. I said no. They let me go.

They put out a bulletin asking for sightings of him, but they came to Langley Hall to search, just in case. They brought sniffer dogs, who paused and barked on the step above the priest hole, only to be told, "Come on, Monty," or Dido, or Samson. "There's nothing to see here. Think the ghosts are getting to them."

---

So it were Lord Langley did it! Mrs. Billings started a thread on the forum. Killed Doug Newman in a fit of jealous rage, then ran away before they could put him in prison.

It does make him look guilty, Mrs. Faulkner replied, and everyone agreed.

When they find him, they should lock him up and throw away the key, Mrs. Chambers said, and that was also received with approval.

Disappointing that Daisy had an affair, though, Mary Bishop wrote. I thought better of her. Lorna would be mortified.

Did you have it out with her, Brenda? Mrs. Faulkner asked of Mrs. Billings.

No, I just left, in solidarity with Jo. I'm doing the season cleaning at the cricket club, then Eric and I are going to retire. We had a little windfall.

The residents of Upper Iffley didn't need the niceties of a trial to come to their conclusions. Had there been one, it would have been for entertainment purposes only. James was tried and found guilty in the forum and would be thought of as an outlaw on the run forevermore. There would be theories as to where he had gone and supposed sightings when people went on holiday. There might even be an exhibition in the village hall, but verifiable answers would forever elude them. I hoped. If anybody noticed, nobody commented on the fact that BigDreams no longer took part in the conversations.

But what happened to Lennie Green? Mrs. Thrussell asked. Did James Dixon kill him as well?

They arrested Daisy Dixon for it, NoseyParker made his first contribution. But now they don't think it was her. The investigation is still open, and James Dixon is the prime suspect.

There were those on the forum who would have preferred a neater ending, but they would have to learn to be content with theories and hypothesizing. Lennie had been avenged, but I could hardly tell them how.

There would be no further speculation on this forum, though. The next time I went to log in, it had been shut down, its purpose served.

---

What followed was a lot of legal wrangling as the Ponzi scheme was investigated. James's assets were frozen, including the contents of the house, but Langley Hall was owned without a mortgage and I was able to stay there, salting James's body every day until the forty days were up.

Then it was time to move on to the bandages stage, and buying the material would raise nobody's eyebrows, so frequently did I buy fabrics. Once wrapped, I took his body—much lighter now, dry and sans organs—to Mr. Billings's shed for temporary storage, until he was ready to meet his public. I hid him in the IKEA bag and put a "No entry" sign on the door, not that there was anyone around to enter.

I had to live on a shoestring at that time, eating little and using the minimum of gas and electricity, just like after my mum died, because without James's money, there wasn't enough in my account to cover the day-to-day running costs. I did run up a few debts in that time.

Eventually, enough money was found in what remained of James's business, the classic cars, and the sale of a tenant farm—not the Newmans'—for warehouses to repay the investors who hadn't already withdrawn their money. I didn't have to sell Langley Hall.

The life assurance paid out on the life of Mr. Newman, and Jo made an offer on the farm. The money was enough for me to continue with the renovations James and I had planned all those years ago.

I hired builders, roofers, carpenters, plumbers, electricians, plasterers, decorators, and historical experts and began restoration. I told them I thought there was something strange about the grand staircase and asked them to look into it; we subsequently rediscovered the priest hole. It made the local news, and schools all over the county asked if they could come to see it.

"Yes," I emailed back to them. "Just as soon as Langley Hall is ready to reopen to the public."

When it was time, I made James some priest's robes and a mask. I dressed his mummified corpse as a sixteenth-century Roman Catholic priest. He was slightly potbellied because of the overstuffing I had done, but I wasn't concerned. I put him back in the priest hole.

Now, he is the star attraction on the tours as Mary Bishop leads our visitors around, flinging the step open to reveal him and shouting, "Do not touch!" every time a curious customer gets too close, without ever knowing why that is so important. Every night, before I close the step up and go to bed, I check that his costume is still on tight: I do not want that mask to slip. Then I wish him good night and leave him to his eternal, infernal rest.

A couple of times Mary Bishop has asked, over tea and biscuits, to borrow James to use as a prop for an amateur dramatics production, but I have had to say no. The issue has the potential to work itself up to a quarrel at some point—Mary Bishop isn't well acquainted with the word "no"—but that is a problem for another day. I try to hurry through tea and biscuits with Mary Bishop; she's no Mrs. Billings.

The income from the tours and the remaining tenant farms comes close to paying the bills, but only close, now and then I have to sell an antique and replace it with a replica, courtesy of Arty's friend, Freddie. Yet, it's so infrequent, I could go on indefinitely and still, one day, leave the hall in a better state than that in which I found it.

The space where the blank family tree was now has a mural, painted by Upper Iffley Junior School, of the history of Langley Hall. I chose something completely different because I don't need the constant reminder of the children I never had.

I'd be overstating the case if I said I was greeted with enthusiasm in the village these days, the memory of my supposed affair with Mr. Newman continuing to linger, but I no longer imagine whispers behind my back and slights in everyday comments. They can say them to my face if they have the gall; otherwise, I don't think about it.

The bones were reburied in the churchyard, with the slab from the mausoleum wall, cleaned up and listing their names and dates, standing over the site. In years ahead, I shall be laid down with them, but that is a long time away. Meanwhile, the Bone Bonanza continues as an annual event. It has taken on some of the attributes of Halloween, mixed in with some pagan Beltane traditions, and has become quite a tourist attraction. The ruins of the mausoleum were taken away and replaced with stables, and now the field is home to three rescue donkeys.

Now and then I get a postcard from Arty as he and his girlfriend roam across the world. It makes me wonder if I could ever have spread my wings like that, but I can't leave Langley Hall now, not with James the way he is. I am tied to him forever "for better, for worse" and beyond: "Till death do us part."

I recently opened a café for our visitors, using the old kitchen and the space around it. The chef is from outside the area and has agreed to keep it a secret that I do some of the cooking myself. After years of grilling and microwaving frozen products, I have enjoyed learning some new techniques. There has been the occasional stomach upset among our customers, but that is only to be expected when you're learning.

READ ON FOR A LOOK AT *JULIE TUDOR IS NOT A PSYCHOPATH* BY JENNIFER HOLDICH

Available now from Sourcebooks Landmark

# PROLOGUE

SEAN'S UNHAPPY "UMMPH" AS HE BOUNCED DOWN THE LAST FOUR stairs convinced me the pulley system was not going to work. Even with gravity on our side, getting him down had been a difficult job. Getting him back up was going to be a Herculean feat.

I followed him to the bottom of the stairs and looked up toward the bathroom. The distance seemed vast. Still, Sean wasn't in any state to use the bathroom, and my mind strayed grimly to thoughts of adult nappies.

The dangers of keeping him downstairs were myriad. Picture the scene if a social caller dropped by, expecting tea and a chat, only to find this young man—strong and healthy just yesterday—prostrate on my lounge floor. Imagine the mayhem that would ensue. If I was going to keep him downstairs, I would have to be very careful indeed.

"Ugg, gllg, glllg," Sean gurgled, and I looked down to find him choking on his own saliva.

I heaved him to a sitting position and kicked his leg into place. Poor Sean would be covered in bruises at this rate! I straightened up, stretching my back, and he began to slide sideways. I caught him by the shoulder and balanced him against the banister.

"Cup of tea?" I asked, and he gurgled. "Come along then!"

I hitched myself between his ankles, like a horse between the shafts of a cart, and started moving forward. As Sean's upper body slid to the floor, I realized it wasn't going to be as easy as that. After a few jerky steps, I turned around and started pulling backward. But that was worse; I turned again and walked forward.

"We'll get you into the dining room and take tea at the table," I said, to rally his spirits. Although Sean's days of sitting up at a table were almost certainly behind him. "Maybe we could have cake? I've got some left over from your wedding. I froze my piece. You're meant to freeze some and keep it for the christening. Did you know that? Did you do that?" At my age, the chances of having a baby to christen were roundabout zero, but I like to stick to traditions. Though traditions were out of the window now. "No time like the present," I said. "I can defrost it."

Or maybe I wouldn't defrost it. Sean's cake-eating days were also a thing of the past. He would almost certainly choke on the crumbs, coughing his way into the next life, as the tiny morsels tickled their way down his throat.

The kitchen door was open and through it, as I dragged Sean down the hall, I could see the blender sitting on the countertop. It would be seeing a lot of business in the weeks ahead; I may be in the market for a sturdier model. Along with the nappies, this was shaping up to be an expensive enterprise.

Perhaps Sean could eat baby food, although I'd need to buy it in vast quantities. People would think I'd opened an orphanage.

"Aaarggh!" he said. As I rounded the corner into the dining room, something snagged. I looked up from my toils and—goodness me!—what had happened to his arm? Something was pulling it above his head, back toward the hall. On investigation, I found it was still entangled in the pulley, tethering him to the stairs.

I unraveled him, crouching down to untwist his sleeve and giving myself time to catch my breath. I gazed at Sean's woebegone expression, ran my fingers through his hair, and sighed.

"Be careful what you wish for, eh, Sean?" I said.

# CHAPTER ONE

## • 2009 •

ON THE THURSDAY BEFORE *SHE* CAME, I TOOK TWO PIECES OF FISH out of the freezer before remembering: Sean went straight from work to football on Thursdays. I popped one piece back in, then, jacket on, bag over shoulder, I took a quick look round…nearly forgot…

The picture needed turning. My own invention, a reversible picture. On one side was a scenic landscape, copied from a postcard; on the other a rather racy image I had conjured up of Sean and I in the throes of passion. I don't tend to leave that one on display—just in case of unexpected visitors.

I glanced outside into the garden where the guinea pigs were buried in their hutch, checking they were out of sight, out of mind: away from the prying eyes of nosy neighbors.

Then a final look around to make sure everything was shipshape, a peaceful and harmonious haven to come back to in the evening.

When all was well, I headed out to the office.

On the train I gazed out of the window at the mountains around our town and thought how lovely it would be to walk up them one weekend. I imagined Sean and I cresting the top and standing hand in hand, slightly breathless, looking down at the track winding along to Cardiff. Not a care, none of the worries of the day to day. But if we tried, we would probably find ourselves lost. We are city people, after all.

The office was a ten-minute walk from the train station. On that early autumn day, with the sun high in the sky, birds singing and people out in their summer clothes for perhaps the last time that year, the walk was a pleasure.

I passed the security guard at reception and showed him my ID, even though he saw me every day. He grunted and continued his conversation with the receptionist. I caught the lift and headed up to the seventh floor.

I turned right from the lift. I skipped around the bend, through another door then—breath held—there he was.

The office was open plan, with desks on either side of an aisle. The desks were in groups—"pods," they called them—and each pod contained four people, who sat, backs to each other, looking out at the rest of the office.

The decor was muted: the walls a purplish gray, the carpet dark gray, medium gray chairs, the desks were some kind of cheap wood, often with snags that caught your clothes, and stainless steel cabinets stood against the walls. The only color was added by the odd staff member who opted for a bright top instead of the standard white shirts and blouses.

The atmosphere, on the other hand, was upbeat with the hectic sound of people on a mission: heated conversations as we discussed the day's work. From time to time members of our own team nipped across the aisle to confer with their counterparts in the neighboring department. It really was a busy hive.

Sean was frowning slightly as he peered at his PC monitor. Probably another tricky case.

"Morning, Sean!" I trilled as I approached him.

"Eh?" He was deep in concentration. He looked around for where the voice was coming from and saw me. "Morning, Julie," he said.

"Good night, last night?" I asked.

"Yeah, not bad. So-so. You know. Wednesday night."

"Yeah, yeah, Wednesday night. Football tonight, is it?" I said.

"I'm not going. It's the Pink concert tonight."

My heart nearly stopped beating in my chest. I'd thought that was next week! I'd only taken out one piece of fish!

"Didn't think that'd be your kind of thing," said one of The Lads, Dave, giving me time to recover myself.

"Hey-ho, it's give and take, isn't it," Sean replied. "My sister's friend dropped out. Pink and Drink, I'm calling it."

"What will you do for your tea?" I asked, still a little panicky.

"I don't know. Probably get a burger or something, if there's time," he said. "Why?"

"I just thought you perhaps wouldn't want to be drinking on an empty stomach."

"I've survived it before. I wouldn't lose too much sleep over it, if I were you," he said.

"No, no. I won't be losing any sleep!"

"Catch you later, then," he said. "I'm up to my neck in this."

"Catch you later," I said.

I went to my desk, turned my computer on, and watched as, a

minute later, Sean followed another of The Lads, Mike, to the coffee machine. They stood by it, talking and laughing about something, Sean throwing his head back in that carefree way of his.

Sean wasn't good-looking in the Hollywood sense of the word. He wasn't particularly tall, he was slightly chubby, his eyes were a bit close together and now, in his midtwenties, his hair was already starting to thin.

Yet he had a way of drawing everyone to him, a magnetism that pulled people in and held them there.

"He hangs on your every word when you're talking to him," Jayne from the mailroom once said. "You feel like you're the most important person in the world."

The day rumbled on. Cheerful, bouncy Ffion, our representative from HR, came down to announce that new health and safety training was being rolled out across the company. She handed out leaflets and advised us to acquaint ourselves with the differences between trips and slips because we would be tested. I hate to fail a test, so I spent what was left of the morning making sure I was in no doubt.

Thursday morning became Thursday afternoon. And, as sure as night follows day, Thursday afternoon became Thursday evening.

Having seen Pink, Sean came into work on Friday looking a bit green. He merely grunted when I said good morning.

By midmorning, he was talking about going home. Marcus, our manager, said he'd have to take it as a half-day holiday; he couldn't be put down as sick when we all knew he had a hangover. Marcus could be such a killjoy.

I saved the day though, when I said I was going across the street for coffee and offered to get him an espresso. He nodded his gratitude and reached into his pocket for change, but I said it was my treat.

"Thanks, Jools," he said. "I owe you one."

Only he calls me Jools. I would only allow it from him. A few minutes later I stood by his desk, watching him stir sugar into his drink, anticipating a few shared moments together. And sure enough:

"What's the plan of attack for the weekend then, Jools?" he asked.

I giggled; he had quite the turn of phrase. "Well," I said. "I'm in tonight. Might do some painting in the garden since the light's so vivid at the moment. After that, who knows? The evening's my own. I'm not going anywhere. I have a leg of lamb to roast, with veg and roast potatoes. I have wine in, a really nice Australian red."

I'd once heard him describing a wine tasting session and how much he had enjoyed an Australian red.

"I won't be opening it before nine," I said. "I'll probably have a bath first, light some candles, put a film on. I'll be in all evening. Just a laid-back evening. Just me and…whoever."

He nodded, his eyes slightly unfocused. "Well, have a good one, then," he said.

That evening, I followed the routine, exactly as described, but I didn't hear anything from Sean. He probably went home and straight to sleep. I wouldn't blame him. In fact, maybe it was my mention of wine that put him off, in his delicate state.

I started watching Jonathan Ross but it was a bit dull. I picked up my phone: no one had called or sent me a text. I skimmed the news headlines: nothing had happened. I checked my emails: no one had emailed me.

On waking that Saturday, I shook off the disappointment of the previous evening. Sean would have had his reasons. Meanwhile, the world was my oyster, having recently subscribed myself to Sky television.

I had already recorded a few romantic comedies, and I set a few more to tape. In the spirit of harmonious living, I added a few action films for you-know-who. Then, having the house to myself, I sat down to watch *Little Miss Sunshine*.

Halfway through I paused it, fancying a glass of wine.

I don't really know how the film finished. I watched a couple more, but they were unremarkable. When the last of them was over, I turned my attention to cooking.

And that saw me through the rest of the afternoon: chopping, frying, blanching, beating. Pouring, tipping, sipping, swallowing… chatting away about this, that, and whatever. At six on the dot the meal was on the table; I had evolved into the domestic goddess my late sister, Angela, was always expected to become.

The seating arrangements looked out over my garden.

"The roses really were a success this year," I remarked, thinking as I said so that, success aside, it really was time I cleared away their dead heads. "Dessert? I shouldn't really, but we all deserve a treat at the end of the working week."

I cleared away the plates. I was still slightly peckish, so in the kitchen, out of sight of the dining area, I polished off what was left of Sean's portion, which was pretty much all of it. Except for the mushrooms I'd already pinched from his plate at the table.

I returned with two sundaes I had put together and gobbled mine down. By the time I'd finished, Sean's had pretty much melted, so I tipped it away, just picking out the chocolate pieces for myself. I poured the remains of his wine into my own glass: I had my drinking head on by then and felt I could drink until dawn.

The meal over and the washing-up done, it was time to wind down in the lounge, and Sean had assured me that *Pirates of the Caribbean* was very good.

It was alright; the plot was a little hard to follow. Eventually the wine took possession of me, and I drifted off to sleep where I sat. I woke at four in the morning with my mouth hanging open and a crick in my neck—the joys of the weekend—and stumbled off to bed.

# CHAPTER TWO

## • 2009 •

WELL, MONDAY WAS A NEW WEEK AND AS ALWAYS ON A MONDAY WE were insanely busy in the office, catching up with whatever has piled in by phone, email, or post. Sean and I hardly had a moment to speak to each other.

By rights, no one should have a moment. We are meant to be a team and that means all hands to the pump on a Monday morning. But that didn't stop several of the others sauntering round the office as if they were on holiday.

Gareth, my sidekick and desk-mate, and I sat together, the other two desks in our pod empty. I wouldn't have known Gareth was in at all that morning were it not for the pile of personal items—phone, keys, wallet, headache pills—he always poured out of his pockets and onto his desk on arrival each day. I looked around and spotted him talking to someone in our neighboring department—Gareth always seemed to know everyone—waving his hands in the air and doing what looked like a belly dance, to the hilarity of all. It was not yet nine o'clock, but already, his shirt was creased and his hair looked as if it hadn't seen a hairbrush for weeks.

Gareth, it seemed, had had a particularly racy weekend involving an inflatable flamingo and a male model from Basildon. How the other half live. I'd thought I'd seen some sights on my streaming service, but Gareth made Hollywood sound tame by comparison.

Eventually the room settled down, Gareth found his way back to his own desk, and wrestled himself into his seat.

"Does my bum look big in this?" he asked, as the chair seemed to close in around him. He had put on some weight in the time he had worked with us, although he was big by nature. He could probably have been a rugby player, if he'd had any coordination, speed, strength, aggression, or aptitude for sport whatsoever. A big, disheveled rugby player, in bright clothes that always tested the limits of the office dress code.

When he was sat down, you could see that his eyes were very pale blue, his nose rather long, and his skin always very smooth, hardly troubled by stubble. But the main thing you noticed about Gareth was that he was always smiling. Even in the middle of a last-minute batch of scanning that was going to make him late, he was always smile, smile, smile.

Once settled at his desk, Gareth and I were nose-to-grindstone catching up for the rest of the day. I left the office somewhat dazed at having exchanged not a word with Sean.

Consequently, I wasn't my cheery self when I returned to the house. But it was only Monday, and I resolved to have a pleasant evening. Tomorrow would be another day.

The weather was still fine that evening, more like summer than mid-September, so I took my easel and paints out into the garden for an hour before dusk to make the most of the remaining September sunshine.

I set myself up facing toward the back of my small garden, in close proximity to the hutch that housed the guinea pigs, Bert and Mabel Jackson. They had the same names as my next-door neighbors, but that was just a coincidence.

After some time, I heard a wheezing from behind, and when I turned round, Bert—the neighbor, not the guinea pig—was leaning over the fence.

"Evening," he said.

"Evening." I turned back to my painting.

"Beautiful weather."

"It is."

"More like August than September."

"It is."

I paused in my work and stared straight ahead, hoping he'd go away, but he just rubbed a hand over his florid face. Bert once told me he'd had a career in the civil service, but he looked like he'd lived a life in the great outdoors: his hands and face were leathery and weather-worn. He cleared his throat and continued. "You know, if you don't mind my saying, my niece had some dark times. She could put you in touch with someone who could help."

I turned around and he was staring at the picture I was painting.

"I'm not having dark times," I said. "I'm just not very good at painting shrubbery."

"Oh," he said. "Alright. It's just with the talking and everything…"

"Talking?"

"We can hear you. When you're in the house. Alone in the house."

"Mr. Jackson, I have a budgerigar. How will he learn to talk if I never speak to him?"

"Oh," he said. "Oh. I didn't realize. He's very quiet, your budgerigar. I hear you, I never hear him."

"I told you, he's still learning."

"Doesn't he sing? Birdsong?"

"No, Mr. Jackson. Apparently, he does not." I turned my back and dipped my brush to the paint to signal the conversation was over, and presently I heard him whistling on the other side of his garden. Should budgies sing? I didn't know. I couldn't remember. I'd have a look on the internet later.

I'd lost some of my enthusiasm for painting after Mr. Jackson's rather harsh critique, so I went back inside and checked my emails—none. Texts—none.

I think it was the heat that made it so hard for everyone to concentrate. Only a couple of weeks before we'd had a real taste of autumn, and this last flash of warm weather had made everyone a bit giddy. Each time I glanced up at Sean he was gadding about, chatting to a colleague, not the industrious man I had fallen in love with.

But who can blame us? We all knew we had a long, hard winter coming up. There was no harm, for once, in a relaxing of the protocol.

"You not feeling the heat, Jools?" Sean asked me. It took a moment before I realized he was commenting on my jumper. It may have looked a little odd on a hot day, but you never knew what the air-conditioning was going to bring.

"She's acclimatizing herself for hell," Gareth said. Sean seemed to think that was funny and walked away, laughing like a drain. He was called back seconds later though, to look at something on Gareth's phone.

They were fans of the Facebook, and it had uploaded a short video of amusing giraffes. I didn't think they were quite as funny as Sean and Gareth found them, but I was in the minority: within minutes most of the department were huddled around Gareth, guffawing with laughter over it.

"Can't believe you're not on Facebook yet, Julie," Gareth said when the fuss had died down. "My gran's on it. There's loads of stuff like that, and you can see what people you know are up to when you're not with them."

"How do you mean?" I asked. I'd heard of the Facebook but had thought it was just a collection of animal videos. I had no idea it was also a surveillance tool.

Well, it wasn't quite the in-depth insight I'd imagined when Gareth said I could see what people were up to: I couldn't track them minute by minute, I couldn't see into their homes, and some people provided more information than others. But it certainly was an eye-opener. We looked at the profiles of a few of our colleagues and I had to admit, I had had no idea Jayne from the mailroom was a ballroom dancing champion—she looked so frumpy round the office.

"What do you have to do?" I asked Gareth. "Do you have to subscribe? Do you have to apply?"

"No," he said. "Watch." And within minutes he'd set me up an account of my own. All I had to do when I got home was fill in the details and request a few friends.

He showed me how to add pictures to my profile. I had

experimented with the camera on my phone in the past and had taken a few around the office: Sean at the coffee machine; Sean at the printer; Sean at the coat stand.

Gareth stared at them for a moment. He looked as if he was going to say something, but instead of speaking, he just scrolled between them again.

"You can't use any of them," he said in the end. "Julie, you can probably get sued for this." Finding nothing suitable, he said, "Smile," and took a picture of me. He added it to my page next to my name, and I had my first proper look at it. I recoiled: I thought I'd smiled, but it turned out I'd grimaced and the angle made it look as if I had a double chin. My hairstyle is timeless, early Princess Diana but brunette: the light here made it look flat and shapeless. No one who knew me would recognize me from that!

Luckily, Gareth then explained how to change it.

That evening, I logged on to my laptop and opened up my "Pictures" file for a better photo. My options were limited. The only real contender was from Sean's late wife, Susannah's, funeral. It didn't seem entirely appropriate, but I wear black most of the time anyway; you'd have to be pretty eagle-eyed to notice that I was wearing a funeral outfit. It was the best photo I had: glass raised, big smile for the camera, and a great outfit. I'd bought it especially for the occasion; the last funeral I'd been to was Angela's, and I was just a young slip of a girl back then. So up it went. Then I went to the search box, typed in a name: Sean O'Flannery—and there he was!

He's very photogenic, really knows how to pose for a snap. My hand shook a little as it hovered above the "Add Friend" button, but I took a deep breath, stabbed my finger down, and off went my request.

I spent a few minutes scrolling through the others in the office, but none of them really interested me.

I returned to my page, looking for any change, but there was nothing from Sean. I read the news headlines, Tony Blair would be at the Labor Party Conference. Nothing from Sean. I was about to switch off my laptop when there was a ding and a small red circle appeared on the top bar on the Facebook. HE HAD ACCEPTED MY REQUEST! And so quickly! It must have meant as much to him as it did to me.

But when I looked more closely at his page, I found out something else about Sean. Someone had posted on his page the heading "HAIR OF THE DOG!!!!!!!" above a picture of Sean with four other gentlemen of a similar age and state of inebriation. It had been posted the night after Pink. While I was waiting for him and wondering what he was doing.

# READING GROUP GUIDE

1. What is your first impression of the Dixons? What are some ways you would describe each of them?

2. Daisy does several things to make James's life more difficult, including altering his suits to make them tighter. If you were in Daisy's position, what other little ways might you try to irritate or inconvenience James?

3. If you saw Lennie's story on the news, what would you think? Would you have any theories as to what happened?

4. As the story evolves, does your opinion of Daisy change at all?

5. Do you think James and Daisy are equally to blame for their crimes? Why or why not?

6. Daisy often struggles with her confidence and self-worth. How do you think this impacts the way she sees other people? Do you think it shapes her choices?

7. Throughout the story, Daisy often gets angry about James removing the Penney family tree. Why do you think this might be?

8. One of Daisy's favorite activities is watching crime shows, and she often spends entire days rewatching her favorites. Do you have a personal favorite crime show? Or a show that you rewatch repeatedly? Share with your group!

9. When she first meets James, Daisy is struggling with loneliness and grief over her mother's death. How do you think that impacted her opinion of James? How might that have influenced her choice to marry him?

10. After learning about her past, did your opinion of Daisy change at all?

11. By the end, Langley Hall has faced quite a few changes. How did you feel about the ending?

# A CONVERSATION WITH THE AUTHOR

**Where did you get inspiration for this story from?**

Originally from *The Twits* by Roald Dahl. I was a big fan of his when I was growing up, and for this story, I loved the idea of a couple trying to do each other down. I also really enjoy dramas where the characters have some kind of mishap that results in a death, and, for whatever reason, they can't go to the authorities and instead have to cover up the death. Then you watch them digging themselves deeper and deeper in. I wanted to try to re-create some of that.

**The setting of a small English countryside town is so vivid and underscores so much of the novel. Is Upper Iffley based on any particular place or multiple places?**

Upper Iffley is a mixture of the three English villages I have lived in. The village green and the shops around it, including the SPAR, which in real life is a co-op, are from Welton in Lincolnshire, although I made the duck pond up. The stately home just outside the village is near Geddington in Northamptonshire, and there are a fair few thatched cottages in Northants, some of them in Geddington. The sense I had of it as being a contained community, where words gets around pretty quickly, is from Lynton in North Devon, as is karaoke night at the King's Head. All three of them are very scenic and are surrounded by lovely countryside, as well as coastline in the case of Lynton.

**Besides Daisy's character, the secondary characters bring so much color to this novel. Do you have a favorite Upper Iffley resident?**

I like Mrs. Billings and Mr. as well. She's straightforward and pretty loyal to Daisy, although sometimes, with friends like Mrs. B, you don't really need enemies. I'd have liked to have kept the Billingses at Langley Hall at the end, but they deserved their retirement.

**The use of the online forum is a unique element in this novel. What made you include it?**

Although Langley Hall and Upper Iffley are Daisy's world, she's not really part of the community: She isn't in any of the social groups or in anyone's confidence. Even Mrs. Billings only really tells her superficial things. So it was a way of getting an insight into what was going on in the village and what people were thinking and saying about her, Langley Hall, and Lennie.

As well as that, it was a way to give a voice to the village as a whole. The residents, in their general outlook, are quite a homogeneous lot, and I wanted it that way, to have them acting as something of a pack, for example, with them all buying into the Meg-test and subsequent results. So the forum represents the village.

Plus, I love it when you're browsing online and you come across a thread that starts as a rational discussion about one thing and ends in a row about something completely different.

**Despite some of the serious crimes that both Daisy and James are committing, the story has a lot of humor to it. How do you balance the seriousness of what your characters are up to with some lighter, funnier content?**

In all honesty, that is just how I write. I've tried to write serious pieces, but it always ends reverting to humor. Once I have the character's voice, that tends to lead the way, and that is the way they always lead it. In real life I don't have the pressure of having to cover up these crimes or deal with the guilt they might give rise to, so it's fairly easy to take a step back and approach whatever it is with a matter-of-fact, humdrum attitude and put the humor in.

In terms of balancing it, I tend to review to see if something is going to land in the way it's intended or if it could be misconstrued. I think adding little details and having characters focusing on trivial matters when disaster is all around them is often a good way of bringing humor in without detracting from the seriousness of a crime. You can never fully remove the risk that someone will think it's in bad taste because different people will read things differently, but I do have the backstop of editors and copy editors, so I try not to worry too much. I'm just happy if people enjoy it.

# ACKNOWLEDGMENTS

If anyone ever tells you the second book is difficult, believe them. I was going into meltdown a few months before the deadline, and I had to keep reminding myself I once heard that the first draft of *Finding Nemo* was unreadable. If I didn't know before how important a good agent is, I do now: So the first thank-you is for my agent, Ariella Feiner.

Also, thank you to Phoebe Morgan for the first round of editing and Kate Norman for picking it up from there. And to the rest of the team at Hodder: Alainna Hadjigeorgiou, Jazmin Demjan, Claudette Morris, Ami Smithson and Lucy Scholes, Helen Parham, and Annabel Maunder.

Thanks again to Nick Paul for an early beta read, Sara Hayes for medical advice (for Lennie, not me), and Cardiff Writers' Circle for some tweaks that set it right a few times and saved me a lot of rewriting.

And finally, thank you again to friends and family for their enthusiasm for this.

# ABOUT THE AUTHOR

Jennifer Holdich obtained an MA in scriptwriting in 2014, won the Cardiff Writers' Circle Short Story competition in 2021, and has had multiple short stories and pieces of flash fiction published. *Mr. and Mrs. Dixon Hide a Body* is her second novel.

# JULIE TUDOR IS NOT A PSYCHOPATH

---

**Julie Tudor is not a psychopath.**

Julie Tudor is 49 and has it all: a fantastic job (well-maintained spreadsheets are the lynchpin of an efficient office), a beautiful house (some may wonder how she got the money for it, but nothing has been proven), and the man of her dreams.

**Julie Tudor is not a stalker.**

Sean is 25 and the love of Julie's life. The only problem is, he thinks he's in love with someone else.

**And Julie Tudor is definitely, definitely not a serial killer.**

But Julie has found herself in a similar situation before. And if there's one thing Julie knows, it's how to get rid of the competition…

**After all, what's a little murder in the name of true love?**

*"Jennifer Holdich delivers a wickedly funny and darkly compelling debut in* Julie Tudor Is Not a Psychopath. *A masterful blend of humor and suspense that kept me hooked from start to finish."*
*—Joanna Wallace, author of* You'd Look Better as a Ghost

For more Jennifer Holdich, visit: sourcebooks.com